ABOUT

Diana Janney is the author of the novels *The Choice* and *The Infinite Wisdom of Harriet Rose*, which has been translated into four languages and produced as an audiobook. It was long-listed for the Melissa Nathan prize and film rights were sold to a British film company. Prior to her writing career, Diana gained two degrees in Philosophy from University College, London, where she was awarded a First for her Masters thesis on Kant and Hume, and three Scholarships. She went on to convert to Law at the College of Law, London, before qualifying as a solicitor at one of the top City of London international law firms. She then transferred to the Bar and practised as a barrister in London, before turning to a writing career. Diana has received much international acclaim for her writing. She weaves her philosophical knowledge, reflective thought and wit seamlessly throughout her novels.

A MAN OF
UNDERSTANDING

DIANA JANNEY

COGITO™

COGITO Publishing
Published by COGITO Publishing Ltd,
4/4a Bloomsbury Square, London WC1A 2RP

COGITO Publishing Ltd, Registered Office:
4/4a Bloomsbury Square, London WC1A 2RP, England

www.cogitopublishing.co.uk

Typeset in Granjob LT Std by
Palimpsest Book Production Ltd, Falkirk, Stirlingshire

Printed and bound in Great Britain by Clays Ltd, Elcograf S.p.A.

ISBN 978-1-9196053-1-9

www.cogitopublishing.co.uk

For my husband

". . . a man of understanding hath wisdom".

Proverbs 10:23

GRANGA CALLS ME BLUE, so I suppose that's my name now. I don't really see what was wrong with my proper name – Rufus – that my parents had given me when I was born.

"Rufus?" Granga repeated with a frown when I introduced myself to him, even though he knew it was my name. "What sort of name is that? You can't go through life being called Rufus – folk will think you're soft!"

But I wasn't soft, and I'd been called Rufus for the last twelve years. I'd even been chosen for the school rugby team at the age of nine.

"Well, I'm not calling you Rufus," he said as he packed all my suitcases into the back of his old Land Rover at Palma de Mallorca Airport, one on top of the other, until the highest one fell off and wedged itself against a mud-splattered window. "From now on you'll be Blue."

"I've never heard of a boy called Blue before," I said, trying not to sound alarmed.

"Neither have I," he replied, "but it suits you. Blue like cloudless sky on a summer's day."

And it was a summer's day, so I didn't mind too much after that. I liked summer's days – they reminded me of my mother and father and our house in England and homemade lemonade and evenings when I'd stayed up late and had supper in the garden.

It only took us forty minutes from the airport to reach Granga's *Finca Vieja* in the mountains, but that was because Granga drove way over the speed limit, even on sharp narrow bends going uphill, and there were plenty of those. I didn't say anything though – he may have been my mother's father but he was still a stranger to me.

"I like your hat," I commented when we'd travelled so high that my ears were popping. It was the first time I'd spoken since we'd decided on my name.

"They call it a trilby." He took his right hand off the gear stick, where it had been until then, and passed his trilby to me. It was dark beige, like a wild mushroom, with a torn lining on the inside and almost worn-away initials in gold – HRH.

"A hat fit for a king," he said as I put it on and it dropped down over my eyes. But I didn't move it – I liked its smell and I could hide inside it for a while like my old tortoise Freddy used to do when he wanted to be left alone.

By the time we reached the Finca I'd almost fallen asleep. I say *almost* because I hadn't dared to fall asleep altogether, not when I was in a strange country in a strange van, sitting next to a strange grandfather, tucked inside his strange hat and answering to a strange new name.

"Wake up, Blue," he whispered, lifting the brim of his hat above my half-closed eyes. "Hemos llegado!" I was later to learn that that meant "we've arrived" in Spanish, but at the time I thought my Granga was just showing off again.

We left my cases in the back of the van and Granga opened

my door and helped me out with a big wide hand, which he wrapped around mine like a rough glove.

"Come and see where you'll be living now." I think the words seemed as curious to him as they were to me, but we both understood how it was to be.

It took a few seconds for me to adjust to the strength of the Mallorcan sunlight. The first thing I noticed was how far into the distance I could see without my eyes resting on a single building. Our only neighbours were trees of differing shapes – some clustered together like extended families, others standing alone in the dusty ground. Far away on the horizon I thought I glimpsed the sea, just a tiny blue hint of it but enough to make me feel calmer inside.

I followed closely behind Granga as he headed towards the Finca. To reach the front door, we had to walk across a paved terrace almost as wide as a tennis court, lined with clay pots that were overflowing with brightly-coloured flowers – pinks, purples, reds. To the left of the terrace, I spotted a massive palm tree that must have been standing there for a very long time. Its trunk was straight but gnarled, its leaves seeming to wave "hello" to me in the gentle breeze.

The Finca was bigger than our house back home, which surprised me but I couldn't say why. Granga explained that *Finca* was Spanish for *Farm or Estate with a Farmhouse*, but it didn't look like any farmhouse I'd ever seen in England. Its walls were the colour of a sandy beach in the midday sun before the sea washes over it and you burn your feet if you're not wearing flip-flops or trainers.

The front door was tall and grand, curved at the top, and made of brown wood like the bark of the tree my swing used to hang from. We didn't need to open it, because someone did that for us from the inside.

She was an old woman, with skin that reminded me of my school satchel when I didn't have my homework filling it. Yet when she smiled and I saw her small white teeth and happy bright eyes, she made me think of my mother, which my mother wouldn't have liked me saying because my mother was young and beautiful and this woman wasn't, and my mother wore soft, brightly-coloured clothes, and this woman was dressed in heavy black material that hung like old curtains. But when she ran towards me and held me tightly in her short arms and spoke words that were fast and unfamiliar but which somehow I felt I could understand, I knew that my mother would have liked her too so I didn't feel so bad about the comparison.

Her name was Maria, as my Granga introduced her, and she was Granga's housekeeper, which meant that she cleaned his Finca for him and cooked his meals because he was a man and he couldn't be expected to do it for himself, for goodness' sake.

Maria lived on the outskirts of the medieval village nearby that we'd driven through on our way here. She lived with her husband and donkey, but I think she preferred the donkey, because she talked more about him than about her husband. He was an extremely old donkey whom she had looked after even before she had met her husband. He was very intelligent and answered to his name – the donkey, that is, not her husband, although I expect he answered to his name as well when he wanted to.

She told me all this in Spanish as if I would understand, and Granga translated it for me. Granga liked talking in another language and translating, so I let him carry on, even the bits that I understood for myself from Maria's hand movements. There were lots of those. Sometimes they even extended to slapping Granga hard across his arm as if he'd said something she didn't like, but I knew she didn't mind really because she smiled as she was doing it.

I was getting used to being Blue by then, so I didn't mention that I was actually Rufus. And anyway, I think Maria would have found Rufus hard to say. I wondered how much Maria had heard about me, but I didn't ask because I didn't really want to know. She liked me, I knew that much, and Granga liked her, as I liked them, and that was all that mattered to me right then.

At home in England I had only seen photographs of Granga – black-and-white ones that were worn at the edges and pasted into a black leather album that my mother kept in a box under her bed. I wouldn't have recognised it was the same Granga, as he was young and handsome and dark-haired then and dressed in his soldier's uniform, but now he was much older and less handsome with patches of grey hair and dressed in faded brown corduroys that were worn at the knees. His bearing was the same though – upright and broad, with his muscular shoulders pulled right back under a pale-blue shirt and his head tilted slightly towards the sky.

As Granga led the way across a big shadowy hall, brightened only by dozens of vividly-coloured oil paintings hanging on white walls, I noticed that he was wearing odd socks, a black one and a grey one, and I wondered if he had dressed in a hurry to come and meet me. It wasn't that my arrival could have taken him by surprise – he'd known about it for more than a month, as had I, ever since the lawyers had informed him in a letter that they'd copied to me.

The decision for Granga to be my guardian had been an easy one because it was what my parents had wanted, as Hannah had explained. Hannah was my mother's best friend so she had been looking after me at home ever since it had happened. I wished that she could have carried on staying with me, but she'd said that would be impossible. I hadn't completely understood why, but it had something to do with her own children and her husband and that if it hadn't been for them she'd have liked nothing better, so I guessed that meant her family didn't like me as much as I'd always assumed they did.

Hannah was nice though. She smelt of flowers that grow in open fields and country lanes and she talked about my mother a lot and told me what she would have wanted me to do. Of course, I could have told Hannah that, and in better detail, but I let her tell me anyway – I liked hearing her speak. She had a quiet voice, almost a whisper, and she made everything she said sound very important – at least to the two of us.

"You've got to be a good boy for your mother, Rufus," she'd told me as she'd driven me to Heathrow Airport. "And strong and brave like your father. Promise me that, Rufus." I couldn't promise because I wasn't sure I'd be able to keep it, so I'd said nothing.

"Are you listening to me, Rufus?"

"Yes," I'd replied and we'd been silent for a while after that.

I'd expected her to bring her two daughters with her, Katy and Melissa, but she hadn't. They were about my age but seemed younger because they giggled a lot and I never giggled.

As we'd approached the airport I'd worried that I would cry, but I hadn't – I'd wanted Hannah to think I was strong and brave like my father. I'd only ever seen him cry twice, once when my mother and I went away for a weekend break without him, and the other time when Liverpool had lost to Wimbledon in the 1988 F.A. Cup.

"Now you've got my telephone number in your father's wallet. Ring me whenever you feel like a little chat. And write and tell me all about your Grandpapa."

"Granga," I'd corrected her.

"Of course – Granga. He looks like a lovely man. Your mother always spoke affectionately of him."

"Then why did he never come to see us?" It was a question that had only seemed important in recent days, and now I had no one else to ask. Hannah hadn't answered for a few seconds and I'd wished I hadn't asked her.

"Your Granga has always liked to travel," she'd said finally, but I wasn't sure whether this was meant as an answer to my question or just something she knew about him.

"You're wearing odd socks, Granga." I thought I should point it out.

"What's odd about them?" he asked, looking down at a pair of faded sandals with the two odd-coloured socks tucked inside them.

"One's black and the other's grey," I explained, wondering if perhaps my grandfather was colour-blind.

"And what's odd about that, Blue?" he asked with a frown between his wiry grey eyebrows.

"Nothing, I suppose," I replied.

I'D BEEN IN MALLORCA FOR six days before Granga mentioned my mother, and if he wasn't going to, neither would I. It was a Sunday – Maria's day off, when she went to the little old church on top of a steep hill that I could see from my bedroom window.

"Don't you go to church, Granga?" I enquired while the two of us were sitting on the terrace outside the drawing room in the morning sun.

"No," he said, reading from a Spanish newspaper, "I'm not a churchgoer." He hesitated then added: "But your mother believed in God, as you probably know."

I noticed his small blue eyes darting nervously from side to side while he was speaking. And his cheeks were turning pink even through his suntanned skin. I didn't often hear my mother's name – Grace – any more. It was as if no one liked to use it. She had become "your mother" in everyone's vocabulary.

"She always said a prayer to me when she put me to bed," I said suddenly. It felt as if I'd finally managed to get the top off a cola bottle, but I hadn't expected the spray to feel so cool.

"She was a good woman." His eyes were still again as he watched me for a response.

Before it had happened, it had never once crossed my

mind that there might not be a God. My mother had always told me there was and I'd had no reason to doubt her. Not like Father Christmas – I'd thought there was something funny about him from the start.

"So don't you believe in God, Granga? Is that why you don't go to church?"

Granga pushed a hand into his trouser pocket and pulled out a big white handkerchief, which he used to mop his brow.

"I rarely discuss questions of a metaphysical nature before lunch," he told me.

It wasn't a very full answer but I could see it was all I was going to get. If I'd known him for longer than six days I'd have pressed him for more, asked him what *metaphysical* meant, but I hadn't. So I pretended to carry on with my letter to Hannah, which gave me time to think about what had been said. I was becoming used to my own thoughts. I didn't really need other people's answers any more. I could work most things out for myself. And I decided there and then that there was a great deal that my grandfather didn't understand, like how to cook lunch when Maria wasn't there, and where we go when we die. He was lucky I'd come into his life at just the right time. I could see that Granga needed me as much as I needed him and I wouldn't let him down.

"Granga," I said finally, "why don't we go for a walk this afternoon, up that hill in the distance?"

"Good idea, Blue," he agreed, closing his newspaper.

"When you look at it, covered in all those thousands of pine trees, it makes you wonder how the world was first created, doesn't it, Granga?"

I saw a smile in Granga's eyes and I knew I was already making progress.

DEAR HANNAH,
A week has passed since I arrived in Mallorca so I thought you would want to know how I'm getting on. It's sunny here, late into the evening, until the sun disappears behind a forest of pine trees on top of a steep hill. They're not like our pine trees in England – these ones look more lively and friendly, like they've got a lot they want to tell you. Yesterday Granga and I walked up the hill, but we didn't manage to get to the very top because Granga wanted to keep stopping to look back at the view towards the Finca (that's Spanish for Farm). It was as if he'd never walked that way before, which seems unlikely, as he's lived here for so many years. The smell of the pines reminded me of Christmas, which is a funny feeling in the middle of summer. I counted 821 trees as we climbed, but only 500 on our way back because Granga kept talking. He likes talking, although he never says much about himself, which is a pity because I'd like to know more about him. He doesn't ask questions either, like most people do. He probably says the same about me. He's not like a stranger, though. Sometimes his

eyes remind me of my mother's – they're smaller than hers and not as still, and they don't watch me as often as hers did, but they smile like hers, even when he's being serious.

I have a large bedroom with a shiny wooden floor that has a brightly-coloured rug in the middle of it, where my bed is. Underneath the window is a small writing desk and chair where I sit and write my diary every evening. I write it to my mother and father so that they know what I've been up to. They always wanted to know, so I expect they still do.

I have a big creaky wardrobe in the corner of my room where I hang my clothes and line up my shoes underneath, except for the ones Maria takes away to clean. Maria is Granga's housekeeper. She looks old until she smiles, and she makes very good food with lots of colours, which she serves on big thick white plates with a blue pattern on the outside. Usually we eat on the terrace where Granga goes to smoke his cigars in the evening and cigarettes during the day. Maria doesn't like him smoking indoors. She pulls a face then holds her nose and glares at Granga until he disappears. Then when he's gone she looks at me and we both laugh. She only speaks Spanish so I don't understand a lot of what she says, but it doesn't matter that much. She's teaching me some Spanish. So far I can say "Dónde está mi abuelo?" which means: "Where is my grandfather?" I say that quite a lot.

Soon I'm to have a tutor, who'll come to the Finca, then later, when my Spanish is better, I may go to the local school. In the meantime, Granga and I are going

travelling together. You were right – Granga does
like travelling. I don't know whether I do or not as I've
only ever been to Cornwall and Jersey and now
Mallorca. He was meant to be going on his own but I
asked why I couldn't go with him. At first he said, "No,
Blue" (that's what I'm called now – Rufus is too soft).
But after a few days, Maria and I persuaded him to say
yes. It wasn't very hard – we just stopped speaking to
him and as Granga likes speaking, he had to agree in
the end. I'm to pack a small case, as we'll only be away
for a week. He hasn't told me yet where we're going,
but he said I should take a pair of strong walking shoes,
my school tie and a pair of smart trousers.

I was wondering if you could send me a photograph
of my old house so I can put it on my writing desk
under the window.

Love from
Blue

4

IT WAS SPRING WHEN IT had happened, my mother's favourite season, a time, she used to say, for new beginnings and fresh hope and perfectly-created life. I'd been born in the spring, on the fourth of April 1978 – I think that was one of the reasons why she'd liked it so much.

If it hadn't been my twelfth birthday the following day they wouldn't have gone without me – my mother and father. I wouldn't have been left behind at home to finish my homework until they got back.

I knew where they were going. They couldn't keep their plans a secret from me no matter how hard they tried – they should have known that. They were heading for our local department store to buy me a drum kit that I'd admired in the window the day before. It would fit quite easily into the back of their car once the back seats were down.

The following morning my mother would wake me with breakfast in bed, then lead me excitedly downstairs where I would discover my surprise birthday present in the centre of the drawing room, a big blue ribbon probably tied around the drumsticks and perfectly-wrapped gift paper concealing the drums. When I saw it, I'd pretend to be surprised and my mother would believe me, while my father would stand in the background with a knowing smile, then he'd wink at me to tell me that our secret was shared – I'd guessed again, I couldn't help it. I always read my mother's mind.

The drum kit was still intact in the back of the car when they found my parents. It was in the place where I should have been, behind their two front seats. My father was at the steering wheel on the right and my mother belted into the seat only ever occupied by her. Two hundred yards from home when it had happened, just as I was conjugating *amare* in the future perfect tense.

I wished I'd gone with them to choose it. I wished I hadn't insisted on a surprise. I wished I'd kissed them both goodbye before they'd left and told them that it didn't really matter what they bought me, because all I wanted was to share my birthday with them. But I hadn't. And now they were gone. And I never got to tell them how much I loved them. Because another driver was in a hurry to get home.

Hannah's husband Daniel had carried the drum kit into my bedroom. I think they hadn't known what else to do with it. Hannah said it was a miracle it was still intact. But I don't believe in miracles any more. So I never played it, even though it was what I'd wanted. Except for once. I'd picked up a drumstick and hammered the big drum harder and harder until I thought it might break. But it hadn't. I wished it had. But you never get what you want.

5

"**F**OR GOODNESS' SAKE, BLUE, PULL yourself together and be a man!" I bet he'd never spoken that way to my mother.

"I'm not a man," I shouted back at him through my locked bedroom door, "I'm a twelve-year-old boy and my name is Rufus, not Blue."

"Well, boy, I'm leaving for Morocco in fifteen minutes and you can stay behind that damned door if you want to."

He'd never mentioned Morocco before. "You've never mentioned Morocco before."

"A trip's a trip, son, whatever they call it, just like a boy's a boy."

"And I'm not your damned son either!" He needed to be reminded.

"Don't you use that language to me!" He must have been on his knees now because his voice was bellowing through the keyhole. I'd never heard my father shout like that. Someone should have warned me that my grandfather was a maniac.

"Why shouldn't I use that language to you?" I tried to sound defiant, but I was beginning to have my doubts. "I've no one else to use it to. And besides, I only learned the damned language from you!"

There was silence after that, and I feared that Granga had gone to get the shotgun I'd seen in his barn, which he used for shooting poor innocent rabbits.

"Granga?" I said finally. "Have you gone to Morocco?" I just wanted to know where I stood. But Granga made no reply.

It wasn't a sign of weakness that I unlocked my bedroom door. On the contrary, as my father would have explained if he'd been there instead of a maniac of a grandfather, it merely showed a healthy curiosity.

"Fooled you!" Granga's voice echoed across the landing as if he was very pleased with himself indeed. I don't know why – I'd half expected him still to be there. I'd only jumped to give him a laugh, although I hadn't thought he'd find it quite as funny as he did.

"An old army trick," he said finally, wiping tears from his silly old face. "Let them think they've worn you down and you've retreated, then ambush them on their way out. Works every time!"

I hadn't quite seen myself as ambushed until then, especially as I was still in my blue-and-white striped pyjamas, but I suppose he had a point.

"Well?" he said.

"Well what?" I might have been ambushed but he hadn't yet taken me prisoner.

"Are you going to take that miserable damned look off your face and come with me to Morocco or would you rather stay here and be mollycoddled by Maria like a little softie?"

It was an unusual way of putting the choice. I didn't know what to say. It happens like that sometimes, especially when you least want it to. I think that's what made me cry for the first time since I'd been there.

"You're not blubbing, are you?" He was speaking more quietly now and he'd sat down on the floor by the stairs and lit a cigarette. "I called you Blue because you looked like a cheerful little fellow underneath it all. Blue like a cloudless sky on a sunny day, or a deep blue ocean that's steady and strong enough to hold a fleet of ships, not Blue like a melancholy song or a miserable little chap who'll grow up sitting on his own in dark jazz clubs singing into his glass about what might have been."

He was heading downstairs without even a glance in my direction. In minutes he could be on his way to Morocco without me. I wiped away my tears with the back of my hand. I had to say something. "Why do you want to go to Morocco anyway?" I shouted loudly so he couldn't miss me.

"Why do you think, boy?" he replied as he disappeared into the hallway. "For the food of course!"

• • •

It seemed a long way to go for a chicken tagine but Granga said it would be worth it and I believed him. If I'd learnt anything about my grandfather over the past two weeks it was that he loved fine food, and lots of it. Personally, I found Maria's seafood paella good enough for a king, and no matter how tasty an authentic tagine served with currant couscous might be, it didn't seem worth two long drives and a plane flight to enjoy it.

"It's not just a matter of the dish itself," Granga explained as we entered the last lap of our journey in a hire car we'd picked up at the airport in Morocco. "It has to be served in the right environment. Regional food has been created and improved over generations, each one adding some new flavour to the experience."

"I bet Maria would know how to create it just as well," I suggested – I must have been missing the Finca more than I'd realised.

"You're not listening, boy!" he growled, creasing up his forehead into a block of five lines like a stave of music. "Close your eyes and hear the sounds! Inhale the scents around you!" He spoke like he was giving orders to a corporal and I knew not to disobey him. So we both sat silently in our hire car, which Granga had brought to a halt at the side of a dusty narrow lane. To be truthful, which my parents had always told me to be, I could hear very little other than my rumbling stomach, and the only smell except for the diesel was coming from dark-red soil which formed a hilly boundary beside my door.

"I can only smell dirty soil," I said, once I'd tired of keeping my eyes closed and had begun to worry that it might be another of Granga's ambush tricks.

"Aha! You see!"

But I saw nothing, as my eyes hadn't acclimatised to being open again.

"That's clay you're smelling – clay that's been here for thousands of years, clay that creative Moroccan hands form into clay pots in which your delicious tagine will soon be served, clay pots that their mothers and grandmothers have used for decades to feed their families with precisely the right local ingredients. And soon you'll be sitting at a table surrounded by hills made of the very same clay as the bowl you'll be eating from, and tasting the food that these people have perfected over generations. You see, Blue, it's all part of the experience, like a beautifully-created oil painting with layer upon layer of colour and just the right amount of shade. You couldn't cut away part of that canvas and stick it onto another painting without losing something, could you? And that's why you've come to Morocco for your first tagine rather than having it in Mallorca. There are many other culinary dishes for you to enjoy in Mallorca, but sometimes it's important to broaden your aesthetic repertoire."

It sort of made sense, and I was feeling quite excited until he added: "But look out for the snake charmers while you're eating."

We parked the car at the bottom of a steep hill that led to Granga's favourite restaurant. Suddenly we were no longer alone. In seconds, the quiet back street was alive with babbling young Moroccans, all pushing towards us like a rugby scrum on a Saturday afternoon. Somehow they seemed to guess that we were English even though Granga was as dark-skinned as they were, and I had hair so black that I'd been mistaken on holiday in Cornwall for an Italian.

"You want guide?" asked one boy not much older than I. "I show you good restaurant? Bar? Hotel maybe?"

I moved my lips to answer politely, "No thank you – my grandfather knows where he's going." But before I had even got to "No", Granga had taken my arm and was pushing me abruptly up the hill and away from the crowd without a word of a reply.

We hadn't gone far when an older boy tried addressing Granga, in French. I couldn't help being impressed by their language skills. I knew a little French myself from my old school, enough at least to realise that the very same questions were being asked of us in another language.

This time Granga stopped, turned around, walked between me and them, then spoke the following words which I'll never forget: "Pusha noo lipma pik shnil!" I had no idea what the words meant, but they seemed to work – the boys were silenced into an exchange of glances, which amused my grandfather enormously but left me as confused as they appeared to be. Fortunately, we'd reached the door to the restaurant, which was ajar, so Granga ushered me swiftly inside.

"What did you say to those boys?" I asked once we'd been shown to a low circular table in the corner of a large busy room, with orange sofas for chairs. His grin was so wide that I noticed for the first time that he had two back teeth missing on each side.

"I said nothing." He was pleased with himself, I could tell.

"But I heard you," I protested, "and so did they."

"What you heard were words that no tour guides could ever understand no matter how many languages they bombarded us with."

"Then what language was it, Granga?"

"It was the immensely underrated language of gibberish," he replied.

It was the first time I'd laughed so loudly since the day before my birthday when my mother had turned the garden hose on my father and chased him across the lawn with it. I hadn't wanted to be reminded of then, but somehow the act of laughing seemed to bring it back to me and suddenly I'd stopped laughing.

"Not that melancholy Blue again," remarked Granga, "I thought we'd left him behind in favour of the cloudless blue sky."

I tried to look less melancholy and more thoughtful – I'd suspected for a while that thoughtful was the only way to impress Granga. "I was thinking, that was all," I replied, as reflectively as I could.

"Good!" he said. "What about?"

Of course, I should have anticipated that question, but I hadn't. And Granga was waiting. I had to say something.

"About my name, actually," I said. "If I'm to be Blue like cloudless sky, I was wondering if you could explain to me why the sky *is* blue?"

I was thrilled with myself. I couldn't have planned a more thoughtful question if I'd tried for a whole day.

Granga nodded encouragingly: "A very interesting question – it shows an enquiring mind and a keen eye for detail. I can see we're going to get on well together, you and I."

I was so pleased that I nearly fell off my chair. But I didn't say any more – if I had, I might have gone and spoiled all I'd managed to achieve.

"Are you familiar with the Ancient Greeks?" he asked.

I shook my head. "Not yet," I explained, "but Latin is one of my best subjects – that and English."

"Ah! A Classicist! I shall bear that in mind. Let's begin, then, with the Ancient Greek philosophers. Their attitude towards colour was quite different from our own. The words they used that came closest to our *blue* really had more to do with dark and light. Colours for them were more about the *spiritual* than the everyday. They had no concept of measurement of wavelength. Not even *The Philosopher himself* was able to come up with a complete answer to your question."

He must have spotted my frown because he paused then asked, "You do know to whom I refer, don't you, boy?"

I knew it wouldn't take long for me to let him down. "I'm not sure," I muttered. "It could be one of many."

He smiled and applauded. "Bravo – a cunning response that speaks volumes about your intellect! Only a fool judges a fellow's intelligence solely on the basis of *what* he knows, without assessing his ability to conceal what he does *not*. *The Philosopher* is a description used, amongst others, by the revered thirteenth-century Italian philosopher and theologian Saint Thomas Aquinas, to refer to the Greek you may know as *Aristotle*, one of the greatest thinkers ever to have set foot on our planet."

"Oh, him," I replied, "didn't he come after Socrates and Plato?"

"Excellent answer," he said, beaming at me this time – I didn't dare tell him that I only knew that much because my father had told me to remember their order by thinking of the word "SPA".

"Aristotle was one of the first to ask about the sky's colour – although it may have been one of his students who attempted an answer. What's fascinating is that he was able to realise how extremely important a question this was – just as you have done too. Remind me to show you Aristotle's work *On Colours* some time when we're back home."

I was happy with that – not the bit about Aristotle, although I enjoyed that too, but Granga saying "back home" without even hesitating.

"Aristotle started the ball rolling with a consideration

about the sky appearing dark blue when denser rays are seen through colourless air in a deep mass. This led to more reflection about colour being an interaction between the air and something else such as the darkness of space lying beyond it."

It had worked. I'd impressed him with my question. He thought I was up to his answer. He was figuring out the next part of it in his head. As I waited to hear it, I began to think I might have made a mistake – I wouldn't understand his explanation, he'd think I was stupid, he'd stop sharing his thoughts with me. But it was too late. Granga was ready to go on:

"*Scientists* would probably answer your question by quoting what has become known as *Rayleigh Scattering*, named after the nineteenth-century physicist Lord Rayleigh. They would tell you that blue travels as shorter, smaller waves, which make it scatter more than longer ones such as red. They would coat their explanation with technical details about this shortness of the colour blue's wavelength that makes it scatter more. They would bombard you with descriptions of how light collides with particles that digest it, then spit it out again, how the process changes the light and how it comes out at a different angle. They would talk of the atmosphere being made up of various gases – nitrogen and oxygen mostly – which in turn are made up of molecules, how light hits these molecules time and again and by doing so turns them a blue colour, over and over and over, each time more and more blue, until they reach you as you stand looking up at the sky with a wonderful impression of blue in your eyes. They might even go so far as to explain that the sky isn't really blue at all, but violet – a colour that our human eye is unable to pick up because our eyes are more sensitive to blue. They might end by telling you that Einstein confirmed the theory with findings of his own . . . but would this answer your question? I think not."

It seemed like a pretty full explanation to me, as far as I could understand it, but I didn't say so because I suspected that Granga hadn't finished.

"Ever heard of the word *explanandum*, boy?"

I shook my head.

"A philosophical term – Latin for *the thing to be explained*."

I wished I'd taken a guess – I knew it had something to do with explaining.

"You see, Blue, I don't give a toss for the scientist's explanation. To me, an explanation of that kind is like reading the recipe ingredients in the tagine you're about to be served, but not *tasting* it, not *savouring* that explanandum, that *thing to be explained*. When I gaze up at the blue sky, it matters not to me how many thousands of times light has bumped into molecules like a sleepwalker at night, heading off at right angles from where it began, helter-skeltering around the universe until it lands, BANG, in the middle of our eyeballs."

"Then what's *your* answer?" I asked him – when I was going to be called Blue, it was important that I knew.

He smiled at me and I guessed correctly that we'd reached the part of his answer that he *savoured* the most.

"*My* blue sky is blue because it is *meant to be that way*. It is the blue that the late Mallorcan artist Miró described, in his painting of that colour, as *This is the colour of my dreams*. It is the blue that symbolised, for him, a spiritual dimension, a transcendent symbol of unreality. It is the blue that the famous Expressionist artist Kandinsky described as *the deeper the blue becomes, the more strongly it calls man towards the infinite.* It is a typically heavenly colour. Atomic theory may be beautiful in itself, yes, but the *essence* of blue for me, its purpose in the heavens, its influence on artists, poets, writers, philosophers, must surely be beyond reduction to something we might be able to create for ourselves one day in a science laboratory or a jam jar. So, Blue, you can choose for yourself which manner of explanation you prefer. There are many highly-accomplished scientists, past and present, for whom their subject is a fascinating one. Indeed, *The Philosopher himself* is included in that category, as you've already heard, and I wouldn't have a word spoken against *him*."

He paused for a moment as if he was thinking about bringing the subject to an end, before saying:

"Blue is your name now, after a colour that has intrigued and mystified for hundreds of years – Da Vinci, Giotto, Van Gogh, Kandinsky, Miró, Rayleigh, Aristotle, to name but a few. Quite a lot for a boy to live up to, but I have every faith in you."

When he finished speaking, I felt as if I'd been swimming in the waves of a stormy sea that had grown calmer as I'd reached the shore. Part of me wanted to get back in, but the other part longed for a big plate of chicken tagine to comfort me.

I was about to thank Granga for his explanation when an important-looking waiter in a black suit came up to our table. I was glad Granga had made me wear my school tie.

"Ah, Mr. Horatio! How good to see you again! It has been too long."

Horatio? My grandfather was called Horatio? He'd only

ever been described as Granga to me. Granga Hennessy, my mother's maiden name.

"I didn't know your first name was Horatio," I whispered.

"You didn't?" he replied. "Then it's about time you did."

He turned towards the waiter. "A name is a crucial aspect of our character, don't you think? It is the paint that defines the portrait. My parents possessed the good sense to name me after the Latin poet Horace, *Quintus Horatius Flaccus*, born in sixty-five B.C. in the province of Apulia, near the heel of Italy – he of *Carpe Diem* repute."

This last reference seemed to please the waiter a lot, who replied loudly, with dramatic hand movements that attracted too much attention: "Yes, yes, of course! *Seize the Day!* Wonderful! *Carpe Diem!*"

Of course, I knew that this was the translation too, and I'd heard of Horace at school, but I didn't boast like they did.

"Horace was considered by many," Granga went on, "to be one of the greatest poets ever to have set foot on this barbaric Earth of ours." He turned to me: "Some might say that a boy given a name in honour of Horace has even more to live up to than a boy named Blue."

"You were well named, Mr. Horatio," declared the waiter. "Your parents chose exactly the right paint for your portrait."

Then he turned to me, as if he had only just noticed I was there, which perhaps he had. "And who is this young man?"

"May I introduce you to my grandson, Blue Ellerton." It was the first time he'd described me as his grandson. I liked it. It made me feel important. I smiled and it was as if a pale-blue sky had come out from behind the clouds, scattering light.

"Blue," said the man as he shook my hand, "you are extremely fortunate to have such a fascinating and unique gentleman for your grandfather." Of course he was right, but I wished I'd worked it out for myself. Maybe I had, without realising.

"And how long will you be staying in Morocco this time?" He seemed to be addressing me and I was about to answer "a week" when Granga replied, "We're leaving tomorrow."

"Then I hope you enjoy your short stay here," replied the man whom Granga described as the Maître d' and who now knew as much about our travel plans as I did.

"You said we were coming for a week!" I protested once the waiter had gone, fearful that my fascinating and unique grandfather had already grown tired of travelling with his melancholy grandson, who hadn't even heard of *The Philosopher* or *Rayleigh Scattering*.

"No, I didn't. Learn to listen more carefully, boy."

"I'm very good at listening," I argued. "My father always told me I was the best listener he had ever known, so don't you tell *me* to learn to listen! I know what you said, that we were coming away for a week, and that's that."

I hadn't meant to raise my voice – I didn't even know I had until a couple at the next table turned to stare at us. But that didn't matter to me. I'd wanted to impress my grandfather. I'd wanted him to see me as his protégé, someone quick to learn, intelligent . . . a Classicist. But instead of that, I'd turned into a dull boy to be taken straight back to Mallorca, deposited like my mother's unwanted clothes at a charity shop, our holiday cut short and all because of my ignorance.

"Keep your damned voice down!" Granga whispered into

a big white napkin. "I said we were travelling for a week and so we are. We're leaving for France tomorrow morning."

I sat without speaking another word after that. When my chicken tagine arrived, I barely noticed. I ate it without even tasting all those flavours I'd been so looking forward to. Granga was right, that's what a bad temper does to a boy.

6

W E WERE TO SPEND THE night in a one-bedroom apartment above the restaurant, which was fortunate because I'd eaten so much I couldn't have walked any further. It surprised me to find that Granga had brought his own key with him from Mallorca, but surprise didn't last long with Granga.

"You're frowning, Blue," he said as he opened the apartment door whilst stamping out his cigarette. "Have you never seen a bachelor pad before?"

I hadn't thought of Granga as a bachelor. I knew he'd been married to my grandmother, of course, but I didn't remember hearing anything about her, except that she was no longer alive. There were no photographs of her in my mother's album that she'd kept under her bed – all of them were of Granga. I should have asked more questions while I still had the chance. But I'd had everything I'd wanted of a family in my mother and father so I hadn't bothered.

We entered a white-walled apartment with a multi-coloured floor that looked like a jigsaw puzzle made of pieces of broken glass. The sitting room smelt damp, like it had been empty for a long time. There were two white sofas facing each other on either side of a fireplace with ashes in it. On a small wooden table beside one of the sofas I noticed some sheets of paper with untidy writing and crossing out all over them that I assumed was Granga's.

"You take the bedroom," Granga ordered, "and I'll make up the sofa bed in here."

Mine was a comfortable bed with a big white duvet. It almost filled the whole room. Above it there were two book-shelves crammed with books whose foreign titles I didn't understand. I'd never slept under books before and I worried that one might fall on my head while I was asleep. Not that they were heavy books – most of them were paperbacks. But there was a particularly large one with a cream leather cover, right in the middle of the lower shelf directly above where my head had to go. I couldn't take a chance like that. I owed it to my parents and Granga to carry on the family name. My head had to be safe at all costs, especially in a foreign country when I hadn't even brushed my teeth or washed my face.

I stood cautiously on the bed and lifted down the large book that threatened my safety. I hadn't intended to read it. I hadn't imagined it would be in a language I would under-stand. But it was. And by an author whose name was familiar to me. Its gold-lettered title read *Verses of a Solitary Fellow*. The author was Horatio R. Hennessy.

I opened the book at the first page. Five words marked the Dedication: *To Sophia, my beloved wife*.

Underneath the Dedication, there was a verse in Latin by Horace from The Odes, Book 2.16:

> laetus in praesens animus quod ultra est
> oderit curare et amara lento

temperet risu. nihil est ab omni
parte beatum.

Horatio R. Hennessy's English translation of his namesake's
Latin verse was printed beside it:

Bless'd is the heart that lives for now; what lies beyond
it does not care to know, and softens misery
with a tender smile. There can be no such thing
as untainted joy.

I turned the page. Then, with the forefinger of my right
hand, I scanned the first lines of Granga's poems, all listed
under the heading CONTENTS. Which poem should I
choose to read first? I couldn't decide.

I noticed that about a quarter of the way through the
book someone had placed a burgundy silk bookmark. I
opened it there as if I was opening a treasure chest. The thick
off-white pages felt as if they hadn't been opened for a long
time. I found myself staring at a poem entitled "Flesh on
Flesh". Dare I read it? Would it be an intrusion? What would
my mother think I should do?

Flesh on flesh
Warm
A happy memory.
Flesh on flesh
Soothing,
Sheer ecstasy.
Flesh on flesh
Bleeding

A punctured artery.
Flesh on flesh
Holding
The pain away.
Flesh on flesh
Hearing
A comrade die.
Flesh on flesh
Hoping
He sees the sky.
Flesh on flesh
Moving
His eyelids down.
Flesh on flesh
Smoothing
Away his frown.
Flesh on flesh
Waiting
'Til break of day.
Flesh on flesh
Orders
You cannot stay.
Flesh on flesh
Tears
As you walk away.
Flesh on flesh.
Flesh on flesh.

My grandfather was a proper poet, and not just any old poet – Granga was a feeling, suffering, knowing poet. I couldn't wait to turn the page and read the next:

No more combat
No more injury
No more orders
In the name of liberty.
I have suffered
I have conquered
I have let men
Lose their destiny.
All for medals
All for heroes
All for men who
Call it unity.
What of mercy
What of empathy
What of seeking out humanity
What of waking in the night
And fearing your foes may be right
And wondering if they fear it too
Or is it just that you are you
And man is man and seeks to fight
And battles seem like pure delight?
I'll not give up
I'll not let go
Of principles I've sought to grow.
For in the end
They're all we are
Save for the pain
Of battle's scar.

I longed to discover each poem that my grandfather had
created, to turn each page and know him more and more . . .

was I too sounding like a poet? Could my Granga make something of a poet out of me? After all, his blood was my blood, wasn't it? I was a part of what he was and is and will be, even when he'd gone – gone like his daughter, my mother, gone like my father, gone like his wife. But we were living in the now, Granga and I, just like Horace had described, *softening misery with a tender smile*. We would carry on what the others had left behind . . . wouldn't we?

I had to read just one more poem before I turned off the light:

Heartbeat
Constant
Like a drum
Faster
In the height of pain
Pulsing
Through a throbbing vein
Praying
That the pain will ease
Hoping
That there's no disease.

Heartbeat
Pounding
Like a drum
Telling you no lie
Soothing
Like a lover's sigh
Never knowing
When or why

Surging
With the weight of hope
Wondering
If the will can cope.

Heartbeat
Warning
Like a drum
Danger
That we can't avoid
Pause
And you will be destroyed
Less
And life will be devoid.

Heartbeat
Pain and joy in one
Heartbeat
Hear it or you're gone
Heartbeat
Sounding like a song
Heartbeat
Never tells us wrong
Heartbeat.

I closed the book and placed it carefully beside me under the duvet, then switched off the light. "Did you hear that poem? Are you still here with us?" I whispered to my parents. "Pain and joy in one, like a heartbeat, constant, pounding, warning like a drum – your very last present for me. We're listening, Granga and I, to the heartbeat. I think I'm starting to hear."

7

"**I**S IT ALRIGHT IF I put my walking boots in your case, Granga?"

As he was distracted by a black coffee and digestive biscuit, I thought it a good time to ask.

"Why can't they stay in your own case, Blue?" He wasn't as easily distracted as I'd hoped.

"It feels a bit heavy, that's all."

"Then put the wretched boots on!"

If he asked to look in my case, all would be lost. So I put on my big black leather walking boots and packed my trainers on top of Granga's book of verses when he wasn't looking – upside down, of course. I didn't want the cover to get dirty.

"Where in France are we going anyway?" I'd only just realised he hadn't told me.

"Didn't I tell you?" he frowned.

"No, or I wouldn't be asking." Just because he was a famous poet that didn't mean I'd be star-struck.

"We're flying to the South of France – *Nice* to be precise. Heard of Nice, Blue?"

I couldn't say that I had because I hadn't, but I didn't want Granga to think I was ignorant, so I replied: "My mother may have mentioned it." Which was true – she may have done and I'd forgotten. I hadn't expected Granga to stare at me though, as if I'd just said something very important.

"What was it you just said?"

That really startled me. I racked my brains to remember the exact words I'd just used, hoping that I hadn't said more than I'd meant to. "Only that my mother might have mentioned Nice to me, that's all."

"And what precisely might she have said?"

It was almost as if I'd made him cross, but I had no idea why. I wished I hadn't said it, especially as it might not even have been true. But I had, so it was too late. Granga's stare was exhausting me and the Moroccan sun was beginning to make me feel too warm, and I'd noticed that the shoelaces of my left walking boot were undone.

"There's no point in trying to distract me with shoelaces, young man." He was on his knees doing up my shoelaces himself. "Grace mentioned Nice, you say?" He sounded softer this time, as if he felt he'd spoken too harshly to me.

"She may have done," I whispered, "I can't remember."

Now that I spoke the truth more clearly, he didn't believe me. Poets must be strange like that, always looking for hidden meanings. Perhaps I wasn't cut out to be a poet after all.

"Let's leave it at that, shall we?" he said as he tied a second knot in my shoelaces. But I knew he wasn't talking about the shoelaces.

The car was by the side of the road where we'd left it, and with all the tyres still in place, thank God, as Granga said. It surprised me that for someone who didn't believe in

God he thanked Him quite a lot, but it wasn't the right time to mention it.

Before long, we'd reached the airport. I was getting used to planes by now, even though I'd only been on two. The trick was to pretend you were at a fairground with your father beside you, patting you on the back like a man as they strapped you in to the big dipper, your mother on the ground waving at you as she blew you kisses which you hoped the other boys hadn't noticed.

The part I liked least about being on the plane was the stewardesses. They talked to you like you were a child through big toothy grins and offered you sweets, which I'd never enjoyed anyway, and gave Granga encouraging looks as if he needed them. I could tell he didn't like them either by the way he sighed as they walked away and then pretended to be asleep when they came back.

"Have they gone?" he asked me with his eyes tight shut.

"Yes," I replied.

"Thank God for that."

"I've noticed that for someone who isn't religious, you thank God for a lot of things that happen, Granga." Now that we were in the air and closer to Him it seemed like the right moment to raise the subject.

"Figure of speech, boy, that's all."

I couldn't believe that he would speak so disrespectfully, especially with pure white clouds floating past our window.

"Don't you think you should be more cautious?" I asked – there was no point in holding my tongue when my grandfather's soul was at stake.

"I've said it for years and I've come to no harm," he said with a laugh, which really worried me.

"Have you never believed in God?" I wasn't going to be put off by laughter. Granga looked sombrely at me as if he'd realised suddenly that there was no escape from me without having to walk past a stewardess.

"I did once upon a time, when I was young and deluded and believed in miracles and happy endings."

"You speak like a poet sometimes." I couldn't help myself. Part of me hoped he would say, "That's because I am" and then I could have told him that I had his leather-bound published book of verses in my travelling case underneath my trainers and I wouldn't have felt so guilty about it. But he didn't. Instead he replied:

"Poets are fools."

Then he reached for a newspaper that was on the floor and I knew to ask no more.

• • •

My feet felt particularly hot in their walking boots in Nice Airport. I noticed other boys in more suitable footwear staring down at mine as if I was an astronaut. I wondered whether to take them off and go barefoot but then I'd have had to carry them and that would have been much worse – someone might have stopped and searched me at Customs in case I was trying to smuggle something inside them into their country, like an English plant or a hamster.

We weren't hiring a car this time, which was a relief as Granga wasn't the safest of drivers. Not that that meant anything – usually it was the good driver who lost his life and the bad one who got away without even a cut and went home to his family while the good driver lay dead with his wife at his side and a drum kit in the back of his car for his son's birthday, only his son never played it.

Our French taxi driver drove as fast as Granga up a road that was steep and narrow like the road to our home in Mallorca. Home. I'd only ever had one of those before. And now I had another.

I should have said a proper goodbye to the other home in England. I should have gone into every room and touched the walls that my parents had painted while I held their tins of paint and told them which bits they'd missed. I should have run around the garden pretending that I was chasing my father once more, then sat on my swing and pictured my mother pushing me higher and higher. I should have explained to my bike that I couldn't take it with me because where I was going it was too steep and bumpy and they drove on the wrong side of the road. I should have rung my best friend, John Thompson, and explained why I wouldn't be able to help him with his homework any more.

"Granga, when we get to the hotel may I make a telephone call?"

He seemed surprised, as if he'd assumed that everyone I'd have wanted to phone was dead.

"Is it a local call?"

Who on Earth did he think I'd be ringing in a country I'd never been to before? "No, of course not!" I snapped, studying his expression to see if he was joking. He had lots of expressions but I couldn't understand all of them. This one I'd never seen before. It made his eyes seem smaller, as if a fierce wind was blowing into them and causing his eyelids to tighten.

"Maria wouldn't answer the telephone if that's what you're up to," he said, still staring suspiciously at me. "She thinks the telephone is a flat iron."

"If you must know," I replied, "I want to telephone a friend of mine in England."

"You didn't tell me you had a friend." Granga could be so clumsy at times.

"I have several actually." I could feel my cheeks reddening as I exaggerated unconvincingly.

"Not a good sign," he said in a whisper. "Never trust a fellow with too many friends, I say."

"Why ever not?" I asked, wondering if this was the right time to confess that in truth I had only three – and two of those – Piers and Richard Jackson, the twins, were only friends because my mother knew theirs so the family came over when my parents held one of their parties and Piers, Richard and I had our own pyjama parties upstairs.

But John Thompson was a proper friend, one I'd chosen all by myself and I didn't care what anyone else thought about him. None of the others understood John Thompson as I did. They all thought he was stupid just because he came bottom in every exam except Art. And there was nothing wrong with being good at Art. Art wasn't only for girls, as Marcus Finnegan had stupidly suggested when John Thompson's name had been read out first. Most great artists were male, and no one ever laughed at Van Gogh or Picasso – or if they did, it was just because they didn't understand them. In my opinion, John Thompson was at least as good at painting as Van Gogh or Picasso anyway. He could paint anything you wanted, and with such detail you'd think you were looking at a photograph, only it was more beautiful. He had a way of picking out what it was he wanted you to notice most, but then when you came back to study it again, you'd notice something else you hadn't seen before.

Once he painted a picture especially for me. It was a birthday present because he'd forgotten it was my birthday until I told him – I knew he would. Then he felt so unhappy about having forgotten it that he spent all month on a painting and handed it to me. It was of lavender fields with a small house in the centre the colour of sand with birds flying all around it as if they'd found somewhere very special. When he gave it to me I'd never seen lavender fields and I wondered if perhaps John Thompson had used the wrong colour. But when I took it home my mother explained that John Thompson had painted a picture for me of Provence, where lavender grows in fields and houses are the colour of sand. And now here I was in Provence with my Granga, surrounded by lavender fields and wishing I'd said goodbye to John Thompson and brought his painting with me.

"What's wrong with having several friends, Granga?" I asked again.

"If a fellow has too many friends, it means he doesn't speak his mind enough, or if he does, he plans too hard what he wants to say. And I don't trust a fellow like that."

I hadn't thought of fellows that way before, but I could see that Granga knew a lot more about them than I did. That was probably why he was a published poet – he knew how to observe and think about what he saw. I wished I could be more like Granga, but it wasn't easy knowing what you were supposed to be looking for.

"Come to think of it," I said after a suitably convincing pause, "I don't have very many friends at all."

"Good man," said Granga. Then he pulled the brim of his hat down over his eyes and fell asleep.

8

THE DRIVE LEADING TO OUR hotel was as long as the lane my parents and I used to live in. On either side, a symmetrical line of trees stood like tall, regimental soldiers on parade, there to herald our arrival. I was pleased with such a poetic description and wondered if I should say it aloud to Granga, but he was too busy rearranging his blazer and straightening his tie.

Our hotel was the colour of the building in John Thompson's picture, only much bigger. I counted eight windows across the first floor, each with a set of pale-blue-painted shutters pinned open to let in the bright sunshine.

I wasn't surprised to find that all the staff seemed to know my grandfather. It was obvious that he'd been here many times before.

"Follow me, Blue," he announced as we entered the hotel's massive entrance hall and walked across a shiny-white marble floor in which you could see your reflection.

He led me up an impressive staircase at the back of the hall to the first floor and opened a pair of double doors onto the largest bedroom I had ever seen. It had three of the eight windows I'd counted from outside, and the bed was big enough for a family of six. A beautiful blue-and-gold eiderdown matched the long heavy curtains identically, and the walls were covered in blue-and-white striped wallpaper that felt soft to touch. All the furniture was antique. Some of it reminded me of ours at home – in England not Mallorca. My mother loved to collect antique furniture. It suited our old house with its high ceilings and thick walls and creaky floorboards. But this furniture looked more expensive than ours, with lots of gold paint and carved wood – there was even marble on top of the matching bedside tables. I almost felt as if the bed was too good to sleep in, that it needed a Sleeping Beauty to fall asleep and wake up to a handsome prince, not a twelve-year-old schoolboy who'd lost his parents and lived with his grandfather and whose walking boots were making his feet wet.

"D'you like it?" roared Granga, throwing his hat onto the yellow velvet seat of a small chair in front of a writing desk that looked as if it might belong to royalty.

"It's like a fairytale," I whispered, not knowing where to put myself.

"I'll be in the room next door." Then he was gone and I was alone, just me and my small suitcase in the centre of a palace.

I tiptoed cautiously to the corner of the bed, where I sat down to remove my boots. The bed creaked like it was saying "hello" to me, or "go away", I wasn't sure which. It wasn't fair of Granga to leave me here like this. He should have known I'd be nervous.

I took off my school tie, which Granga had told me to wear, and undid the top two buttons of my shirt. I felt better once I'd done that. It was the sort of thing John Thompson would have done in a situation like this.

John Thompson! I'd forgotten all about my old friend again. Hadn't I asked Granga if I might phone him? It was the perfect opportunity, but where would I find the telephone?

I searched the room from the corner of my bed until I saw it – surprisingly modern it was – on the writing desk. I threw Granga's hat onto the bed and sat down on the chair. It was surprisingly comfortable. It made me feel like a writer to be sitting on it, a poet even. I searched the desk for paper and a pen to write down the thoughts I intended to share with John Thompson. I didn't want to forget anything – there was so very much to tell him. It would have to be clear and precise so that he understood it.

I hoped one of his parents wouldn't answer – they always called me "love" rather than Rufus, which made me think that they couldn't be bothered to remember my name. I wondered about introducing myself as "Blue" then waiting to see how long it took John Thompson to realise it was me. No. Too confusing all round. I'd stick to Rufus.

I looked up the code for England in a booklet by the telephone and dialled the number I'd only ever dialled from home. The tone seemed unfamiliar. I wondered how it sounded at the other end.

"Hello." It was John Thompson himself.

"Good afternoon, John Thompson!"

"Rufus – is that you?"

"Not exactly – I'm called Blue now." I put a tick against the word *name* on the list of things to tell him.

"It suits you better than Rufus."

"That's what Granga said too."

"Who's Granga?"

"My grandfather, of course."

"Then why don't you just call him that?"

"Because my mother always called him my Granga, that's why." I wished I hadn't mentioned his name.

There was silence after that. I consulted my list but felt suddenly that *chicken tagine in a Moroccan restaurant* might seem a bit boring to John Thompson.

"I'm in the South of France." He'd like that. Otherwise he wouldn't have taken so long to paint it.

"Where's that?"

"In Europe – next to Spain. It's where you painted – with the lavender fields – you remember – for my birthday."

"I made that up."

I should have guessed. What experience could John Thompson have had of the South of France?

"Perhaps you saw it in a photograph," I suggested.

"Nah, in my head," was John Thompson's reply. I knew not to disagree.

I crumpled up my list of topics and threw it in a waste-paper basket beside me. "I wanted to say goodbye properly."

"Goodbye."

"No – wait! Don't hang up! I meant I wished I'd said goodbye before I left England."

"When're you coming back then?"

It had never once crossed my mind that I might return. It was as if England was a stamp album and I'd reached the end, positioned my last stamp and closed the book ready to start a new Volume Two. "I'm not sure yet," I said, partly to reassure John Thompson.

"You're not coming back, are you?"

I couldn't hide anything from him. He seemed to read

my mind with his funny little brown eyes that darted around in their sockets like torches in the dark.

"If I don't go back, will you come and stay with me?" It wasn't on my list, but I had to know.

"In the South of France?"

"No. In Mallorca."

"You said you were in the South of France, where the fields are lavender."

"I'm only on holiday here. I live in Mallorca. It's a Spanish island. We live in a finca. It's big and made of sandstone with green shutters on every window. You could do a painting of it. It's called *Finca Vieja* because that's the Spanish for *Old Farmhouse* and that's what it is. We're going back there at the end of the week."

"How will I find you in Mallorca? Is it big like school?"

"Even bigger." John Thompson always managed to make me laugh.

"Then you'll have to look out for me. Mallorca, you say. What colour are the fields there?"

I had to stop and think about it for a moment. John Thompson would have known straight away if he'd been staying there, and he'd have been able to paint them too. "Some of them are red with thousands of poppies growing in them, others are green and filled to bursting with trees covered in olives. Then, way up in the mountains in the north, near where we live, there are forests of green pine trees that smell like Christmas. And the soil is reddish brown in places where it shines through patchy grass from underneath it."

"I'll be there next week."

Then he hung up. I continued to hold the receiver against my left ear as if I thought he would come back. I knew he wouldn't. Yet there was so much more I'd wanted to say.

As I replaced the receiver I suddenly felt guilty. A son who'd lost both his parents and hadn't even mentioned them to his best friend – what sort of a son was that? I'd talked about Granga but I hadn't said a word about my mother or father – not that I missed them, not that I was unhappy without them, I hadn't even asked if he'd heard about what had happened to them.

I closed my eyes tight shut to stop myself from crying then opened them again. I don't know what I expected to see. I couldn't say what was in my mind. But I wouldn't have guessed in a million years what I saw in front of me, there on the desk, slightly hidden behind a lamp, but clear enough for me to see, now that it wanted me to see it.

I picked it up and held it in my hands. Then I drew it to my mouth and kissed it over and over again. Then I put it back in its place on the desk and studied it from every angle, from every part of the room. Then I returned to the desk and picked it up again. Because that was what it wanted me to do. Because it followed me everywhere I went. Always had. Always would. It was a photograph of my mother.

• • •

My grandfather's room was smaller than mine but just as beautiful. He was lying on his bed reading a French book when I walked in. I expected him to be alarmed by the way I barged into his room without even knocking. I should have known not to expect anything about Granga.

"What's it doing here?" I shouted. "What haven't you told me? Why don't you tell me anything about yourself?

Why haven't you said you were a poet? Why is my mother's photograph in a bedroom in a French hotel?"

Horatio Hennessy closed his book and stood up. I hadn't really noticed how tall he was before. As he walked towards me I wished I hadn't asked him so many questions all at once. One would have done – the last one. So I repeated it just to let him know that that was the most important one. When he reached me, he placed a hand on my left shoulder and spoke the following words, which I'm sure no one would blame me for misunderstanding:

"My life, my flesh, my eyes,
Your mother's nose –
Will I ever see your little face again?
God only knows."

Granga was crying. I didn't know what to do. If I went back to my room, he would think I was rude and he might even blame my parents for that. Perhaps he'd feel better, comforted, if I joined in and cried too? It was what I felt like doing. But that didn't seem right either. And Hannah had told me to be brave like my father. I had to speak, say something to my grandfather, anything.

"Why mightn't you see my little face again? What do you mean?"

Granga stopped crying and looked at me as if he'd forgotten I was there.

"You're quite right, Blue. I am a poet. Or I was once upon a time. I don't know how you found out. That was one of my poems you've just heard. Written many years ago, before you were even born."

I shouldn't have assumed it was about me – what would Granga think of me now? "Then who was it about?"

"It was written for your mother, for Grace, when she was about your age – how old are you, boy?"

"Twelve."

"Sometimes I forget you're so young," he said. "The photograph in your room – I knew you would see it – I wanted you to. But it's not your mother."

Could it be that my grandfather was going senile? He'd asked my age but I had no idea of his. There was no doubt that the photograph was of my mother. Did he think I wouldn't recognise my own mother? "What are you saying, Granga?"

"The woman in the photograph was my wife, Sophia, your grandmother, and this was once our home. Your mother was born here, in the very room I gave you. Symmetry, you see, appeals to poets – the circularity of events, beginnings in ends, ends in beginnings."

"But why do the owners of the hotel still keep your wife's photograph?"

"Because, you little fool, I am the owner of the hotel and that photograph will not leave here as long as I draw breath."

9

MY MOTHER HAD BEEN BORN in France and I hadn't even known. What was more, she looked so like her mother that not even her own son could tell them apart. And on top of that, my grandfather owned a hotel like a palace in the South of France. How much I had to tell John Thompson when he arrived!

We were treated like royalty at dinner, which was to be expected when your grandfather owned a hotel like a palace and his initials were HRH. It was a very formal restaurant, much grander than the one in Morocco. A waiter in a black suit showed us to a table in the corner of the room, covered with a white tablecloth and heavy silver cutlery. We passed a dozen tables and two hanging chandeliers on our way there. By the time the waiter drew back a shiny wooden armchair for me to sit on, I was feeling dizzy. If I'd known the floor of the restaurant would be made of white marble like the entrance hall, I'd have polished my shoes before I'd left my room, like Granga had done.

We'd only just sat down when the waiter took my napkin from its place in front of me on the table and swept it across my slightly trembling knees. Then he handed me a large menu handwritten in French, a lot of which I couldn't understand. I left it to Granga to choose for me. He was used to menus like this. I was more concerned not to knock over one of the giant wine glasses with it.

I learnt from Granga that the flavours in French food were "subtler on the palate" than the spices we'd enjoyed in Morocco. Granga could pick out all the herbs in our main course and knew every other ingredient too. Our beef was cooked in a "red wine and truffle reduction", but truffle wasn't made of chocolate like I was used to – it was a kind of fungus that was a very expensive delicacy.

Granga had walked with me round the grounds before dinner and insisted that I inhale the aromas of Provence so that I would remember them while I was eating, and I was confident that I could pick out some of the herbs in our food that we'd inhaled earlier.

I'd never thought of food this way before, even though my mother had been a fantastic cook and I'd always enjoyed eating, we all had. But, until Granga explained it, I'd never thought that whatever we eat or drink or smell or see or hear or touch all become a part of us, and so it is "damned important that we make the right choices out of respect for our bodies and our minds".

Of course, my choices weren't actually mine, they were Granga's, but they felt like mine all the same, especially when our desserts arrived and I recognised at once a big apple tart and vanilla ice cream. At least, I thought I recognised what I was eating until Granga told me that it wasn't apple at all, but pear – "pear tarte tatin" he called it – and the flavour of the ice cream was actually cinnamon. Apparently I should have recognised the cinnamon because I'd already tasted it in my Moroccan tagine, only it was subtler in the ice cream so I was forgiven this time for having missed it.

After dinner we "retired" to the library for Cognac and a cigar, except that I had sparkling mineral water and a paper straw. I liked this room more than the dining room. It was quieter and less bright and I didn't feel so out of place and stared at. There was only one couple in the library apart from us, and they were far too interested in each other to notice me.

Each wall was covered from floor to ceiling with books, many of them very old ones, others quite new. I had always been interested in books, even ones I couldn't understand. It was the feel of them I enjoyed, and the excitement of opening one and discovering its contents like the mind of a new friend.

"I like a man who enjoys a good book," remarked Granga from a cream-and-gold striped sofa under a window where he'd settled himself with his Cognac and cigar. "It shows an enquiring mind."

I grabbed the opportunity I'd been waiting for and asked: "What sort of book is your favourite, is it poetry?"

He didn't answer straight away, but swirled the Cognac round his glass in circular movements, then inhaled it, before tasting his first mouthful contentedly. He stared into the glass as if a secret was hidden there.

"Poetry is a highly underrated means of expression," he remarked finally. "Some might agree with Aristotle when he said in *On Poetics* that poetry demands a man with a special gift for it, or else one with a touch of madness in him."

I waited for him to go on, to expand on a subject so close to his heart, but he appeared to have no more to say. But I did.

"Isn't it easier to miss the point in poetry, though, than in a novel?"

He looked over at me where I was stooping beside a lower bookshelf. I was pleased with that. It meant I had interested him more than his Cognac and cigar for a moment. So I carried on: "I mean, isn't poetry so personal to the poet that others might not understand what he's feeling?" I had in mind the poem he'd recited to me earlier about my mother, which I'd assumed mistakenly to be about me.

"Therein lies its beauty," Granga answered. I could tell there was more this time. "Think of the written word as food and you'll understand. Many novels – not all, mind you – hit the palate at once like the spices in a curry, or a tagine – remember how that felt?"

I nodded.

"But poetry, good poetry, possesses the subtlety of the flavours we experienced this evening: delicate herbs, intense reductions, sharp contrasts. The words of poetry must be held longer, savoured, in order to enjoy them. And they leave an *aftertaste* once they've been digested. Whereas, with some novels – too many, I fear – one loud burp and they're gone, if you're not left with God-awful indigestion, that is."

He was enjoying himself now. I knew from the way he was kicking the air with the foot of his crossed leg. "Or gout – even worse. Know all about that. Overindulgence. Too many damned adjectives, and that's the price you pay."

I liked it when Granga talked this way and I didn't want him to stop. So I dared not move from my stooping position beside the bookcase for fear of distracting him. How my legs ached! I began to grow anxious that they would become so stiff that I would have to walk to my chair in a crouch.

"You ever written a poem, Blue?" It was my chance to stand up before the damage was done.

"Not a proper poem. Only childish ones when I was younger."

"Would you like to write a proper poem?"

I hadn't meant the conversation to be about me. I'd wanted to find out more about him. "Could you teach me, Granga?" I was sure it was what he had in mind. Why else would he have taken a pen from his inside pocket and be picking up a piece of hotel writing paper from the coffee table?

"To be a true poet, you must have something to say. Do *you* have something to say, boy?" He was searching my face for a sign of something – but did I have it? I feared not.

"What sort of thing are you meaning?" I whispered, afraid of being overheard by the couple at the other side of the library.

"What *matters* to you, boy? What *moves* you? What shakes your soul?"

I longed to say, "You write it, Granga, you show me what to say." But I didn't want to let him down. So instead I thought and thought for what seemed like hours but was probably only minutes.

What was it that moved me? At first all I could think of was rugby and cricket and football, but Granga said that wasn't the kind of thing he had in mind. Sometimes music had moved me, I told him, especially when I listened with my father to Max Bruch's violin concerto – we both loved that one. But how could I write a poem about a piece of music? There must be something else. And Granga was still waiting.

"Take your time, Blue. There's no hurry." I feared that

Granga was getting bored until he went on: "It sometimes helps to begin with the title. Painters often do the same. Joan Miró, for instance, whom I told you a little about – remember him?"

I nodded. "Yes – he said that blue was the colour of his dreams."

"Quite right. *Ceci est la couleur de mes rêves*, he wrote below his splash of blue on a canvas. Do you see how he created poetry with that title and the simplicity of his creation? He captured the mystery of blue, a spiritual quality that calls out to the imagination. You can't live in Mallorca and be ignorant of one of the greatest artists who ever lived. The Spaniard made his home in Mallorca for many years, until his death on Christmas Day in 1983, a tragedy of a day . . . now why was I talking of him?"

"You were explaining about the importance of titles in poetry like in art."

"Ah yes! Excellent student! Just testing. Miró described his work as *poetry in paint*, and once you see his work, you will understand why. And because he was such a poet, his titles were similarly poetic, like a line of poetry. I'll give you another example: *The Flames of the Sun Make the Desert Flower Hysterical*. Now how about that for a title? Doesn't it conjure up a *feeling*, a *sense* of something before you've even seen the painting – the pure emotions of the sun and the earth and the vibrant flower in the female shape that sets the earth alive? Do you see the clever use of metaphor in that title?"

"Yes," I said excitedly, "I've learnt a bit about metaphors at school."

"Well then, you'll understand what the good poem title

requires also. Aristotle was another fine thinker to recognise the importance of the metaphor. He wrote that the greatest thing by far is to have a command of metaphor. He thought it was the mark of genius, for to make good metaphors implies an eye for resemblances. *For the purposes of poetry*, he wrote, *a convincing impossibility is preferable to an unconvincing possibility*. But for now, let's concentrate on the title. Miró put it well when he said that when he had found the title, he lived its atmosphere – the title for him was *une realité exacte*."

Granga looked at his watch and replaced his pen in his inside pocket. "But it's getting late. Sleep on it, boy. Reflect on a title that matters to you. Perhaps in the form of a metaphor."

"I think I shall," I replied. I needed a night's sleep before I could find the right title and start my poem.

My first evening in France was almost over. I wished my parents had been able to share it with me, all of us together like a real family should be. But Granga was my family now. So if I had an important question on my mind before I went to bed, then he was the person to take it to.

"Granga, there's something I want to ask you."

He looked hard into my eyes. I hesitated.

"Speak up, Blue! Or do you want me to guess? Is that it?"

He was growing impatient. I had to be brave like my father.

"I was wondering why you never visited us, why I never met you until . . . until now. I mean, I saw your reaction when you mentioned my mother in your room, and I heard the poem you wrote for her. So why didn't you want to see her, even if you weren't interested in meeting me?"

I tried to look hard into his eyes, just like he'd looked into mine. I had to observe him carefully before he spoke, I had to savour his expressions slowly, like reading good poetry – isn't that what he'd taught me? The trouble was, I couldn't read anything in them. It was like looking at a page written in a foreign language that no one had bothered to teach me.

"Dear Blue," he said finally. "Do you truly believe I had no desire to meet you, little man?"

Now I could read his expression – it wasn't difficult. "I didn't mean to upset you, Granga. You don't have to explain if you don't want to."

We were alone now in the library. The only sound I could hear was the ticking of a grandfather clock. Granga was reflecting. He looked older when he wasn't speaking. Suddenly an answer to my question didn't seem so important. But I got one anyway – or sort of a one, or maybe not one at all.

"We see others in many ways, Blue, not just with the eyes. Our senses can be unreliable sometimes."

"But haven't you been teaching me how important our senses are?"

He smiled at me warmly – that much was easy to understand.

"Bravo! You listen well for one of your few years. Our senses are extremely important, yes. They take us on a journey, a fascinating, colourful journey – but they are not a destination."

"Then what is more reliable, Granga? Do you mean the brain – thinking about someone? Is that more reliable?"

I frowned as I waited for him to explain.

"Recall in your imagination the Max Bruch violin concerto

you told me you loved to listen to with your Papa. Your ears took you on that wonderful journey. But was it your brain that told you how to love it? Is it an analysis of the notes that remains in your memory . . . or is it something more than this?"

He was urging me on with the expression in his small restless eyes. I thought and thought until my face grew red and hot. I wanted so much to find the right answer, *his* answer.

"Something more," I agreed, afraid that I wouldn't be able to explain exactly what it was.

Granga nodded encouragingly. I grew more confident.

"I loved the music in my heart. I didn't understand it all, but that didn't matter. It made me want to cry, like when you lose someone special – or when you find someone you thought you'd never find."

Granga nodded knowingly. "You *felt* the music. It moved your *soul*." He patted the centre of his chest where his heart was. "It's still there, is it not, even without the actual music playing in your ears? It's hard to forget."

"Yes," I replied quietly, remembering.

Granga got to his feet. I feared he was leaving without me, so I stood up too.

"I trust that answers your question, Blue."

I T WAS THE HOTTEST MORNING I'd ever known. Granga told me to put on a smart pair of shorts and a T-shirt and he changed into a blue shirt, cream trousers and a blazer. He undid the top buttons of his shirt, which I'd never seen him do before. His face and arms were browner than ever, but the skin I could see where the shirt was undone looked extremely pale and loose, like a turkey neck. It made me wonder just how old he was.

"Are you ready for a treat, Blue?" He seemed pleased with himself, like Father Christmas in a big French grotto. "We're going on a short trip!"

"Which country this time?" I asked, but Granga just laughed as if I'd meant to be funny.

"I'm taking you to the most beautiful village you'll ever see. Not far from here. Fifteen minutes at the most if we get a good driver."

I was relieved that we were staying in France. Secretly I wished that we could have remained at the hotel and swum in the pool I'd noticed on our evening walk. But I didn't want to disappoint Granga, not when he was so eager to show me his favourite village.

After ten minutes in the taxi, I began to feel nauseous.

We climbed a road so narrow there was barely enough room for two cars to pass. And the higher we climbed the winding road, the more nauseous I became. It didn't seem to bother Granga though: "Quite something, isn't it?" he exclaimed, which forced me to open my eyes again. "There it is! Lean forward! Don't just sit there!" He grabbed my arm and pulled me nearly out of my seat. Excited or not, he was taking our adventure too far.

"Granga," I began, "don't you think you're being . . ." But I didn't finish my sentence, for that was when I saw the medieval village, perched high in the sky like a giant sculpture carved from a rock. At its top, an ancient church reached up towards the sky as if to point the way towards the next life for those who learn this one's lessons well. I wanted to share my first impression with Granga, to impress him with the poetic soul I was developing. But I feared that I wasn't good enough for him yet. So I sat in stunned silence, my mouth slightly open, my eyes fixed firmly on our destination and let Granga do the speaking:

"Where time is but a mode of thought
And life eternal has one moment caught."

As we continued to gaze at the village together, I tried to understand exactly what his words meant. I had the beginnings of an idea, but I knew there was more for me to learn, maybe not with my brain, but with the *something more* we'd been talking about in the library the night before.

"I wish my mother was here to see this!" I half-whispered – I didn't want to disturb my grandfather's mood. "She would have loved it."

"She did," was Granga's only reply.

The taxi driver pulled up outside a large wooden door with a big golden door handle at its centre. The door formed part of a high wall that hid what lay behind it. I pictured a secret garden, perhaps with a poets' corner at one side and a statue of a great philosopher, Aristotle maybe, beside it. I hoped we were about to find out, but Granga took my arm and led me to the other side of the road where a group of men were standing talking. There must have been ten of them at least, all about my grandfather's age. One or two waved when they saw us approaching, the others turned to see who it was. Then there was shouting and French chatter and lots of excited hand movements, all of which made me feel quite self-conscious in an English sort of way.

"You wouldn't find better men than these if you searched the whole world thrice over!"

I began to think that Granga was prone to slight exaggeration from time to time, especially when his spirits were high as they were now. But I hadn't expected that even he would actually throw his arms around grown men as he did – and kiss them on both cheeks! It was quite embarrassing. If any of them had bothered to notice me at all, they'd have seen my cheeks turning crimson. As it was, I was left stranded in the centre of a pit of flat sand, surrounded by abandoned silver balls.

After what seemed like several minutes had passed and I was thinking that I may have the beginnings of sunstroke on the back of my head, I pushed past a group of laughing Frenchmen and tugged hard at the back of my grandfather's blazer. "Ah, mon petit!" he said, as if I'd suddenly changed my nationality.

"Yes, grandfather, it is I!" I replied harshly. He knew what I meant, even if his "copains" didn't.

I don't know what I expected to happen next – a small, polite introduction might have been nice. Maybe even a handshake. But no – these were Granga's friends, and I was his companion, which meant it was my turn to be the centre of their attention. "Bleu", as I'd now become, needed no proper introduction – or if I had been introduced, I'd missed it amongst all the noise and cheers and hand movements.

I think it was Henri who decided I'd be able to watch their game more easily from his shoulders. "Pétanque" they called it, which was like our bowls only much more animated. I'd only ever been once to our local bowls club in England, but I'd never heard anyone there shout out and make a fist when someone else's ball touched theirs. But the most dangerous part of the game for me was the end. That was when Henri leapt in the air, forgetting all about his little friend perched on his bony shoulders like a speechless parrot.

"Enjoy that, Blue?" Granga called up to me, a silver ball in each hand.

"I was wondering if I might have a citron pressé?" I suggested.

"Not up there."

It seemed more of a relief to Henri than to me when I was back on firm ground. Granga found a small round table for me to sit at and watch their next game, and a waiter brought me a citron pressé with lots of ice in it and a straw. I felt a lot better after that, and by their fourth game I was enjoying myself. That was the one Granga won. I knew he'd won even before *he* did – he was too busy talking to Pierre to notice. I raced from my seat across the sand and threw my arms around Granga French-style. He liked that. He picked me up with his big strong arms and swirled me round and round in the air.

"Listen!" cried Granga, cupping a hand around his left ear. "Hear that? Music, Blue!"

He was right. It was coming from across the road, behind the big wooden door, which opened to let in a group of smartly-dressed diners. I could just make out tables and chairs on a vine-covered terrace. It was a restaurant, not a secret garden. Guests were arriving for a sophisticated lunch at tables that were neatly set, from which there were views over miles of Provence far below.

Now that the door was ajar, I could smell the aroma of beautifully-prepared food just like at our hotel — I picked out garlic and rosemary and grilled fresh fish, probably caught that morning. Overhanging the tables, vine leaves created natural shade for the midday guests, and black-suited waiters made sure that silver wine buckets stood firmly on their stands beside the tables, bottles popping their heads out of them like luxury liners on the Mediterranean Sea. As I watched, more guests arrived, dropped off at the large wooden door by drivers in long limousines, who seemed in no hurry to get away. None of the guests looked in our direction. They were too busy waving to friends already gathered on the terrace.

"There must be a private party at the hotel," suggested Granga, following my gaze. "I wondered why I couldn't reserve my usual table for lunch this afternoon. Not to worry, we'll make our own party here, you and I."

He felt inside his blazer pocket and I thought perhaps he was about to pay for our drinks and take me somewhere else.

But it wasn't a wallet he took out. It was a mouth organ – silver with red wood along the sides. Granga put it to his mouth, tilted his body forward slightly, closed his eyes and began to play.

It was the most beautiful sound I'd ever heard, and Granga played it as if he was part of the music. His left foot tapped in time to the tune, which was his own version of the music already playing across the road only much cleverer, with lots of different notes highlighting the beat like small colourful details in one of John Thompson's paintings. As he gathered pace, his friends joined in with hand clapping and singing and before long a huge crowd had developed around us. Granga didn't care though – his eyes were still tight shut.

If only I could be unselfconscious like Granga, I thought. If only I could entertain others without really having to try. If only I could lose myself so completely in what I was doing that I forgot about everything else.

The music from the restaurant grew louder, but that only made Granga play his mouth organ with more force. Some of the tunes I recognised. Granga's friends seemed familiar with them all. I knew because they began to sing along to them – Henri first in his deep French voice that sounded very strong for a man of his age. Later I learnt that Henri had been a famous singer in France many years before. It didn't surprise me. I could have listened to him all evening. It was obvious that he had sung to Granga's playing before. His voice glided in and out of the notes like dancing. Pierre joined in next. He wasn't as steady as Henri, but that didn't bother anyone, and once all ten of them had joined in, their different voices – good and bad – sounded right together. The whole crowd applauded at the end of each song. All, that is, except for me. I sat at my small table, sipping citron pressés and still wishing that I could be as confident and unselfconscious as these men.

It wasn't just my age that made me shy – John Thompson was the same age and he knew how to forget himself when he was lost in something he liked to do. So why couldn't I?

A teenage boy and girl who'd been listening beside me took a few steps forward and started to dance. It was a slow song this time. The girl put her arms around the boy's neck while he held her at the waist and they swayed to the music as if no one else existed in the whole world. They blocked my view of Granga, though, which I didn't like.

I stood up and crept along the back of the crowd until I found a gap from where I could see Granga and the others clearly. The mood had changed again. The beat was faster now. Much of the crowd had begun to dance. It was as if two parties were taking place at the same time, to the same music but in two very different ways. Occasionally the mighty door across the road would open and I could see some of the guests standing on the terrace, sipping champagne and talking as if the music wasn't even there. At our party, there was no talking, only singing and dancing and clapping as Granga played on.

He couldn't have known it was my mother's favourite song that he was now playing, but I did. She often sang it as she was driving me to school. I couldn't remember the words, but hearing it again made me shiver as if I'd just dived into cool water on a summer's day. Granga must have heard me humming the tune, because he opened his eyes and stared at me out of the corners of them. I think it was the first time he'd noticed me since he'd begun to play. I liked that. It made me feel warm again. I smiled at him. He winked back as he carried on playing. I liked that too. I took a step closer. His eyes had gone back to being closed. Henri alone was singing, but all I could hear was my mother's voice.

I stood silently watching as everyone danced to my mother's favourite tune. She'd have been dancing too if she'd been there, and my father, although he wasn't very good at it. I wanted so much to join in, but I was afraid I would make a fool of myself. I couldn't dance like my mother. I didn't have my grandfather's rhythm. I wasn't confident like my father.

The song was almost over. I tapped my left foot to the beat as I'd seen Granga do, and wondered if that counted as joining in. Granga opened his eyes again. Perhaps he'd heard my tapping. Perhaps it was off beat. Perhaps I'd put him off. This time his eyes were wider open and he didn't wink. He was staring at me, just like my mother used sometimes to stare when she was encouraging me to do something I was afraid of doing.

In seconds the song would be over – my mother's song played by her father. This time it wasn't Granga but I who closed my eyes to take in the last notes of the music. I'd forgotten till then that I liked it too. It was exactly the kind of song to dance to, first with your feet, then with your arms, until your whole body was moving to the music.

I'd done it! What did it matter if my eyes had been closed? I didn't think anyone had noticed me – except for Granga. I knew he'd noticed because he winked at me again.

I wanted that moment to go on forever:

Where time is but a mode of thought,
and life eternal has one moment caught.

Suddenly I understood Granga's words completely, not just his words, but the feeling, the emotion behind them. Because I felt it too – deep inside me, where I'd left all thought behind.

He played on, capturing the attention of more and more passers-by, until it was as if the whole village was part of our experience. But I didn't care about that. I'd dared, and that was what mattered to me.

• • •

By the time we'd said goodbye to all Granga's friends it was starting to get dark, which Granga said meant only one thing – supper time.

We walked to a café high up in the medieval village, by the church. We sat outside at a table with a red-and-white striped tablecloth for almost two hours, just the two of us, with no one who knew Granga to disturb our conversation.

It began with a discussion about "the love of life", which was Granga's favourite thing to toast to. I asked him what he loved most about it and he replied, "Its infinite finality," which I said sounded like a contradiction to me. That led on to a conversation about how something can have "an end" but also be "endless", or be "purposive" but "without purpose", or "constantly changing" but "changeless". And he told me about great philosophers such as the German eighteenth-century philosopher Immanuel Kant and the pre-Socratic philosopher Heraclitus, who had "propounded thoughts such as these". I asked Granga whether "death" might be an example of something with an end but yet endless. I was thinking of my mother and father at the time and wondering whether they were still watching over me as I sat there eating and drinking with my grandfather.

"You're referring to that most tedious of subjects – the *afterlife*, are you, boy?" he asked, with a heavy sigh. I said that I was, which caused Granga to raise his eyes heavenwards, but in a disapproving sort of way.

"Whether the soul is capable of independent existence, or whether it is but a material entity which ceases to exist once the body is no more." I merely nodded this time.

"The subject referred to by philosophers as the mind-body problem. The *Frenchman*'s favourite topic."

"Which Frenchman is that?" I asked, wondering whether Granga was meaning one of his old pétanque companions.

"René Descartes, of course." He said it as if it was obvious to whom he was referring, but I'd never heard of him.

"Oh, him!" I replied into my glass of mineral water.

"The seventeenth-century dualist," he added, casting a sidelong glance at me.

I couldn't bring myself to tell him that I'd never heard of René Descartes, nor did I know what a dualist was, although I suspected it had something to do with swords. So I put down my glass and looked him hard in the face with what I hoped was an intelligent expression and said: "Go on."

"He believed he could prove that the soul was capable of existing independently of the body, and he also came up with a series of arguments to persuade lesser mortals that God existed by necessity."

It struck me as more than a coincidence that such a conversation should have taken place under the shadows of the old medieval church, and I said so.

"There's no point in philosophical discourse," he replied sternly, "if you cannot keep your metaphysical feet firmly on the ground!"

I pushed my metaphysical feet further under my chair, uncertain whether they'd just been insulted or not.

"Granga," I whispered, "can you explain why it is that you love life for its infinite finality if you don't believe in God or an afterlife?"

"Poetic licence," he mumbled.

I feared I'd upset him a little.

THE SWIMMING POOL WAS EMPTY, the surface blue and still and waiting to be enjoyed by the first morning bather, which was me, first with my feet, then with the rest of my body. After twenty-two lengths of crawl, I decided to float on my back so that I could face the pale-blue morning sky and inhale Provence.

That was when I thought of an idea for my first poem. It didn't yet have a title, but it was to be about my adventure the day before. It began like this:

Yesterday I dared.

I felt it left more of an "aftertaste" than the other poems I'd started. Then I tried to think of words that rhymed with *dared*, but didn't know what to do with *cared* or *prepared*, although I played around for some time with *scared*. Secretly I hoped that my swimming might inspire line two, but it didn't.

After a few more lengths I climbed out of the pool, careful to avoid a tiny lizard who was asleep in a gap between two concrete paving stones. I settled myself onto a yellow lounger and waited for the sun to warm my soul. I could feel its strength drying out my skin and swimming trunks as I lay quite still, half-asleep. Then suddenly, from nowhere, line two popped into my head:

Today I am awakened.

I liked the word *awakened*. It sounded adult. And it was how I was feeling – ready for a new day, prepared for what it held, a conqueror, a hero . . . a dualist.

Like a lizard by a pool
Sleeping but alert
Still but in motion
I am ready.

I read my poem over three times. It said what I wanted to express. It was part of me, just like I was Granga's grandson, perhaps not as clever as he was, perhaps a shadow of him, but linked all the same.

"I thought I'd find you here."

I hadn't seen Granga in shorts before. It made him seem frighteningly old. I didn't like that, so I turned away and closed my eyes.

"What are you writing, Blue?"

"Just a postcard to my friend John Thompson."

It wasn't exactly a lie – I had written a card to him earlier, with my new address on it. But this wasn't the right moment for Granga to hear my first poem.

"When you're ready, boy, there's something I'd like to show you."

He spoke more quietly this morning than he had the night before.

"Do I need to change?" I enquired.

"Only into your flip-flops," he replied, kicking them towards me.

I followed behind Granga like a corporal being led to battle, not knowing what lay ahead. The morning was silent except for crickets and the sound of my flip-flops. I wished I could have left them behind, but where we were heading the ground was spiky with pine needles and stony soil.

Granga used his muscular arms to fight back any over-hanging branches, so the upward path was easier for me.

"Are you keeping up, Blue?" he called out without looking back. "It's easy to lose a small fellow in a tangled labyrinth such as this."

"I'm with you, Granga," I replied.

I discovered that the trek was easier if I swung my arms in time with my steps and kept my chin up high like a proper soldier. Occasionally the scent of lavender wafted over me like one of my mother's soaps that she'd kept in a small bowl in the guest bathroom. I don't remember it ever having been used. It was for atmosphere, an aesthetically pleasing touch, as she'd explained when I'd suggested that I clean the pedals of my bike with it. It had seemed to me that leaving soap in a bowl was a waste of a perfectly good soap, and I think my father had agreed, but he hadn't said so. He was the only one of the three of us to use the guest bathroom, because it was downstairs and he hadn't wanted to wake us when he got ready in the mornings.

He never knew it but sometimes I got up and watched him from my bedroom window as he climbed into his car and drove off down the lane. He was at his most serious in the mornings, when he thought no one was watching him. I knew what he'd be thinking in his great big brain – he'd be running through the arguments he'd prepared the night before, checking that he'd covered every point, making sure he expressed himself the right way so that the Judge would be persuaded by what he had to say.

I'd only ever been allowed to see him once in court. My mother and I had sat up in the public gallery and at first I hadn't recognised him in his wig and black gown. But then he'd turned round, looked up at the two of us and winked. I think everyone else in the gallery realised he was my father after that.

When it was his turn to speak, he stood up, quite slowly, and held the lapel of his gown with his left hand. The man in the witness box looked uneasy as he waited for my father to ask his questions. Sometimes they weren't so much *questions* as *suggestions* that the man disagreed with. When that happened, the man sweated a lot and his cheeks turned red and my father was silent and looked hard into the eyes of the Judge.

The Judge was quite an old man, who watched people a lot. But not just ordinary watching – wise, thoughtful, deep watching, like you imagined God to do. In a way, I suppose that was what he was at that moment – listening to both sides of an argument, then later deciding the sentence.

My father's voice sounded louder and clearer than it usually did. He had a way of making every word he spoke sound important. As I listened, I wondered what it must be like to be him. Could I ever sound that confident, or express myself so well? Was it an act or did he truly believe what he was saying the way he seemed to? And if so, could he be certain that he was right?

The man in the witness box was still sweating. His gaze left my father and roamed around the courtroom as if he was a trapped animal looking for an escape route. When it was my turn to be noticed by him, I looked down at the concrete grey floor until I felt sure that his gaze would have passed to someone else.

We didn't stay to the end of the trial, my mother and I. I think my mother must have been growing restless, because she fidgeted a lot in her seat and said she'd had enough. I'd have liked to stay to the end and hear what the Judge said but my mother had explained that she had some shopping to do and that my father would tell me later when he got home. So we'd crept quietly out of the gallery and chosen my favourite food for supper that night, which was fillet steak stuffed with chicken liver pâté and served with thick chips. My parents drank red wine with theirs, out of a decanter that they usually used at Christmas. My father had said that this was a celebration because he'd won his case, which meant that the man in the witness box had been found guilty by the jury, and the Judge had sentenced him to several years in prison.

My steak was just how I liked it – well done, so that no blood seeped out of it at the edges onto my chips. Secretly I was quite relieved that I hadn't stayed to the end of the trial. I never asked to see my father in court again and he never suggested it. I was glad I'd gone, though. It meant I could imagine what he was doing when he went off every morning. It's important to imagine. That way people never really leave you.

"Are we nearly there, Granga?" The sun was growing hotter and I felt faint all of a sudden.

"Nearly where?" Granga asked, still marching ahead of me.

"Wherever we're going," I replied impatiently.

"I'm not sure. Can't remember. It's been a long time." Granga sounded out of breath too.

"Are you sure this is the right path?" I asked. "I'm slipping out of my flip-flops."

"A good soldier never blames his uniform." It was alright for him to say that – he had on a sensible pair of walking shoes.

We'd reached as high as we could climb. "What exactly are we looking for?"

"You'll know when you see it," was his only reply. Then he turned to his left, lifted a large branch and held it while I crept under it to the other side.

It was the smallest church I'd ever seen, white with a pointy steeple to one side and a rough wooden cross above an arched entrance door that reminded me of the front door to the Finca. A tiny path led to it, overgrown with weeds and colourful wild flowers. Beside the church, a low sandstone wall protected it from a sheer drop down to the winding hills of Provence. A wall not to be sat on, as Granga pointed out.

It had been built as a private place of worship for the original owners of the estate. That was why there were several very old and worn gravestones on either side of the pathway. Granga and I treaded respectfully between them, reading aloud names such as "Honoré de Ville" and "Mathilde Constance Bretton", as if they meant something to us, even though they'd died nearly a hundred years before. Honoré had been seventy-five, poor Mathilde only twenty-one. I stooped beside her small worn gravestone and with my fingernail scraped moss out of the carving of her name. She deserved that much. No one should die so young. It wasn't fair.

"Don't start your blubbing again!" Death didn't seem to matter to Granga. "It happens to us all, boy, sooner or later."

"It's the sooner that I don't like," I replied, wiping away my tears with the back of my hand. "Why did you bring me here anyway?" I wished he hadn't. Not when I'd only just created my first poem. He'd spoilt everything.

He walked away and I knew to follow him. When we reached the side of the church where the ground was sheltered by the shadow of the steeple and the old wall, he stopped.

I could see only one gravestone here. It was newer than all the others, grander. I didn't even need to stoop to read the name:

SOPHIA HENNESSY
BORN 15TH MARCH 1920, DIED 20TH MARCH 1955.
BELOVED WIFE OF HORATIO R. HENNESSY.

There was a small verse underneath. I guessed at once who had written it:

MY SOUL, MY EVERY WAKING THOUGHT, MY LIFE.
GONE YOU MAY BE, BUT STILL, ALWAYS, MY WIFE.

Granga was facing away, looking towards the wall and the steep drop beyond. "My grandmother's grave," I said in a whisper. Granga made no reply. "*Sophia* – it's a beautiful name."

"For a beautiful woman," he said quietly. "*Sophia* is Greek for *wisdom*, and she certainly lived up to her name."

"Is that where the word *philosophy* comes from?" I asked.

"Indeed," he answered, turning to me like I'd impressed him. "It is made up of the Greek word for love – *philos* – and, as you spotted correctly, *sophia*, meaning wisdom. So philosophy is *the love of wisdom* . . . but to me it is also the love of my Sophia. I love them both, you see."

I waited in case there was more, but he was silent again.

"I wish I'd known her," I persisted – I needed him to speak to me again.

"You did," he replied, "in your mother . . . in Grace."

"Nineteen twenty to nineteen fifty-five," I read the words aloud this time. "She was only thirty-five when she . . ."

"The same age as Grace when she . . ."

"My mother was only thirty-three," I corrected him.

"Always excuse a woman for a lie about her age," he said with a smile in his eyes. "It shows a healthy interest in life."

"So you're saying that my mother was born in nineteen fifty-five and not nineteen fifty-seven?"

He nodded, then looked away again, as if he feared he had given away my mother's secret. "I thought you knew that," he said. "It was why I brought you here – for you to make some sense of it all."

But Granga wasn't making any sense and I told him so.

"The dates, Blue! Read the dates, for God's sake!"

My heart was pounding faster. I could hear it in my ears. I did as Granga commanded. *Born Fifteenth of March Nineteen Twenty. Died Twentieth of March Nineteen Fifty F . . .*

I didn't need to finish it. Suddenly I understood.

"My mother's birthday!" I exclaimed. "My grandmother died on the day my mother was born!"

Granga helped me to my feet and put his arm around my

shoulders, not like I was a child, more like I was a friend, an army comrade.

"Don't ask me why it was such a difficult birth, for I have no answer. God knows, I've asked myself the question a million times. Some said it was her age – that thirty-five was too old for a first pregnancy. Perhaps that is the answer. Perhaps we . . . perhaps I made her wait too long." He paused, but I didn't speak. "And yet my Sophia was so young, so healthy, so strong . . ."

It was as if he was beginning a poem. He removed his arm from my shoulder and looked at his watch. "These things happen," he said in a different, firmer voice. "I thought you should know the facts."

But I didn't want any more facts. I'd had enough of facts. Facts were what had taken my mother and father away from me. Facts were what had changed my life forever. Facts were what explained that my mother had never known her own mother, and that no one had told me. Facts were what made my grandfather about seventy if he was the age of his departed wife. And facts told me that that was dangerously old.

"Sod facts!" I shouted at the top of my voice.

I know I shouldn't have said "sod" in a churchyard, especially at the grave of my grandmother, but it was how I felt right then. Not a fact, but a feeling. And that was what I wanted.

"Poets don't care for facts, do they Granga? And that's what you are – what *we* are, isn't it? Poets! And bloody good poets, too!"

I shouldn't have said "bloody" either. But, as Granga explained, sometimes a bloody good swear word is necessary to clear the soul.

"I've an idea!" Granga looked pleased with himself all of a sudden. "Why don't we write a poem together, you and I?"

We were sitting on a bench beside the church. Granga was smoking a cigarette, I was staring at the back of Sophia's gravestone.

"What about?" I asked, uncertain.

"You choose," Granga replied, "but don't make the subject too wide. It's a mistake that many make. Seldom works. It's like trying to paint a wide landscape – you'd struggle to capture that breathtaking view of Provence out there," he said, pointing over the wall. "But if you focussed on a single aspect of it – something that captures the *soul* of what you see, then you'd create a painting worth looking at."

I remembered John Thompson's lavender fields and the small building at their centre. He would know what Granga had in mind.

"What part of it would *you* choose to paint, Granga?" I hoped his example might help with my topic for a poem.

"Me?" he said, inhaling deeply on his French cigarette and gazing into the distance of Provence.

Several minutes' silence went by and I feared he'd forgotten my question until he stood up, placed a hand on each hip, shoulders broad, feet firmly apart and said, "I would choose to paint that wall."

"That old crumbling wall you told me not to sit on?"

"That's the one!" His eyes were darting from side to side, creating the painting in his mind as he spoke.

"But it's broken in the middle!" I couldn't hide my disappointment at his choice.

"Precisely!" he exclaimed, as if he was pleased with my observation. "Right bang in the middle of it. That's the part I'd paint – observe the textures, the colours, Blue! See how it changes where uneven slabs of sandstone have crumbled away over time. There's not a single one that isn't different from another. No twentieth-century concrete symmetry in that old wall. No perfect pointing, no polished edges. Pure unadulterated imperfection!"

I have to admit, I hadn't seen the wall that way until then. It had just been something to avoid which had protected my grandmother's grave from too much sun. But now I looked harder at it I could see the colours and textures of so many of the buildings I had seen in Provence. Not bright, lively colours like John Thompson's lavender, but faded colours that changed with the light and the passing of time. It was obvious that the wall should be chosen for a painting – obvious to a genius like my grandfather.

"So, Blue, now for our poem. What's it to be?"

He'd told me to capture a moment and he'd shown me how it should be done. I couldn't let him down. But which moment was I to capture amongst so many? I thought first of Sophia's grave and of death, but then, thank goodness, I remembered that Granga had described death as the most tedious of subjects. I couldn't copy his wall or he'd think me an untrustworthy fellow. There was no doubting that he admired travel, but hadn't he said that too wide a subject seldom works? And what could be wider than travel?

"You in difficulty there, Blue?"

He didn't ask it as if he was disappointed or impatient, so I felt safe in replying, "Yes." Then I told him the subjects I'd dismissed and gave him my reasons why.

"I think I know where you're going wrong," he said thoughtfully.

"You do?" I replied, encouraging him with my eyes to go on.

"You're trying to think of a subject that will please *me*. That's not how to create a poem. It should be for you and you alone. It's an expression of yourself, Blue, no one else. Poems are the embers of a brightly-burning life."

"Then I know what I should like our poem to be about!" I exclaimed with new certainty.

"What's it to be?"

"It's to be a poem about you!" He hadn't expected that.

"*Me?*" I was sure he was reddening. "Why would you want to create a poem about a decaying old fool like me?"

"For the same reason that you would choose to paint that wall!" I replied. Then we both laughed and laughed until I thought I saw tears in his eyes.

"Does it have a title?" he asked me.

I reflected for a moment then said, "Yes – we'll call it 'The Crumbling Wall'."

"Excellent use of metaphor. As it's your choice of subject, you have to create the first line."

It wasn't easy, especially as it was to be a joint effort. I looked at the wall for inspiration and, with fingers crossed behind my back, began:

"A man of many colours."

He smiled. I breathed a sigh of relief. His turn now:

"His favourite colour's Blue."

Did he really mean it, or was he being kind? It was my go again:

"A father to my mother."

"A grandfather to you."

It took me a little longer to think of the next line, I don't know why:

"I want to understand him."

I was pleased with that. It expressed all I felt at that moment. Granga already had his next line – I could tell by the way he stamped out his cigarette:

"An inconclusive task."

Was it what he truly believed? I wondered. But I had little time for reflection – it was my turn again:

"Discover what he's hiding."

I hadn't meant to make him feel uneasy, but I could see I had. I wished I'd thought of a different line, but then I remembered that Granga had told me to write for myself, not to please him. I waited for him:

"The man behind the mask."

So he did recognise this part of himself in my words. I carried on:

"He must have loved my mother."

The words almost slipped out of my mouth without me thinking. But how would he react? He was taking longer this time, rubbing his left temple with the fingers of his left hand:

"A precious, gentle child."

"But why did he not see her?"

He stood up, his back to me as he answered with:

"The man should be reviled."

"He must have had a reason."

"Does reason tell us why?"

"He can't say she's forgotten."

He sighed, then said:

"For that would be a lie."

Suddenly I realised how important this poem was to me. I had to go on, however difficult it was for both of us. It was poetry. And poetry shouldn't be easy.

"Through loss he gained a daughter."

Granga bowed his head low until it was nearly touching his chest:

"Sophia was my life."

He said it as if he was talking to himself rather than creating a poem and I wondered if our poem had come to an end. When he said no more, I decided to go on and see:

"The image of her mother."

His hands were over his eyes now as he cried aloud:

"She robbed me of my wife!"

"So he could not forgive her?"

I said it like a question rather than a fact, and he answered:

"The girl was not to blame."

"Then she was a reminder?"

At last I was beginning to understand, even before he added:

"Her face, her voice, the same."

"Granga," I said suddenly, "are you sure you want to go on with our poem?"

"A poem must have an ending," he replied, wiping his eyes.

"But you have the hardest part," I suggested, "your lines all have to rhyme. Why don't you go first this time?"

He nodded and continued as if he was happy with my suggestion, relieved of a burden:

"I tried to be a father."

This was the piece that was missing. I would have to tread carefully:

"Alone it must be hard."

"I gave her all she asked for."

"Two people both left scarred."

It wasn't as good as Granga's rhymes, but it was the best I could do. And besides, it was what I felt. Granga was ready again:

"I should have kept her with me."

He was right. He should have kept my mother with him. But somehow, suddenly, I couldn't blame him. I spoke:

"She had a happy life."

"A boarding school's no answer."

So he had sent her away from France to boarding school in England. It was what I'd guessed had happened. Would he do the same with me?

"She was a well-loved wife."

I had to point it out. How would he have known otherwise? I knew it was Granga's turn, but I felt I must carry on:

"Although you lost a daughter,
Through her you still have me."

Granga took my hand in his and said:

"A mighty consolation."

Then I ended the poem with:

"For both of us – you'll see."

We'd created our very first poem together. No more words were needed. We descended the same path in silence.

"**B**urro! Burro!" I could see that Maria was becoming impatient with my lack of Spanish, but it was no use – my tongue wasn't built for the Spanish *r*, especially double ones.

"Donkey!" I said finally, perhaps a little too defiantly. Maria had as much trouble with "donkey" as I'd had with "burro". I couldn't think why – "donkey" was such an easy word to pronounce, you barely needed to move your tongue at all.

"He's a beautiful animal." As I spoke, I stroked the top of his big, grey head, right between his pointed ears. He seemed to like that. I felt in the plastic bag that Maria had given me for another carrot. He crunched it in seconds with his few remaining teeth, then burped as he swallowed the pieces in one gulp. I showed him my empty hand to let him know there was no more.

"Finished," I said loudly – I sensed he might be a little deaf.

"Finito," Maria agreed, and I wondered if her donkey only understood Spanish.

Maria had walked him on his lead all the way through the village and up our long drive just to introduce him to me. I say "lead" but really it was a rope with a small rusty bell hanging from it. I'd never stroked a donkey before. His mane was coarse and wiry, matted here and there with dried mud. He wasn't a very big donkey, but he seemed sturdy nevertheless, especially his hooves. They looked like hooves that had walked a lot, and stood even more.

"Venga!" said Maria, handing me his rope and beckoning me to follow her. I didn't even need to tug for him to know what to do. The three of us walked slowly in a line towards the Finca, me sandwiched between the two of them, like a BLT made with crusty old bread.

I'd never seen Maria from behind before. I couldn't help thinking that she looked very like her donkey – her cropped hair black and grey and wiry, her legs thin but strong and used to lots of walking, her back long and straight but broad at the rear. They even walked the same way – casually but with determination, as if they were carrying something important on their backs, but they didn't want anyone else to know.

By the time we'd reached the Finca, Maria and the donkey were panting. Maria disappeared inside and came out with a large white bowl of water for her donkey and two glasses of her freshly-squeezed lemon juice for me and for her. We all stood in a circle beside the front door, silently enjoying our drink in the midday sun.

El Burro found a beautiful pink flower growing on the wall of the Finca to eat. Its last remaining petal was stuck to his wet nose. He could see it with his brown popping eyes but his tongue couldn't quite get the right angle to reach it. Like me with my Spanish *r*, I thought as he tried once again.

When Maria noticed what he'd been up to, she was horri-fied. I knew because she covered her face with her bony rough hands and then peeped out between her fingers to take in the damage to Granga's climbing flower bush. That was when El Burro decided to relieve himself on Granga's porch. It looked as if he'd been waiting to do it for some time. The bowl of water couldn't have helped.

Maria babbled to me in Spanish as she did when she was so concerned about something that she forgot for a moment that I didn't speak her language. I took a guess at what she wanted me to do and led the donkey back towards the field from which we'd just walked.

At first he didn't want to go without Maria and kept stopping to look back at her as she mopped up the porch with a large scrubbing brush almost as tall as she. I don't think he realised he'd done anything wrong; he certainly made enough noise complaining to her.

Back in England, no one had ever thought to educate me about the art of leading a stubborn old donkey with only the help of a thin rope and a plastic bag empty of carrots. The more I tugged the less he wanted to move. I tried telling him what I wanted him to do, but then I remembered that English wasn't his natural language.

"Burro!" I shouted. "Venga!" He looked away from Maria to where I was standing as if he'd only just noticed I was there.

"Venga!" I shouted again.

To my astonishment he began to move, slowly, cautiously at first, his big hooves clicking on the drive like the castanets I'd heard while we were driving through the village one evening.

"Good boy," I said, as my father used to say to me when I'd done something he'd been trying to teach me. El Burro nuzzled his hairy chin into the side of my neck, then looked me straight in the eye to see how I responded. I remembered my father again and winked at him as he would have winked at me. Then the two of us walked on in silence, lost in our own ways of thinking of things.

He seemed pleased to be back in the little field. There wasn't much grass for him to graze, and what there was seemed rather dry and brown to me. But donkeys probably see the world differently from twelve-year-old boys, especially as not even twelve-year-old boys see it the same way as each other.

Take Sebastian Hamilton, for instance. About the same age as me, just six months older, but his interests could not have been more different from mine. Girls, girls and more girls were all he ever talked about. I even saw him kiss one once! He was standing with her under the big oak tree on the lawn in front of our school. I don't know what the girl was doing there – maybe she was someone's sister. It was after school. I was waiting for my mother to collect me – she was late as usual. Everyone else had gone home. Then I saw him – Sebastian Hamilton – at least, not him exactly, but the back of his head leaning over the girl, his hand resting against the tree behind her shoulder. I expected her to run away, but she didn't. She carried on standing there, looking up into his eyes as if she couldn't see his spotty forehead or greasy blonde hair at all. Then he did it, right on the lips. And she let him. I tried to turn away but I couldn't. Fortunately my mother had the good sense to arrive just then. I climbed into the passenger seat and didn't say a word all the way home, except for "Nothing," when she asked me what was the matter.

It wasn't that I didn't like girls. Some of them were quite

good-looking, although I hadn't met many. We only had boys at our school, except for a few of the teachers. I wasn't keen on girls who giggled a lot like Hannah's daughters. They seemed pointless to me. If they'd been more like Hannah I wouldn't have minded them so much. Hannah never giggled. And whenever she spoke, she tried to make sense. If I were to have a girl for a friend, she would have to make sense like Hannah. And not talk too much either. And like rugby and music and poetry. Especially poetry. And she'd have to understand donkeys. They're not easy to get to know. But then neither are girls. I'd never trust a girl who didn't like a donkey. She could be afraid of donkeys – that's not the same. Then I could teach her what I knew about them – their favourite things to eat, like carrots and flowers, and how they shout their heads off when you take them away from someone they like, and the best way to speak to them in their own language and by using your eyes to send them pictures they can understand of what you want them to do.

"Stay there!" I told El Burro, picturing him plodding around the field but going no further. "Maria will come for you soon."

Then I imagined Maria hurrying up the drive to fetch him and walk him home. El Burro twitched his ears as if he could hear her coming, and stared down towards the Finca with new hope and excitement. "Not yet," I added, "in a short while. After she's cleared up your . . . when she's ready." I patted him on the back like a comrade and waved him goodbye. He grunted quietly and contentedly and looked away into the distance. It must be nice to be a donkey, patient and strong and unaware if people are never coming back.

13

MY TUTOR WAS TO BE a retired teacher from England. That meant she'd be at least sixty. Granga had met her at a tapas bar in the village one evening. She'd been dining alone, which he said was fine for a fellow like him of advanced years, but entirely inappropriate for a lady, so he'd joined her. She was only staying in Mallorca for the summer months, in a villa owned by her godson who didn't use it very often, as he travelled a lot with his job. Granga had learnt all this over a shared bottle of Rioja with Mrs. Bainbridge. He didn't know her first name, so I assumed that he would be Mr. Hennessy to her.

"What else do you know about Mrs. Bainbridge?" I'd asked when he'd first informed me of her arrival. He reflected for a while, then answered: "She's a woman who would never dance barefoot on a table."

"Why not?" I'd asked, wondering if perhaps Mrs. Bainbridge was too self-conscious to be my tutor.

"Because the damned table would break clean in two, that's why not!" Then we'd both roared with laughter and I didn't hear any more about Mrs. Bainbridge until she arrived the following morning.

"How do you do, young Blue!" As she held out a hand

of fleshy fingers for me to shake, layers of skin rippled along her upper arm. "I'm Mrs. Bainbridge, I shall be your tutor for the rest of the summer."

We decided to study outside on the terrace that morning. There was a gentle breeze that Mrs. Bainbridge said reminded her of Bournemouth at the height of summer. Bournemouth was where she'd lived for thirty years, after she'd married her late husband.

"I've never been there," I remarked, as I opened *Far from the Madding Crowd* at page one.

"Whereabouts in England are you from?" she asked over her reading glasses.

"Wiltshire," I replied, wondering if Mrs. Bainbridge had decided to abandon English Literature in favour of Geography.

"A fine county, Wiltshire," she went on. "I have cousins who live just outside Salisbury."

I hope Granga isn't paying her by the hour, I thought, so I said: "Thomas Hardy is one of my favourite writers."

"Then you'll know that most of his books were set in Dorset, won't you?"

"What did you teach in England?" I asked – I had to know whether I'd guessed correctly.

"Geography," she answered proudly.

By Chapter Two, it was clear that Mrs. Bainbridge didn't approve of Bathsheba, which was a pity, as I liked her. She was brave and strong like my mother and beautiful like her. I didn't tell this to Mrs. Bainbridge though – I thought she might dislike Bathsheba even more.

We spent the rest of the hour discussing the importance of the landscape in Hardy's writing and the relevance of the seasonal changes to the plot. I could hear Granga's voice outside the window. He was talking in English so it couldn't have been to Maria. I stopped listening to Mrs. Bainbridge, which wasn't difficult as she was only telling me what I already knew about Sergeant Troy and the manifestation of his traits of unreliability early on in the story. Granga was still speaking. He sounded surprised and it wasn't easy to surprise him. He said my name, I was certain of it. First Rufus then Blue. Who could it be? Mrs. Bainbridge was drawing to a conclusion: Bathsheba had deserved all she got for allowing her vanity to influence her judgment and pursuing a relationship with the inimitable Sergeant Troy on the basis of his highly-pleasing appearance. "Books, young Blue, are never to be judged by their covers, remember that." She pulled in her several chins as she spoke, then nodded at me as if she was dotting an exclamation mark.

Granga was bringing the visitor into the house. I could hear two sets of footsteps crossing the hall, although the second was more of a scurry to keep up with the first. I had to say something, or Mrs. Bainbridge would guess I hadn't been listening properly:

"Don't you think she found Sergeant Troy exciting to be with as well as good-looking?"

Mrs. Bainbridge closed her book with a thud, which told me our first tutorial had come to an end. As she did so, the door behind me was flung open and Granga walked onto the terrace. Whoever he'd been talking to hadn't come with him from the hall.

"Mr. Hennessy!" Mrs. Bainbridge blushed and I hoped she wasn't judging this book by its cover.

"Good day, Mrs. Bainbridge, apologies for the interruption."

"We'd just finished, hadn't we, Blue?"

"I shall telephone you to organise your next visit."

"I look forward to it." Bathsheba tucked her blouse back into her elasticated waistband and pulled in the stomach that had forced it out. Sergeant Troy held open the door for her to pass.

"A monthly cheque acceptable?"

"That would suit me fine."

Granga beckoned for me to follow them out. It was a strange procession – Mrs. Bainbridge at the front, Granga behind her copying her walk, and me at the back trying not to laugh. What would the visitor think of us?

The hall was empty except for a trail of muddy footprints leading from the front door, which was ajar. My eyes followed them to see where they'd gone. I traced them as far as the foot of the staircase, where they disappeared. The visitor had either gone upstairs, which seemed unlikely, or had removed their muddy footwear and returned to the front door. I studied the marks on the floor more carefully until Mrs. Bainbridge disturbed them, as she was busy arranging her cloth handbag over her shoulder. They were large footprints with horizontal ridges here and there. As I approached the front door, I could see the footprints across the porch, the gaps between them lengthening until they disappeared. It was as I'd thought. Our English-speaking visitor had left.

In my hurry to run outside, I almost collided with Mrs. Bainbridge, who shouted after me to slow down, or calm down, I couldn't be sure which, but it ended with "down" and was followed by "boys!" in a tone that made me think that Granga wasn't around any more.

The drive was empty and there was no sign of a car. It

didn't make sense at all. All I could see was Maria's donkey tied to the big old tree beside the drive.

"You're looking very old and tired this morning!" I called over to him – I thought he needed cheering up – "Haven't you had enough carrots?"

"I don't like carrots," came back the voice. Unmistakeable: "I don't like carrots." I walked a little closer to the beast with new admiration. I'd never heard of a donkey who spoke before. And in English too!

"What did you just say?" I watched his mouth for an answer. It was slightly open, I could see his remaining teeth sticking up like a line of old gravestones.

"I said, I don't like carrots, Rufus – I mean Blue."

It was a miracle! "How . . . How do you know my name?" I was right up to him now, patting the crown of his head, where his great big brain must have been.

"I might not be good at exams, but I'm not stupid!"

I was about to fetch Granga and Maria as witnesses to this incredible event when I saw his face – John Thompson's – peeping out from the other side of the tree. "It's you!" I exclaimed, "I thought you were a donkey."

John Thompson shrugged and said, "What's his name?"

"I call him *Donkey* or *Burro*, that's Spanish for donkey."

"Is he yours?"

"No, he belongs to Maria – she's Granga's housekeeper."

"I've met your grandfather. He asked to see my passport with my name on it and photograph."

"I wonder why he did that," I said, sitting down next to John Thompson. "He didn't ask to see mine."

"Old people can be funny like that sometimes," suggested John Thompson.

"He's not that old," I replied.

John Thompson pulled on his dirty old Wellingtons that had left their mark all across our hallway, and stood up.

"How long can you stay?" There was so much I wanted to show him, to tell him, to discuss with him.

"I don't know," he mumbled. "Will you show me my room?"

But which room was he to have? There were five in total, which meant three of them were empty. "I'll have to ask Granga."

It seemed silly to dirty Maria's floor again, so I decided to knock on Granga's study window from the flowerbeds. He jumped when he heard me, then lifted the sash window and stuck his head out. "I see you've found each other," he said with a smile. I think he was pleased there was somebody else for me to talk to.

"I was wondering which room John Thompson was to have."

He hadn't thought of that – I could tell because he rubbed the centre of his forehead with the fingers of his left hand before saying: "I know – show him the rooms and let him choose. Better that way." Then he slammed down the window and continued with his reading.

He hadn't let me choose my room, I thought, but I didn't say anything.

14

I LEARNT SOMETHING NEW ABOUT JOHN Thompson on his first night with us – he cried in his sleep. Not just ordinary crying into his pillow like I sometimes did when I thought about my parents and how I would never see them again. John Thompson's crying was loud sobs like a lamb that can't find its mother. The noise of it woke me up. Granga must have been sleeping with his good ear against the pillow or he would have woken too. I didn't know what to do. At first the idea of going into his room and nudging him out of whatever nightmare he was having felt like an intrusion. But the longer he went on, the more it seemed like the only solution.

That was when I discovered something else new about John Thompson – he wore his vest in bed, and not a very clean one either. My mother would never have let me wear my vest in bed, no matter how tired I'd been and how reluctant to change into my pyjamas. I crept up to the side of his bed and stood there for a few minutes wondering how best to wake him without giving him a scare. His straight black fringe was pulled back in strands of perspiration, revealing a high forehead with a hairline that pointed down in the centre like a V. Tears had saturated the pillow that Maria had taken so long to iron before she left. His bare arm clung onto it as if it was a lifejacket and his bed the sea.

"John Thompson," I whispered, tugging gently on the corner of his duvet. "Wake up!" The sobbing subsided, but his eyelids remained closed, the eyeballs darting underneath them like the two mice my mother had trapped under a towel when she'd found them nesting in the corner of our garage.

I'd never thought of John Thompson as being a crier – nothing had ever seemed to bother him, not even Sebastian Hamilton's jokes about his weight and low marks and his father being a lorry driver. If it hadn't been for John's red cheeks, anyone would have thought he hadn't heard Sebastian at all. I was the only one who spoke in John's defence – even though I realised that that might make Sebastian worse. When I'd told my father about it, he'd said that it would be better for John if I let him sort it out for himself, and that he wouldn't learn otherwise. My mother had added that people like Sebastian Hamilton only picked on those whom they secretly admired for something they lacked in themselves. Then she'd packed an extra jam doughnut so I could give one to John the next day. He'd loved that. We ate them together by the side of the outdoor pool in our morning break. John got jam all over his tie and I said he looked like he'd been shot in the chest, which gave him a good laugh. The jam stain lasted until the end of term.

His breathing was steadier now and his eyes had stopped darting. So I tiptoed out of his room and went back to bed. Over breakfast next morning I asked, "Did you sleep well?" with the stress on the *well*.

"I dunno, 'cos I was asleep," he replied through a mouthful

of Maria's freshly-made fruit salad. It sort of made sense in a John Thompson way and I said no more about it.

We were having breakfast in the kitchen rather than outside, as it was an unusually cloudy day with a few drops of rain, as Maria pointed out with vertical finger movements. As we were finishing, Granga arrived with, "What day is this?" aimed directly at John Thompson. I did what I always did when someone asked John a question – kept quiet and prayed that he'd know the answer.

"Saturday, I think." And it was Saturday, so I nodded and smiled confidently at Granga.

"It may well be a Saturday, lad, but my question entails a far more significant *explanandum*."

I stopped smiling. "My grandfather often speaks in a way that no one but he understands," I said, casting a look of disapproval in Granga's direction, only he didn't notice as his eyes were still fixed on John Thompson. "But I think he means that there's a thing to be explained about this day."

"Don't know?" he was saying, "Then I shall tell you. This is the day that you two boys will never forget. Today is the day you will talk about for years to come."

We two boys exchanged a glance that said without words, "What *is* he talking about?" mixed with "I can't wait to find out."

• • •

I'd glimpsed it from my bedroom window when I was standing on a chair trying to coax a bee outside, and if you stared very hard, you could see a bit of it from the drive. From such a distance it was barely distinguishable from the sky. Only a darker shade of blue let you know it was the sea. But today as we three drew closer, it seemed the sea was grey. And by the time we felt it tingling our toes and loosening our grip of the sand, it had no colour at all.

As we hadn't known where Granga was taking us when we'd set off, we didn't have our swimming trunks with us. Granga rolled up his flannels to just below the knees and kicked off his shoes, while John Thompson and I, both in shorts and white T-shirts, raced each other over the waves like hurdlers. Of course, it wasn't a proper race or I'd have won easily being at least a stone and a half lighter than John and twice as agile. It was more of a competition against the waves than against each other. By the time we were some thirty waves out, I thought I'd better stop and check on Granga. It wasn't like him to hang back when an adventure had begun. I turned round so abruptly that the weight of a wave upset my balance and if it hadn't been for John Thompson's steadying hand I would have fallen headfirst into the water.

"Beat you back!" I cried into the salty air and, with eyes half closed, we splashed our way back to the shore.

Granga was easy to spot on an empty beach with his rolled-up trousers and white cotton shirt and old trilby to protect him from the clouds.

"Why do you need to be protected from clouds, Mr. Hennessy?" John Thompson had asked as we'd left the van and set off down the rocky slope towards the sea.

"So that they cannot intrude on my sunny disposition, lad," he'd replied, which had given John Thompson a thoughtful look I hadn't seen on him before.

I wondered why Granga referred to John Thompson as

"lad" when I'd always been "boy", but I didn't ask in case "lad" was a lower rank than "boy", and John Thompson might not have noticed.

Granga had his back to us when we approached him, and he was dragging his right foot heavily through the sand.

"Granga?"

"Come no closer, or you'll destroy the whole damn thing!"

We peered down to his feet to discover what we were in danger of destroying. He was standing where the word ended and we were at its beginning. Between us read the word he'd carved with his heel.

"*Sophia*. Can't walk on sand without writing that name. Done it for too many years to stop now. Only wish she could still add mine."

I stood staring at the name as if it were her grave again, Granga's trilby tipped lower over his eyes, his heel digging out a full stop, until John Thompson brought us back: "*Sophia*. Nice name. Sounds foreign."

"Sophia was my grandmother," I whispered respectfully. "She was named after the Greek word for *wisdom*."

"So she's dead then." Perhaps Sebastian Hamilton would have made a better friend after all. I shot a glance at Granga, unsure what I'd find, but certainly not expecting laughter:

"You've chosen a fine fellow for a friend, Blue!"

Was he being sarcastic, as my mother had described my father when he'd said how much he'd enjoyed her celebrated tarragon chicken after she'd left it too long in the oven and it had tasted like mush?

"Too much sentimentality blurs what is there in front of your eyes, isn't that right, boy?"

I moved my lips to answer, then realised he was addressing John Thompson. "Yes, sir," beamed my best friend.

"Shall we?" asked Granga.

I was about to ask, "Shall we what?" when John Thompson nodded and he and Granga set about tracing their own names on either side of Sophia's, John's in big block capitals, Horatio's in swerving joined-up loops like a signature.

"That's just what I was going to do," I muttered, but neither of them heard me – they were too lost in what they were doing.

I didn't have to work out what to do next, the sky did it for me – it started to rain. Three minutes it took to wipe out all that they'd created. We sheltered between two big rocks that met at the top, and hoped it was only a passing shower. But after a while we realised that the rain was getting heavier and we were likely to be in our sort of cave for some time.

"Do you know what soldiers do in situations such as this?" Granga asked us.

"Polish their guns?" John Thompson suggested.

"Write letters to their families?" asked I.

"They tell stories," Granga exclaimed, his voice echoing slightly in our stone shelter.

"What about?" John Thompson enquired.

"About whatever comes into their heads first." He seemed far away as he spoke.

"Were you a soldier, Mr. Hennessy?"

"A lifetime ago," he replied.

I remembered the first of his poems about war that I'd read in his *Verses of a Solitary Fellow*. I'd never really thought of him as solitary until that moment.

"Why don't you tell us a story now, Granga?" I felt it was what he wanted me to say.

We waited eagerly, John Thompson and I, cross-legged on the hard, sand floor – two corporals and a general killing time while raindrops hammered against the landscape like gunshot.

Meanwhile my grandfather stood before us, sandwiched between our two rocks so that what daylight there was almost disappeared behind his upright frame, which was reduced to a silhouette of a man and a trilby and a right arm leaning against a rock with a cigarette between two fingers.

"There was once a young man not much older than you two boys. He lived with his parents and sister and brother in a small fishing village by the sea. They weren't a wealthy family by any means, but they managed to get by the best way they could. Work was sparse in those days – the father took whatever work he could find and their mother managed their resources like a bird with a nest to make."

Granga paused to draw on the remains of his cigarette, then he went on: "Our boy was the middle child – old enough to be bored by his schooling but young enough to be protected by his family from employment. A fellow of the half-whiskered, balls-dropped variety, low in voice but high in expectation – too late to be a choirboy, too soon to be a fisherman, too proud to be a labourer, too humble to be an officer, too slow to be a scholar, too quick to be a loafer, too wise to stay behind, too naïve to run ahead, too admired to be forgotten, too poor to be acclaimed."

The raindrops were beating louder than before and a wind was whipping foliage against itself as a background beat to Granga's voice.

"So what do you think he did, boys?" We didn't want a question, we were longing for an answer. "I'll tell you then what he did – he joined the Army."

That got John Thompson to his feet, but his head banged against the overhanging rock and he sat down again: "Were there guns, Mr. Hennessy, and battles?"

"Most certainly, Mr. Thompson, and our young man excelled at weaponry like no other. So much so that it wasn't long before he was put in charge of artillery."

"Did he kill people, Granga, with his guns?" I had to know, in case this young man was my grandfather. He hesitated just long enough for me to think I'd guessed correctly.

"He'd killed before – rabbits, game, no more. He understood the meaning of a gun. It held no mystery, no fear:

He sought, he aimed, he fired,
'Twas but a sport.
A natural consequence of being man –
Or so he thought."

"So what happened to him, this bloke, did he die?"

"Of course not, John!" I snapped. "Let Granga tell his story."

"The young man survived many a battle until he was a young man no more, his only disability a bit of deafness in his right ear from a shrapnel wound." He stooped down to our eye level: "Does that seem fair to you, Blue? That a man should rob his fellow man of a right to live, to feel, to breathe – not evil men, not cruel, spiteful men, mere young men full of courage and false hope just like himself?"

I could see him clearly now that he no longer blocked the

entrance with his frame. The rain had abated and sunlight was pouring into our cave over Granga's shoulders like a halo. "You're a boy of principle, Blue. What would you have done if you'd been . . . that young man?"

I hung my head to avoid his eyes and noticed there were goose bumps on my knees. He was waiting for an answer, but did I have one for him? I'd already seen two dead bodies more than I should have done, left without the chance to fight for survival that those men had had. They'd been lying in their coffins when I'd seen them. They looked as if they were sleeping until I touched their faces and their flesh was cold and stiff like the defrosting turkeys my mother used to cook at Christmas.

"There's only one person that I would ever kill," I declared with the pain of a wounded soldier, "and that's the man who killed my mother and father!"

"You can't say that! It isn't fair!" It was John Thompson now, not Granga.

"It's their death that isn't fair and he caused that!" The words came out of my mouth like bullets. I'd never mentioned their death before to anyone – except God, and I didn't really know if He could hear me.

"But he didn't mean to, Rufe!" implored John Thompson. "You can't blame him if he didn't mean to do it!"

"Let the boy speak, John Thompson. It's why I brought you both here." I'd never heard my grandfather so stern. He was an officer again. John froze and so did I.

"Go on, Blue. Tell me. Tell us." Suddenly I feared he'd ambushed me again with one of his old army tricks. His story hadn't just been about him, it was for me too.

"They were too young. I was too young. I couldn't even

say goodbye. I thought they might come back somehow, that's how stupid I was!" I pulled my T-shirt out of my shorts and wiped my eyes and nose with it. "They never even got to see me win a rugby match."

Now I was a crier too – and in front of John Thompson! What would he think of me? I didn't dare meet his eyes. All I could manage was a sidelong glance as I tucked my T-shirt back into my shorts. His hands were covering his ears and his eyes were tight shut. He reminded me of Freddy when his little head retreated into his shell. Only I'd never seen Freddy with tears on his face.

"It's alright John Thompson," I said, removing his hands from his ears. "I've finished now."

15

W E HAD JUST SEEN THE sea from the street we were strolling along in the old part of Palma when John Thompson asked his question: "What did you do after you left the Army, Mr. Hennessy?"

It wasn't like John Thompson to ask questions – usually he barely spoke to people he didn't know well. Our teachers were always complaining that he should be more outgoing. Once, his parents had come to the school to discuss it with the headmaster – in his study – for an hour and ten minutes – from four p.m. to five ten – John Thompson had told me afterwards. Then John had been summoned by his father to join them. So he'd abandoned the twigs and leaves he'd been arranging into a picture on the front lawn and had gone to the Den – that's what we all called Mr. Collins' study.

"Come and sit with me, love," his mother had said as he entered the room. So he'd sat on the sofa next to her, whilst his father stood by the fireplace and Mr. Collins remained in his usual armchair behind his desk. It had all been very polite, like a birthday tea but without the cake, John Thompson had told me. The Head and his Mum had asked if he liked being at school and who his friends were and which lessons he liked most and what hobbies he had other than painting, and whether he was happy, to which John Thompson had replied, "Not bad; Rufus Ellerton; just Art and releasing caged animals." That's when it had all gone wrong.

"You mean it was you who let out Hamish last term?" Mr. Collins had exclaimed. Hamish was Class 3's hamster – or at least he had been.

"He wanted to be outside in the fresh air," John Thompson had replied.

By the time Mr. Thompson had discovered that his own son was also to blame for the disappearance of Dirk the parrot, whom Mr. Thompson had inherited on his father's death, he'd heard enough. He dragged John outside by the arm "to get some of that fresh air you're so keen to talk about".

John Thompson had talked even less after that – to everyone, that is, except me – and now Granga.

Granga was walking between us, John and I half-running to keep up with his long strides. He knew the history of every ancient building that we passed and he had a way of explaining it that made all of it sound so interesting that whatever he said to you returned to your mind when you were alone.

It wasn't the unexpectedness of John's question to Granga that surprised me – it was the fact that his voice was louder than usual, stronger, like a boy telling his parents he's been chosen to be rugby captain. Granga must have noticed it too, for he stopped in his tracks, turning to face him as if I wasn't there.

"You know I left the Army a very long time ago?" It was more than I'd ever been told.

"How old were you?" John asked – I should have asked him that question myself.

"Can you multiply, John?"

John nodded.

"Take your own age and times it by two, then you'll have the age you're asking for."

It took John Thompson a few moments to get there, but he did. "Twenty-four!" That voice again.

"Precisely." Granga began to walk on.

"But you haven't answered my first question! What did you do after you left the Army?" John Thompson shouted after him so loudly that passers-by stared at him, but he didn't seem to notice. Granga did, though. He increased his pace until he had disappeared around a bend. When we turned the corner we almost collided with him, as he'd stopped walking.

"There!" announced Granga. "Look for a glimpse of my past and you have it!"

We looked to where Granga was pointing. It was standing in the distance many feet high, made from rough, unpolished wood, like something John Thompson might have put together. But so very mighty, positioned with the deep blue of the sea for its backdrop like a curtain behind an altar.

"A cross!" I exclaimed, whilst John just stared in silence.

"A symbol is how the Reverend Horatio Hennessy used to describe it to his congregation."

"You! A clergyman!" I hadn't meant to sound so surprised. Shock is like that sometimes: it jumbles up your thoughts until they don't coincide with your tongue. "But you don't even believe in God!"

"Never confuse the present with the past, Blue. Your grandfather was young once, and look at him now!"

"My Dad doesn't believe in God either," said John Thompson.

"Sounds like a sensible man," Granga replied, looking out to sea as if he owed his grandson no explanation at all.

"But what happened to change your view?" I persisted.

"*Belief* they call it, but *view* will do. What happened? I woke up!"

John Thompson laughed, but I didn't find it funny. My only hope was beginning to fade away. Reverend Hennessy must have seen me as part of his congregation for a second: "That's not to say I'm right, Blue. I don't have all the answers. I used to think I did back then, but I was wrong."

He gestured to a bench where we all sat down, nothing but Granga's past before our eyes, its shadow falling in a dark cross over our feet.

"Where do you go when you want to leave something behind?" he asked us. It was a question that I asked myself a lot too, but I had no answer. "You go back – back to where you once were, before it happened – to a place where you were happy, unscarred, hopeful . . . ". His voice drifted off as he got out a cigarette and lit it. "So I went back – to the tiny village by the sea where I'd been raised. Little had changed over the intervening Army years – but for my parents. They were old by then, and frail. They lived in the same terraced house that had filled my memories whenever I was cold with rain and wind and the sound of bullets. The rest of our family were sprinkled God knows where by then. So Major Hennessy moved back into his childhood bedroom and packed away his old train sets and soldiers and guns."

"Why did you do that?" John Thompson asked, frowning.

"He'd had enough of soldiers," I explained.

"I had no manual skills such as my father possessed, nor a gentleman's degree. My skills were of a very different kind.

So I took what work I could find, and gladly: fisherman, waiter, driver . . ."

"Like my Dad."

"Mr. Thompson's a lorry driver," I explained.

"A solitary occupation," Granga replied.

"Like *A Solitary Fellow*," I couldn't help but remark – I'd waited too long to tell him that I'd read his book.

"You read my published verses?" He didn't seem all that surprised and I wondered if somehow he'd known all along.

"In Morocco," I replied. "But now in Mallorca."

"Aha," he said as if he was thinking of something else. "My progress – if progress it was – began with a visit to our small parish church for want of anything else to do on a sunny Sunday morning. Five years later I was preaching from its pulpit with the fervour and dedication of a man who was lost and is found. And so I thought back then, young fool that I was."

"You weren't a fool, Mr. Hennessy. No one could ever say that about you!"

"Thank you, young man," Granga said with a smile. I wished that I could have thought of something like that to say. But I couldn't. I was locked inside my head, reflecting on how noisier it was than words.

"And then a miracle happened – a beautiful, young, vital French miracle to change my world. She, like me, had been drawn to my church for consolation, although hers was of a different, less angry kind than mine. An only child, like you, Blue, she too had lost both her parents, but, unlike you, she had been an adult when they'd passed away. Their home she found too large to live in alone when they were gone. And so she had decided that she would travel – to the smallest and oldest villages in Europe beside the sea that she could find. Those were the only criteria she had set herself. And there I was, one Sunday, telling her all she wanted to hear and reading words of comfort as if they had been written especially for her. What could she do but fall in love with me? And she did."

"So you returned with her to her home in the South of France that we stayed in, where my mother was born."

"A husband, but a clergyman no more." He had reached an end, for now at least. I could see it in his face.

16

"I'VE A SURPRISE FOR YOU, John Thompson!"
Granga emptied the contents of a white plastic
shopping bag onto the garden table. "I couldn't
decide which colours you would like so I bought a tube of
each one. You'll find turpentine and linseed oil in amongst
them – damned if I know what you do with them, but if you
don't need the turpentine we can always use it on the
barbecue." All I got from Granga was a wink as he disappeared back into the house, and even that might have been
the sun in his eyes.

I'd never seen John Thompson so excited. He held his
very own palette with his thumb through the hole as if he
was a proper artist. It occurred to me that I hadn't received
a single present from my grandfather. In all our travels
together – to Morocco and the South of France and back to
Mallorca – he had never once considered a small token for
me. And we'd passed several shops, not to mention airports
full of books and chocolates, or what about a camera to
encourage *my* artistic flair? Didn't he see that his grandson
possessed flair too? I was fond of John Thompson myself,
but this was taking hospitality a bit too far.

The Artist was dabbing the largest of his many new

brushes into one of the colours he had selected. He said it was *ochre*, but it looked like brown to me, so I think he must have been showing off – perhaps he had more in common with Granga than I'd realised.

"What are you painting?" I called to him from my chair where I was busy trying to read a Spanish newspaper.

"Wait and see," came John Thompson's reply, which I thought was a bit offhand.

"Do you mean you don't know yet?" I asked.

"Of course I know!" he said with a laugh. "You can't start painting before you know what you're going to paint!"

All those years I had defended and protected him and it had come to this! I put down the newspaper and walked casually over to where the Maestro was standing with that expression on his face that I'd once mistaken foolishly for self-doubt.

"Don't look till I've finished," he snapped as he saw me, covering the front of his canvas as best he could with his smocked arm and a rather silly stance.

"I had no intention of looking." I tried to sound convincing. "I haven't time for that at the moment."

"Why? What are you doing?"

But what *was* I doing? I had to think of something. "I'm writing a poem, actually."

"Where are you writing it?" he asked, perplexed.

"In my head first of all." I had to explain – he wasn't a poet like Granga and me.

"What's it about?" He turned to face me as he spoke, and I noticed that he had a splodge of ochre on the tip of his nose, but I didn't tell him.

"You'll see when I've finished," I replied, walking

determinedly in the direction of the pine forest. That'll teach him, I thought to myself. Then I discovered that I was grinning contentedly, which didn't make me happy with myself at all. Especially now that I had to write a poem – a good one if it was to impress Granga – and I wasn't in a creative frame of mind.

It was cooler amongst the shadows of the pine trees. Today, I decided, was a day for new adventure and fresh challenge – I'd been held back by John Thompson's arrival for too long. I was a pine tree, not its shadow after all.

I paused to study what Granga would have described as my "metaphor" in more detail, hoping that it would give me a poet's inspiration, but the only words to enter my head to describe the tree that I'd become were "strong" and "proud". Unsure how I could justify a tree being described as "proud", let alone myself, I walked on, seeking out further inspiration. A singing bird perhaps, or a babbling brook – the kind of sounds that poets' heads are made of.

Instead of climbing up the mountainside as Granga and I had done, I decided to take a different route along a path that led to a clearing in the distance, which I hadn't noticed before. Thinking like a poet, I wondered whether by making my way out of the shadows and into the sunlight, I might similarly rid my mind of self-doubt and writer's block and find the clarity I was looking for.

Encouraged by such thoughts, I hurried on, careful not to trip on "gnarled old tree roots" that "littered the ground like nature's traps for poor innocent creatures such as I" . . . yes, it was working! I could feel it in my bones and in my prose. "Shedding the forest's shadows", with each step I drew nearer to a new creative understanding.

Ahead of me, a fence of posts and wire created a square boundary large enough to house a flock of sheep. Skinny they were, and bony, shorn of their winter coats as if by a barber with an unsteady hand. Two or three were resting under a line of trees in front of the far fence whilst others were grazing what little grass remained.

I climbed a stile and soon I was on their land, hoping that they wouldn't be afraid of sharing their home with another bony creature. The grazers stopped and stared at me through eyes that told you everything they thought: "I've not seen him before. He's a funny-looking creature. On two legs – I don't trust those two-leggers. I hope he won't harm us, or move us on again when we've only just settled here."

I held out the palm of my hand in a gesture meant as friendship. But they read it as a way of capturing them and backed away.

"I wish I had their eyes that tell you what they're thinking," I said out loud, "so that I could tell *them* what *I'm* thinking."

Slowly, one by one, they started to approach me, on thin white legs with mud-encrusted hooves. The one at the front, whose gaze was stiller and bolder than the others, leaned her head towards my open hand. I guessed she was their leader. I barely dared to breathe in case a movement frightened her away. She sniffed my palm with her wet nose as if she hoped to find something nice to eat there. When she didn't, she raised her head and glared at me with pale, misty eyes that didn't flicker. I glared back at her without taking my hand away, wondering if I owed her an apology.

"I'm sorry, Ewe," I whispered, "I'll bring you a treat next time."

The sound of my voice caused her to take a step backwards, her gaze still fixed on me. Slowly I dropped my hand to my side, unsure what to do next. Something must have brought me here – maybe I'd found the place to be inspired.

I counted a dozen sheep. By now they'd formed a semicircle around me, like an orchestra waiting to be conducted. How long we stood like this I couldn't say. The shared stillness wasn't like anything I'd known before – what exactly did these animals think they'd found?

Her shout, their leader, was so unexpected, breaking the silence like a bolt of thunder from a summer sky. I jumped. I wished I hadn't, but you can't stop instinct. And neither could they – they fled, all twelve together, to the far side of their field.

It might have been my cue to leave but I didn't want to go yet. So I found a patch of grass that was clear of their small round droppings, and lowered myself gently to the ground. It couldn't have been a sight that they were used to – a skinny boy sitting cross-legged on their floor.

It should have been a poet's dream, a scene like this to capture. How happy Granga would be, I thought, if he were with me now! His poem, I was certain, would already have been half-formed, the other half just waiting to be given life. But how should I start my poem? How should I give it meaning? I feared I lacked the verbal skills required. All I could do was sit cross-legged and ponder, but how was I supposed to capture a lasting moment that was real?

I closed my eyes, uncertain what I expected from my imagination – perhaps a word or two to keep the scene alive. I inhaled the country smells and felt the warmth of the sun on my shoulders. I heard contented bleating from the ewes.

But what I saw inside my head was not the scene I'd wanted – instead it was an image of my mother with my father by her side.

"Go away!" I shouted. "You're blocking out the present! How can I write poetry with you two standing there?"

I sensed twelve pairs of ewes' eyes watching as I disappeared over the stile and back into the forest. It seemed darker there than it had been before. I should have looked back, waved at the woolly creatures I'd made friends with, but I could barely see – my eyes were full of tears.

"I'm not a poet!" I shouted loudly at the pine trees. "You're just ordinary trees like any others, as I'm just an ordinary boy."

I raced through the forest without any awareness of where I was heading until finally I drew close to the garden of the Finca. I could see John Thompson busy at his easel, his face intent with concentration, as mine had been minutes before.

"Hello, John!" I called as I approached him, but he didn't hear me. "I'm back!" I went on, but John Thompson made no reply. Perhaps he hadn't even noticed that I was gone. Granga had though, I thought, as he waved to me from his sun chair.

"I've been for a walk through the forest," I told him, even though he hadn't asked me.

"And did you find what you were looking for?" he asked, his face turned to the sun like a sleepy old ram.

"I did as a matter of fact," I replied, standing beside him but careful not to cast a shadow that might disturb his relaxation.

"So are you going to tell me what it was?" His eyes looked closed, but I had the feeling he could see me.

"Why don't you try and guess," I said through nervous

laughter, although I wasn't feeling funny. He didn't speak for a while after that and I feared he might have fallen asleep, so I asked quietly, "Granga, did you hear me?"

"Of course I heard you." He raised his head and opened his eyes, shielding them from the sun with a broad bronzed hand across his wrinkly forehead, "I was trying to remember what a bright young boy wants to find."

I would have to give him a clue, I could see that, though I didn't want to: "I was looking for inspiration," I explained, "for a poem."

"Of course!" he said, casting a glance in the direction of John Thompson and his canvas. "We choose our canvas, mix our colours – then we wait. Wait for as long as it takes." Was he referring to me or to John Thompson?

"John says you can't mix your colours and begin a painting until you know what it is you're going to paint." He had to realise that John Thompson had a very different way of thinking from us.

"All artists need inspiration," he replied as he got to his feet. "It isn't easy to predict when it will occur."

"That's exactly what I thought!" I knew we would agree. In fact, we were on our way to explain it all to John Thompson. He must have guessed, for he stopped painting when he saw us approaching.

"Are you ready for us, young Thompson?"

"I think I've finished now," John replied.

"May we?" asked Granga, putting on his glasses. John nodded with a head that was full of smiles. But not Granga's. His was full of serious concentration and silent awe and widening of the eyes. I had to see the subject of such attention. I had to know if John Thompson had been inspired.

I turned my gaze from Granga to the canvas, then stared as if I'd turned into a ewe. I recognised at once John's inspiration – the creation I saw before me was called *Blue*.

"You've painted me!" I exclaimed.

"What better inspiration!" I half-heard Granga say as if I was waking from a dream. He'd painted me in the white T-shirt and shorts that I'd worn on our trip to the beach. I looked happy, carefree, excited to be there. The sea all around me was pale blue, except for the tips of the waves that I was jumping over, which were white with froth as they began to fall. I knew what Granga was thinking, he didn't have to tell me: John Thompson could capture the essence of a soul.

"You're a true artist, John!" I said when I'd recovered.

John's big cheeks reddened. "Thanks!" he said. That was all.

17

FROM THE SMELL OF WINE on Granga's breath, I guessed that he and his Spanish friends had drunk more than they'd eaten for lunch in the village. Now that he was back, we could plan what we would do with the rest of the day. It was too late in the afternoon to go far. I made a few suggestions, then gave up and waited for Granga to decide for us – John Thompson wasn't good at thinking of ideas.

"Got it!" Granga announced finally. I knew he'd think of something once he had a cigarette in his mouth. "We'll have a barbecue, here on the lawn, invite a few of the villagers, make it a celebration!"

"But what are we celebrating?" I enquired, which floored him for a minute.

"What month is this?" he asked, before inhaling again.

"August, of course!" I replied, sensing a plan taking shape in his curious mind.

"The date, the date!" He was growing more excited by the second.

"It's the twentieth, I think." I turned for confirmation to John Thompson, who shrugged.

"As I thought!" Granga beamed. "My birthday!"

When we told Maria she kissed Granga on the cheeks three times, then slapped his arm for not having told her before. Of course Maria would prepare all the food (my mouth watered at the thought of it) whilst Granga selected some bottles of his favourite wines from the cellar.

He returned holding two bottles by the necks in each hand, and another two under each arm, with one more tucked into the belt of his trousers. "That should be enough," he said, carefully placing the bottles on the garden table, which was now covered with Maria's favourite white linen tablecloth.

"How many people are you inviting?" I asked, counting the bottles.

"Let's see." He strode up and down the same patch of grass for a few minutes, carefully selecting the lucky guests in his head. John and I waited excitedly for the outcome.

"There'll be you two boys, so we shall need fruit juices too." I was glad he hadn't forgotten us amidst all that thinking. "And, of course, Maria will be here."

"Of course," I agreed.

"With her husband, Carlos, if he'll come."

"I hope so," I said – I longed to see the man good enough to be chosen by Maria.

"José is sure to have heard about it by this evening." Granga had never mentioned him, but I didn't want to interrupt his thinking.

"Miguel can come if he agrees to leave that wife of his behind."

Miguel I knew. He owned the tapas bar in the village. He was almost Granga's age, not quite, his wife who served behind the bar from time to time was much younger. They hadn't been married long. Too damned long, Granga said. I'd only seen her once. Granga had ordered some *gambas al ajillo* from a waiter for us to share as an appetiser before supper. Then suddenly, just as Miguel's wife arrived with the food, he'd thrown money onto the table and said in a loud voice, "We're leaving, Blue!"

"But why?" I'd protested – gambas had become a favourite of mine.

"I never stay where I'm not welcome," was his reply.

As we'd walked home I'd asked Granga to explain – I knew he wouldn't unless prompted. Apparently, the wife, Conchita, had been a waitress in Miguel's bar for a year or so before they'd married. During that time, Granga had visited his amigo Miguel regularly. Conchita had always seemed polite and respectful towards the two men although confidentially Granga had never trusted her smile – he said it revealed too many teeth, at the top as well as the bottom, and as far back as the "incongruous wisdom teeth", which was a bad sign indeed. Once she and Miguel were married, everything had changed. Conchita barely revealed as far back as her molars and Miguel wore a constant frown. Then one day, Granga had taken his dearest friend Archibald, his black Labrador, to the bar with him as he was in the habit of doing in winter months when it was too cold for Archibald to wait outside. The damned woman had flown at them from across the room like a mad thing, shrieking for Granga to take Archibald outside, using Spanish words that meant "dirty" and "ragged" and "old". To make it worse, Archibald had died quietly in his basket a few days later, and Conchita's words had never been forgiven.

"What about inviting Mrs. Bainbridge?" I suggested.

"Good thinking, Blue," he agreed. I was relieved to have distracted his thoughts from Conchita and Archibald.

"How many's that?" he asked.

"Eight, including us, if they all come," I told him.

"Not enough," he said, still pacing. "How could I have forgotten my dear friend Juan Antonio?"

"Is he the one you play dominos with?" I remembered the name, I'd heard it often, but I'd never met him.

"That's the chap!" Granga replied happily. Then, just as I thought we'd reached the end of the guest list, and Granga was grinding the remains of his cigarette into the ground with the heel of his shoe, he added, "And, of course, when she hears there's a party, my sister will insist on coming."

• • •

Her name was Lucy – my great-aunt, Granga's sister – short for Lucinda. She was his older sister but I didn't ask how old she was. That would have been bad manners. "How old is this sister of yours, then?" John Thompson hadn't been blessed with my sensitivity.

"Can you keep a secret, John?" Granga whispered into John's big red ear.

"Yes," he replied excitedly.

"Well, so can I!" said Granga.

At first I couldn't understand why a relative living only fifteen kilometres away would not have come to visit us before, but then I remembered that she was, after all, a sister of the grandfather I hadn't met for the first twelve years of my life.

"Should I call her Aunt Lucy?" I wanted to sound respectful.

"God, no!" he guffawed. "She'll never speak to you if you do. She answers best to *Lulu*."

All the guests he'd mentioned had said they were coming, and there were more he'd met on his way to deliver his invitations. In short, we were to expect seventeen guests and three dogs. Fortunately, it was a particularly sunny evening with only a slight breeze, not even strong enough to sway the tops of the palm trees.

It was too late to buy Granga a birthday present, so John and I made our own cards with pages from John's sketchpad and some pastel crayons. Of course, John's was the better drawing, but I had the brainwave of writing my first poem, which I'd composed in the South of France, "Yesterday I Dared", as I'd decided to call it, inside my card, so I was confident secretly that Granga would prefer mine. Although there was no metaphor in the title, I thought that Granga would approve of its poetic sound, and it expressed what I'd been feeling at the time.

At about six o'clock, after preparing several bowls of salad and paella and gambas al ajillo especially for me, and fish pasta and tortillas and fried calamari and fresh fruit and a surprise chocolate gateau, Maria went home to fetch her husband. I didn't like it when Maria left because Granga always started to panic about things he couldn't find and John Thompson and I had to spend all the time we should have been using for getting ready on hunting for Granga's favourite brogues from Madrid, his best trilby from a hat shop in Barcelona, his old Army tie, his bespoke London blazer with gold buttons, a missing gold button, navy thread, a needle that didn't have a "piddling hole the size of a blackhead".

It was easy for John to decide what to wear, as he'd only

brought one spare pair of trousers and a clean shirt with him. I decided on the outfit I'd worn to travel to Mallorca on that first day. Hannah had helped me choose something smart that my parents would have been proud to see me in, as it had been such an important day for my grandfather and me. The trousers were navy linen, my polo shirt white with a logo the same colour as the trousers. Maria had ironed them for me before she left. The trousers were still warm when I put them on.

Mrs. Bainbridge was the first to arrive – early. John Thompson was still in the bath and Granga couldn't find his mouth organ, so I had to answer the door to her myself. When I opened it I couldn't see her face as it was hidden behind the massive cake she was holding. It was a birthday cake, in three layers with a mountain of cream and strawberries on the top. I hoped Maria wouldn't be offended.

"I thought I'd make him something special," she said, peering proudly round the side of it. "Men like a nice cake."

We placed it in the centre of a table on the terrace where Granga could see it when he came down.

"What a glorious evening for a barbecue!" she exclaimed, eyeing up Maria's bowls of food. "Someone's been busy."

"Yes – Maria. She's a wonderful cook."

"Oh," replied Mrs. Bainbridge, in a tone that made me realise she hadn't heard about Maria.

"She's Granga's housekeeper," I explained. Mrs. Bainbridge's face lit up again.

"Yes of course," she said. "And a very fine one too by the look of all this."

I knew I should have offered her a drink, but the trouble was I'd never uncorked a bottle before. My father had always done that at home. Although it looked easy, I wasn't going to risk wine all down the front of my freshly-washed polo shirt.

I didn't have to worry for long – Miguel was the next to arrive, and a man with his own tapas bar knows all about corkscrews. He introduced himself to Mrs. Bainbridge with a flamboyant bow, which revealed a small bald patch on the crown of his head – probably through living with Conchita, I thought, relieved that he'd shown the good sense not to bring her with him.

Miguel hadn't brought a bottle of wine for Granga – he'd brought a whole case. In no time he and Mrs. Bainbridge were sipping white Rioja and discussing the geographical importance of the island's forestry. I was surprised at how good Miguel's English was. He spoke with barely an accent, as Mrs. Bainbridge commented after her second glass of wine.

"My father was a diplomat," he explained. "We lived in London for several years when I was a child. I was educated there."

"How fascinating!" exclaimed Mrs. Bainbridge, fingering her string of pearls. "And what brought you back to Mallorca?"

"I fell in love," he replied to a blushing Mrs. Bainbridge, "with my restaurant."

"Ah yes – your charming tapas bar! I've been there a few times. I don't suppose you remember me . . ." As she spoke she did something funny with her eyes that was supposed to be flirting, but looked more like she was about to faint, especially as her cheeks were bright red.

"Are you alright, señora?" Miguel asked. He wasn't used to her expressions like I was – I'd seen this one whenever

Granga was around. I did as Miguel suggested and went to fetch her some *agua sin gas* (which is Spanish for still water) while Mrs. Bainbridge joked: "I don't want any bubbles – they might go to my head!"

While I was gone, some other guests arrived, mostly men, one or two had women with them. I decided that I preferred watching the party, as I used to back in England, from afar, rather than being a part of it, so I gave Mrs. Bainbridge her still water, then pretended to be rearranging the tableware.

There was a lot of Spanish talk that I didn't understand. Even Mrs. Bainbridge was now chatting away in Spanish to a lady I hadn't seen before – her back was to me, she was small but wide at the hips, dressed in a beautiful blue silk dress and around her shoulders she held a matching shawl. So elegant, I thought, so . . . "Maria?"

It was her voice I recognised first, although even that was softer than usual. When Granga finally emerged from the Finca a few seconds later, all clean and pressed and glowing, instead of slapping his arm, she kissed him on both cheeks. Her husband, Carlos, was about six feet tall, but seemed even taller next to his wife. His right arm lingered gently around her shoulders as if it was very used to being there, and whenever Maria spoke, he turned his bronzed craggy face towards her and listened attentively to her every word, his thick white moustache lifting at the corners now and then.

"Encantado," he said, when Maria introduced us, then he removed his arm from Maria's shoulders and shook my hand. Maria rested between her husband and Granga like a warm, comforting summer hammock between two sturdy oaks. I liked it when she tidied my hair with her fingers – it told everyone else that ours was a special friendship. It was John

Thompson's turn to be introduced to Carlos next. He couldn't have had any idea who he was being introduced to, as he was staring down at his shoes throughout.

José crept up on Granga from behind and surprised him with a head butt between the shoulder blades. There was such a loud roar from my grandfather that everyone else was silenced. Then the two old men greeted each other as if they hadn't met for years, rather than having had lunch together earlier that day. José was the only guest I'd seen to arrive without a birthday present for Granga, which surprised me, as they seemed like the best of friends.

Judging by José's appearance, he'd probably only just got up from an afternoon siesta. He didn't bother with wine, but made straight for the *cerveza*, which was Spanish beer that Juan Antonio had brought in a crate. Then he stuck his forefinger into the cream on the top of Mrs. Bainbridge's birthday cake and licked it clean. I'd never seen behaviour like that at any of my parents' parties! I wondered what Aunt Lulu would make of it all.

Granga caught my eye with a look that said: "Don't just stand there, boy! Circulate, for God's sake! Enjoy yourself!" But I *was* enjoying myself, only not in the same way as Granga, that was all.

I searched for John Thompson amongst the growing crowd and found him stooping to stroke a black-and-white dog that was tied to a tree by the side of the terrace. It was an old, skinny dog but friendly, with a long pink tongue that fell out of the side of its mouth where teeth should have been. A stream of dribble had run down the pink chute onto John Thompson's left shoe. I poured some water into a bowl for the dog and took it over.

"He doesn't like being tied to a tree." It was a mystery to me how John Thompson knew this, but he seemed quite certain.

"He might jump up at the guests if he's let loose," I suggested, remembering just in time Class 3's hamster and Mr. Thompson's parrot Dirk.

"Shall we help ourselves to something to eat?" I knew how to distract him.

We strolled towards the table covered with Maria's carefully-prepared dishes, discussing whether or not Granga had remembered to light the barbecue. Once we'd reached the table, a delicious aroma of chargrilled meat wafted from somewhere, so we tucked into the salads and waited for Granga to announce that the barbecue was ready.

"Any sign of Lulu yet?" asked John Thompson.

"Don't think she's arrived," I replied. "Maybe she won't come at all."

"I hope she does," remarked John through a mouthful of olives.

"Why?" I asked.

"I like your relatives," John replied. "They're happier than mine."

It was his use of the word "relatives" and the present tense to include my parents that shook me, as if somewhere right then they were carrying on with their happiness, just like Granga and me. Suddenly it didn't seem fair that we should be enjoying ourselves, not now, like this, celebrating a birthday when they weren't allowed celebrations any more.

"At least your parents are still alive," I muttered, not caring whether he heard me.

"But I don't have a grandfather," John Thompson replied,

putting down his empty plate and walking away. I was about to follow him when I heard clapping and realised that Granga was about to address his guests.

"I have a confession to make," he announced, first in English then in Spanish. "My birthday isn't really until tomorrow."

There was much laughing from everybody except Mrs. Bainbridge, who gazed uneasily towards her birthday cake.

"But why have one celebration when you can have two?"

José cheered and raised a half-empty glass.

"And besides, how can you celebrate a new age without first saying goodbye properly to the old one? It would be disrespectful, wouldn't it, like welcoming a new guest to your party and ignoring the one who's just leaving."

Behind him, Maria was busy wheeling a black barbecue into place. I hadn't seen it before and guessed that Granga had bought it that afternoon. It was much bigger than ours at home in England, with a hood that covered the food and protected it from the gathering mosquitoes. I wished John Thompson would hurry up and return. He was missing all the fun. Surely the smell of barbecued food would bring him back again.

"Now where's that grandson of mine?" Granga continued. I hadn't expected that. "Come here, boy, where everyone can see you." I shuffled to the front, careful not to catch anybody's eyes. He could be so embarrassing sometimes.

"Has everyone met Blue?" What sort of question did he think that was? I raised my eyes to meet their nods of approval – I was Horatio's grandson after all.

"No one's bothered to introduce him to me!" I heard her booming voice – how could anyone have missed it – but at first I couldn't place where it was coming from, until she went on: "Stand him here under the light so I can have a proper look at him."

That was when I saw Lulu for the very first time. She was lying on a lounger by the French windows; she'd put the chair to its furthest recline so that all I could see of her until I drew closer was her big floppy straw hat and the soles of her stockinged feet.

"I didn't think the other boy could have been him," she shouted to Granga, whose speech had come to a sudden halt. "Too chubby to be a relative of ours."

Now all the guests were staring in Lulu's direction, even those who spoke only Spanish, transfixed by her. "So you're Blue," she said, raising her chair to the upright position and removing big black sunglasses that had covered most of her tiny face.

"Hello, Lulu," I said nervously.

"Well now that you've met him," bellowed Granga, "would you mind terribly if we got on with my party?"

"I'm not stopping you," Lulu replied. "It's about time you gave us some proper cooked food to get our teeth into."

Lulu put on her sandals and together we headed to the barbecue. Or rather, I walked – Lulu floated in a long colourful dress that touched the ground and made me worry that I might tread on it. "I don't normally like children until they reach about twenty-one," she confided, which left me unsure how to reply.

"Sorry," I said finally, then wished I hadn't and added: "I'm quite adult for my age."

"I can see that," she said with a smile that softened her face and made her pale-blue eyes twinkle.

"Your eyes are a bit like my mother's," I remarked.

"We were related!" she replied, which made me feel really stupid – somehow I hadn't thought of that.

"She'd have liked you," I went on. "She wore bright colours too."

"He told me." She pointed a finger towards her brother, who turned to me and smiled.

"Shall I carve or will you?" he asked me. I wasn't sure if he was joking or not, so just in case I said, "You do it!" It was all going so well, Granga's birthday party, just as I'd hoped it would.

• • •

The last words I remembered were Granga's: "Dig in!" he shouted as Maria pulled back the hood with pride to reveal the sizzling meat. I don't know who carried me inside – probably Granga. When I came to, I was lying on the sofa in the drawing room, with my head on his lap, Lulu kneeling beside me.

"Get him to tell you his seven times table," she was saying in a loud whisper to Granga. "That's always a good test."

"Can you hear me, Blue?" came Granga's voice, mixed with Lulu's: "What's seven times eight? It's the hardest."

I knew it was fifty-six, but I didn't say so. I opened my eyes, though, just to let them know I was still alive. I hadn't expected tears to be pouring from them, nor sobs of despair gushing from my mouth.

"What's the matter with the child?" shrieked Lulu. "You should know – what sort of guardian are you?"

"There was nothing wrong with him until *you* arrived," Granga replied.

"That's enough!" I screamed through my tears. "It has nothing to do with either of you."

I couldn't block it from my memory any longer – the smell, the sight of baked brown-crusted sheep. "The meat!" I summoned from somewhere the strength to say. "Where did it come from?"

Brother and sister exchanged a quizzical glance, "You mean the barbecued mutton?" Granga asked.

"Of course," I shrieked. "What else?"

"It was perfectly fresh – couldn't have been fresher – my birthday present from José," he replied. "He keeps a few sheep in one of my meadows."

I sobbed, then fainted again.

18

I WOKE EARLY THE NEXT MORNING with a throbbing headache and a rumbling stomach. But worse, my mind was full of memories of the night before. I was surprised to discover that I was not only dressed in my vest as if I was John Thompson, but I still had on my trousers and polo shirt. There was a glass of water on my bedside table and a biscuit beside it.

I got up, pulled on my walking shoes and crept downstairs. It was quiet, no sign of last night's party. The tables outside were in the same places but the plates and glasses had been cleared away. All that remained of the food was a basket of bread and a serving plate stacked with apples. When my eye caught the barbecue, my heart began to pound and I was afraid that I would faint again. It stood there all shiny and clean and empty, no longer the crematorium I remembered. I picked up the basket of bread and placed an apple in each pocket. "They'll like that," I said out loud whilst inwardly I was praying all twelve ewes would still be there.

I didn't know what time it was – a mist hung around the mountains like breath on a cold English morning. Birds were singing as they did when it was early, like it was their favourite time of day. I hurried on, longing but frightened to arrive there, at the meadow where twelve sheep should be.

Hastily I climbed the stile, standing on it to give me the height I needed to count them properly. I counted twice, both times the number was the same: once upon a time it had been my favourite number, I liked its symmetry, the way it read the same backwards as forwards, just like the word "ewe".

"Eleven!" I cried. "Eleven because one of them is missing – their leader!" I threw the bread on the ground. I'd known last night that she would have been chosen – the perfect birthday present for the hungry guests. Selected by José, full of good intentions. A tasty, bold ewe slaughtered for a special friend. I pictured him standing in the field where I stood now, searching for the one he'd take away. When they'd spotted him coming, they'd have been all excited, expecting he was there to give them food. They'd have gathered round him in a woolly, hopeful circle, shouting their heads off, butting each other in order to get close. But he would have noticed only one of them, the one to be cooked on a barbecue as a special gift.

"Why?" I cried. "Why does it happen to everyone I care for? Why choose the ones who want so much to live? Why can't You pick on those who have displeased You? Why always the lives that have the most to give?"

"That rhymes," came a voice from somewhere behind me. "Is that the poem you were writing yesterday?" I didn't need to turn round to know whom I'd find there.

"Go away, John Thompson!" I spoke loudly enough for him to know I meant it, but not so loud that I would frighten the sheep.

"But I've only just got here!"

I hadn't intended to hurt him, so I turned to him, hoping

he wouldn't notice that my face was wet, and said, "Sometimes I feel like being alone, that's all."

"I know what you mean," he replied solemnly, "I feel like that most of the time when I'm at home."

His loneliness was so different from mine that I didn't know what to say next. I stood there, thinking how seldom I'd have chosen my own company over that of my parents – or Granga's – and wondering what it must be like to be John Thompson. "I suppose now you're here we could go for a walk," I suggested finally, climbing the stile to where John stood on the other side.

John wanted to lead the way so I followed him along a narrow track of clay, where footsteps had worn the grass away. I hadn't paid attention to how he looked from behind before – his knees brushed together every time he took a stride, and he used his arms to move himself on more than I did, and his head moved backwards and forwards like a hen. "It's a bit steep here," I said when I noticed he was panting. But he made no reply, so I was silent again. I didn't dare look back to where the eleven sheep would be quietly grazing.

"Did you eat from the barbecue last night?" I found myself asking.

"No, it had all been cleared away by the time I got back," he replied.

"Got back from where?" I asked – I'd assumed he'd been in his bedroom.

"I took that dog for a walk," he explained, "I don't like crowds."

"The dog with a floppy tongue and lots of saliva?"

John nodded. "It didn't want to be caught once it was off its lead."

We'd reached the top of the hill. John stopped and looked around him. "It must be around here somewhere," he said. "This is the way it went."

"You shouldn't have let someone else's dog off its lead!" I cried.

"Why not?" he answered. "He wanted to run free so where's the harm?"

I was about to explain the harm in losing other people's animals that they care for, when John shouted out in excitement, "There it is! Over there! I knew I'd find it!"

No creature could have seemed happier to see us than she was. As she raced towards us she leapt and turned in the air as if she was still a lamb, calling out to let us know she'd found us, with eyes that said, "I'm so glad you're here!"

"The missing sheep!" I threw my arms around her neck and drew her to me, stroking the curly tuft of wool between her ears. "I thought you were . . . gone," I whispered into her pointy ear that looked pink with the sun shining through it.

"So did I," said John Thompson, "when that dog got into their field. It chased all the sheep around in circles, then jumped the fence and lay watching them from the ground."

"So what happened to the dog? I thought that was who you were looking for."

"I took it back with me last night. It was easy once I'd put its lead on again."

"But how did this ewe get out?" I asked, imagining what his answer would be. "Don't tell me that you left their gate open in case any of them wanted to go and explore?"

"Of course not!" he replied. I thought he seemed quite hurt. "Why would I do that when they told me they were happy where they were?"

"Then how is she here?" She was jumping up at him now and he was tickling the base of her ear.

"You didn't tell me you were a girl sheep," he whispered to her, then turned to me. "She'd had enough of being chased around by the dog," he explained. "She ran at that fence like she was in the Grand National. You should have seen her land on the other side!" John patted her back proudly. "You've got bloody long legs for a sheep! I knew I'd find you if I came back this morning. You wouldn't wander far from your mates."

The sheep followed us down the hill and back to her flock. She seemed happy to be reunited with them all, and they with her. There was a lot of excited talking together before they settled back down to their grazing.

"What do you think they're saying?" I asked John as we returned home.

"Probably that they're lucky to have good mates," he said.

"Or to be alive," I suggested. "I'm glad I didn't eat any meat last night."

"So am I," agreed John.

• • •

"You should listen to your sister – I told you that you were worrying about nothing."

"Forgive me, dear Lucinda!" replied Granga. "I'd forgotten for a moment that I was in the presence of the Omniscient."

"I've forgotten more than *you* ever knew, and that's a fact!"

They were walking together across the lawn to meet us.

"Where on Earth have you two little fools been?" snapped Granga. "You've had your great-aunt frightened out of her mind!"

"We went for a walk," I said, pointing in the vague direction of the forest.

"That would have been the first place I'd have looked for them," Lulu told Granga with a sharp tone of criticism. "Didn't it even cross your mind that that was where they would be?"

"And I suppose *you'd* have combed the entire forest by now on those little skinny legs of yours," Granga suggested to his sister.

Lulu raised her long skirt to just above the knees to reveal a pair of straight thin legs which looked short but strong: "These legs," she announced proudly, "have been admired the world over."

Granga chuckled: "They look like sparrows' ankles to me."

John and I struggled to restrain our laughter, but it was no use. Lulu took off across the lawn at a speed that was more of a run than a walk, shouting ahead of her as she went, "I'd like to see *your* legs move at this pace, Horatio Hennessy!"

"I've invited my sister to join us for a birthday lunch on the lawn with Maria – two old women are always easier to endure than one!"

With all my concern over the missing sheep, I'd completely forgotten that today was Granga's real birthday.

"Happy birthday, Granga!" I exclaimed, kissing him on his cheek as I used to do with my father on his birthday – only he would hug me back in return, whereas Granga stood firm like a statue and said, "Sentimental nonsense," which was not how I'd thought of a birthday kiss before.

At lunchtime we gathered round the wooden rectangular garden table – John Thompson and I sat on one of the long sides, Maria opposite us, and Lulu faced Granga at the head – or vice versa. Maria had set the table with big hand-painted bowls of cold salads left over from the night before. Thankfully there was no sign of mutton that I knew I would never be able to bring myself to eat again.

John and I drank peach juice, whilst the others shared a bottle of champagne left by one of the guests. Lulu was the first to raise a glass: "To Horatio!" she announced. "God bless you and grant you many happy returns – not that you deserve them."

"Good health, happiness and prosperity to us all," Granga added, standing to meet Lulu's champagne flute with a clink.

"Feliz cumpleaños," joined in Maria, smiling.

"Happy birthday," I said, careful not to kiss him this time.

I turned to John – he would need a prompt – but he was leaving the table.

"John!" I called after him.

"Back soon!" was all he replied.

We helped ourselves to a little bit of everything. Granga and I discussed the party whilst Maria and Lulu chatted away in Spanish like old friends, which perhaps they were.

When I caught a glimpse of John returning, I hoped that he might manage a simple birthday greeting, at least to please me. I continued talking to Granga as if I hadn't noticed he'd been gone. I'd found that was always the best way with John Thompson. He sat down forcefully in his chair and crossed his arms determinedly over his chest. I passed him a bowl of cold pasta mixed with seafood and said, "Save room for the *birthday* cake." I thought that might be the subtle reminder he needed.

John didn't seem to hear me – he was too busy fiddling with something by his side. I nudged him with my elbow, hoping none of the others had noticed that he still hadn't wished Granga a happy birthday. It worked. He spoke.

"This is for you, Mr. Hennessy," he mumbled. "Happy birthday." Then he passed Granga the present he'd been fiddling with. Granga removed John's bed sheet that covered it to reveal what was underneath.

"Blue," he whispered staring at the canvas he'd so admired the day before. "You've given me your painting of Blue!"

Then Maria fanned herself with a napkin whilst my great-aunt ran round the table to see for herself "what all the fuss is about".

The three of them stood transfixed with admiration, exactly what a work of art should do – capture, as Granga said, "the essence of a moment, beyond the eye, right to the soul of Blue".

Just then the soul of Blue seemed happy with not moving. I knew, if I joined them, exactly what I'd find. After all, I was an artist too, if only they would remember. It was just that mine was of a different kind.

The artist, the genius, didn't respond to their approval. I could hear him beside me tucking into his plate of food. He'd given his birthday present, he didn't care what they were thinking. He knew Granga liked it, and that was all that mattered to him.

My grandfather stood up. He was walking to our side of the table. Perhaps this was the time for him to open my card. He was standing behind me.

"Thank you, John Thompson, dear boy. Thank you for my *Blue*."

I was certain that his voice had quivered as he'd spoken. I'd never heard him speak like that before. I moved my lips to tell him to open his birthday card. Too late – he was kissing John Thompson on the cheek.

"You're a funny little thing," Lulu said, peering over her sunglasses at John. "To look at you, you wouldn't think you had the sense to paint a picture like that."

Of course she was right, but only she could have got away with saying it. And in a way, it was a compliment, especially compared to the kind of remarks John was used to receiving at school.

"You're in the company, sister, of two very talented young men." At least my grandfather had remembered I was there.

"Well you can't be talking about yourself," laughed Lulu, "so you must mean Blue."

She turned to me just as Granga said, "He has the makings of a fine poet."

"Open your birthday card, Granga."

It was the perfect opportunity to show off my first poem. I pushed the white envelope into his hands and waited. He seemed pleased with my drawing of a birthday cake on the front. Everyone watched as he opened it to read what was inside, in my best handwriting. "Yesterday I Dared" was about to have the recognition it deserved.

"Yesterday I dared." It sounded even better when Granga read it, more thoughtful. I hoped he wouldn't see the smile on my face.

"Today I am awakened
Like a lizard by a pool
Sleeping but alert
Still but in motion
I am ready."

Granga looked at me with admiration – no words were needed between two poets such as we. John's painting was history, the moment was all poetry – until Lulu spoilt it with: "I can't stand poems that don't rhyme. Now Betjeman – he makes all his poems rhyme. Proper verses they are. You should copy one of his next time."

"I didn't copy 'Yesterday I Dared'," I protested solemnly, "I made it up. It's one of my poems."

Aunt Lulu wasn't the least deterred by this news, "*Yesterday I dared*, dared what? It doesn't make any sense to me at all. *I am ready*, what are you ready for? I haven't the faintest idea what you're talking about."

It wasn't the response I'd expected. I turned to Granga, who was still holding my card. He would explain.

"In poetry," he said, and already I could have jumped up and hugged him, "it's not so much the words we use as the ones we leave out." He'd put into words exactly what I'd been thinking.

"Sounds like a lot of nonsense to me," Aunt Lulu replied, "like baking a cake without the eggs."

To my surprise, Maria, whom I'd always believed not to speak a word of English, began to laugh! No one had laughed at John's painting, and he'd left out all sorts – the rocks we'd sheltered under, the writing in the sand, even Granga was missing, for goodness' sake! But Lulu hadn't finished: "How are we supposed to know which words you've left out anyway?"

"It matters not which precise words are omitted, you old fool." Granga was growing impatient. Impatience suited him, like a general waiting for battle to begin, giving last-minute instructions to his soldiers, none of whom possessed the intelligence to grasp them – but one. "The important thing is *that* they're left out, not *what* is left out – like the silence between musical notes – get it?"

Lucinda placed her champagne flute gracefully on the table and whispered, barely audibly, to her brother, "I see – what matters is *that* the words are unspoken."

"Precisely!" Granga roared, mopping his brow with a big white handkerchief with an embroidered "H" in the corner.

His sister stood up, adjusted her floppy hat with a demure gesture of her left hand and said: "Then perhaps, dear brother, you might follow your own advice and keep your words to yourself!"

She gathered herself up and glided across the lawn like an old actress who has just delivered her last line. We watched her go, Granga included, absorbing the silence between the words just as Lucinda, I suspected, had wanted. But Granga had another verse to add. He shouted after her:

"There once was a woman from Mallorca
You wouldn't believe what a talker!
She thought she knew best
So much more than the rest
But she didn't know half what she oughta!

There you are, woman – is that rhyme enough for you!"

19

"**J**OHN," I WHISPERED WHILST GRANGA and Lucinda were busy discussing the hanging of *Blue* above the fireplace in the drawing room the following day. "Would you like to see another work of art, something very special?"

"Yeah!" enthused John, so I beckoned to him to follow me out of the drawing room and upstairs to my bedroom.

"What is it?" John asked impatiently.

"You'll find out in a moment," I replied, kneeling beside my wardrobe and pulling out the old leather book I'd hidden underneath it.

"*Verses of a Solitary Fellow*." John read the words slowly. "*By Horatio R. Hennessy* . . . your Granddad's poems!"

"Every single one!" I beamed proudly. "Open it up."

I hadn't dared to read it again since we'd left the South of France. At first, I'd thought it was because I hadn't told Granga that I'd taken it from the bookshelf in Morocco. But then, once I'd confessed to him, and he hadn't seemed concerned, I'd realised that there must have been another reason why I'd left it hidden all this time.

It hadn't taken me long to work it out – I was frightened of what I might find in the other poems. Each night, as I lay in bed waiting to fall asleep, I would glance over to the wardrobe and picture the big leather book with its thick, off-white pages and old-fashioned black print, and wonder what other revelations it contained. Already I'd discovered how he felt about his wartime experiences, but there was so much more to my Granga's life than that. And I hadn't felt ready to hear it.

But now that I'd shared *my* first poem with *him* and I knew how that felt as a poet, I wanted to share everything that Granga had created in his book. I wanted to see how he'd "captured the essence" of being not just Granga, but Horatio R. Hennessy, the poet, the preacher, the philosopher, the man.

"Anywhere you like, John. Just open it up and read what you find!" I sat on the corner of my bed. John Thompson took the book to the window so that the sun's rays fell on the open page like spotlights on a stage. "Hurry up," I urged him, suddenly impatient to hear more. "What does it say?"

John traced the words of the poem with the forefinger of his right hand, which was stained with blue paint.

"What can I tell you?" he said.

"Tell me what's written, of course!" I replied.

"That's what I'm doing," snapped John, raising his eyes from the book to look at me. "The first line says: *What can I tell you?*"

I was quiet after that, all the way to the end of the poem.

"What can I tell you?
You've seen all my faults
Didn't I lay them at your feet
Like stepping stones

To a murky pond
That waits patiently
For fresh drops of rain
To cleanse it?

How can I show you
I'll do you no wrong
That my past is gone
Drowned
By your reflection
In the clear water
That is now my soul?

Speak!
Come back to me!
Without you
Life holds no mystery
I am floating on my back
Staring at a cloudy sky
That once was blue.
I breathe the air
I fill my lungs
I live
I wait
I die
. . . Without you."

John Thompson had reached the end. He took a deep breath and sighed, "Blimey!" It wasn't the word I'd have chosen, but I knew exactly what he meant. "So who do you think had left him?"

"I expect it was my grandmother, Sophia." I tried to speak with the thoughtfulness of a published poet's grandson.

"I'd like to have met her – why do you think she went off then? Met another bloke?"

"Of course not!" His brashness was getting on my nerves. "They probably had a small lovers' quarrel, that would be all," I explained, wondering if I should broach the subject with Granga.

"Some quarrel!" John exclaimed. I wished I'd left him to his own art form instead of trying to educate him to ours. "You read this one!" he said, thrusting the book into my hands.

I hesitated, just like I'd done before. Was it right what we were doing? Were we prying into my grandfather's private, most personal feelings? Yet hadn't I already decided that that was what poetry was all about? And hadn't he had them published, after all?

I opened the book where it chose to fall, just as John had done. It was a short poem this time. I cleared my throat and read:

"Criticise me if you will
Tell me I'm a fool
But speaking ill behind my back
Is but the devil's tool."

I knew John Thompson would like that one, but I hadn't expected him to applaud and shout, "More!"

I closed the book and opened it again as if it was an ancient oracle. The next poem was longer.

"Are you ready, John?" I asked. John nodded enthusiastically from his cross-legged position on the floor.

"*To* . . ." I paused to take in what I was seeing, reading it again in case I'd made a mistake:

"*To Rufus*

Somewhere
Out there
In the small vastness of it all
You grow
Like a thought
Moment by moment
Stronger
Wiser

Further
From my understanding
Known but unknown
Distant but close
Mine but your own
Linked but a stranger
Imagined but real.

How does your smile
Alter your face?
Do tears
Ever blur your vision?

Have you heard
My name
From your mother's
Sweet lips?

Does it cause you
To wonder
As I do?

Are there days when
Explosions
Of happiness
Lift your spirit
Far, far away
To a place
That no one knows
But can only
Feel?

Am I there, child?
Do our spirits
Clash
Like cymbals
In an infinite
Now?

You
Who are
Part of me
In the curious continuum
Called life.

I close my eyes
I see
A child

Filled to the brim
With beginning

And end
You and I
Where the sea meets the sky
Two contrasting
Shades of blue

Divided
One
You and I."

When I reached the end, there was silence until John broke it with, "You lucky sod! I wish someone would write a poem like that for me."

I didn't know what to say. Words seemed for other, wiser, more creative people right then, not for someone like me. If I'd tried to express myself, all I'd have managed would have been the briefest picture – a verbal sketch. It would have said I wanted to cry, to throw my arms around Granga's neck and thank him for what he'd written. I wanted to tell him how proud I was to have him as my grandfather, and that he meant everything to me. But those words wouldn't have been enough to capture what I was feeling inside – "the essence", as he would describe it – not the way he had done. Each silent sentence I tried unsuccessfully to create in my mind left something out. Granga was right – feelings were much more than just our words, our thoughts. Like crying to a piece of wordless music, our hearts know sometimes what our minds can't describe – unless you are Granga, and your heart and mind are one.

"I'm going downstairs to see Granga." I passed John the book of verses. "You carry on reading them if you like."

"Thanks," he replied. "I will."

I had no idea what I'd say when I found him, but somehow that didn't matter. Once I was near him, I'd think of something, like opening up his book at exactly the right page to discover a poem dedicated to me, the grandson he hadn't needed to visit in order to meet in his heart. And besides, it didn't have to be something special I said to him because I wasn't special like Granga, but he seemed to like me for who I was anyway.

He was alone, standing on a kitchen chair, when I walked into the drawing room.

"Does that look straight to you?" he called to me, hanging the painting.

In its heavy gold frame, which Granga had selected from his collection in the room above the garage, the painting looked pretty spectacular. "Perfect!" I exclaimed. "A real work of art!"

That led me to wonder what a good work of art really was, and whether I was able to recognise one. Of course, I might *think* I knew, like when I admired John's paintings or Granga's poems, but how would I know if I was right?

I waited until Granga had finished admiring *Blue* to ask, "How do you know if a work of art is a good one, Granga?"

"Ah!" he sighed. "The complex subject of aesthetics, debated by great philosophers for generations."

It was news to me, but I nodded and he carried on, "You're

wondering whether the judgment of taste is merely a subjective one."

I told him I supposed I was.

"And if that is so, how we are able to claim that a judgment of taste is true intersubjectively, rather than being a personal preference."

I didn't want my response to disappoint him, especially as I'd hit upon a subject in which he seemed particularly interested, so I said, "Yes – that was what I was wondering."

"And you're not alone in wondering it," he replied, "Immanuel Kant, the great eighteenth-century German philosopher, addressed it, David Hume too. They both wanted to make room for intersubjectively valid judgments of taste and they approached the subject in a similar way."

I wished John Thompson would come into the room – I feared I wasn't up to this conversation alone. But I liked Granga explaining it to me anyway.

"Hume – the Scot – eighteenth-century, like Kant – charming fellow – claimed in his celebrated essay *Of the Standard of Taste* that certain judgments of taste are absurd, which they would not be if there were no intersubjectively valid judgments of taste. *Whoever would assert an equality of genius and elegance between Ogilby and Milton*, Hume wrote, *or Bunyan and Addison, would be thought to defend no less an extravagance, than if he maintained a mole-hill to be as high as Tenerife, or a pond as extensive as the ocean.* A little harsh on Ogilby and Bunyan, perhaps, but never mind, you get the point."

"It would be like saying that I was as good a poet as you," I suggested cautiously, which made Granga grin and pat me on the back.

"Kant makes a stronger claim in his *Critique of Judgment*. He believes that it is integral to the notion of a judgment of taste that our attitude to disagreement is that other people ought to react as we react. For Kant, the solution lies in discovering what is involved in seeing the world how it is, not just for a particular group of talented special people, but for each and every one of us. For Hume, on the other hand, the problem is solved by describing a group of people – the *true judges*. The true standard of taste and beauty is identical with the joint verdict of these *true judges*."

"How does he describe them?" I asked, wondering if I might be one of them.

"He believes that a true judge is a *rare* character indeed: *strong sense, united to delicate sentiment, improved by practice, perfected by comparison, and cleared of all prejudice, can alone entitle critics to this valuable character; and the joint verdict of such, wherever they are to be found, is the true standard of taste and beauty*."

He quoted Hume's words as if he was giving a talk to an audience of very important and intelligent people, not to a twelve-year-old boy struggling to keep up. "You'd be one of Hume's judges," I said, slumping into an armchair.

Granga smiled again. "I've certainly had many years to be improved by practice. Hume would have told you that the way to establish these principles of taste is by experience. You, Blue, have the beginnings of a strong sense and good judgment, as does young Thompson. In time, you will possess all the characteristics that Hume describes. I'm certain of it."

I sensed my face was lighting up. "Do you really think so?"

"I wouldn't say so if I didn't. There's no point in

encouraging a fellow with false hope. That would be a waste of everyone's time. It's one of the reasons why I took you to Morocco for your first tagine – it was your initiation into ascertaining a delicacy of taste, picking out flavours, ingredients. Then, in the South of France, we broadened that experience, if you recall, to subtler ingredients. Hume recognised the importance of a good palate. He wrote that in like manner, a quick and acute perception of beauty must be the perfection of our *mental* taste. So, you see, your delicacy of taste and experience, your practice in comparisons has already begun."

I picked myself up from the armchair and walked confidently towards *Blue*. I may not have understood everything that Granga was trying to explain to me, but I'd impressed a true judge with the beginnings of my good judgment. That was more than enough for me – at least, for now.

"One day," I said, full of new confidence, "I'll create a poem all for myself. It'll express what I truly feel about something or someone. And when I've finished it, true judges of taste might even appreciate it." I turned abruptly to face Granga. "I won't have written it for that purpose, though," I explained, just in case he was interested – but even if he wasn't, it mattered to me, so I said it anyway. "It'll be my greatest ever achievement." I smiled contentedly at the thought of it somewhere not too far into my future. "And I'll dedicate it to you."

"I look forward to it very much," he told me. "I shall read it with pride."

"Good," I replied without even a moment of hesitation, "because that's how I felt just now when I read the poem in your book of verses that you'd written to *me*."

That took him by surprise – I could tell by the way he turned away from me to fiddle with the frame again. Maybe I shouldn't have told him I'd read it. Maybe some feelings are best kept to yourself. But I'd started, so I had no choice now but to go on:

"*To Rufus.* I forget most of the time that I used to be called Rufus. It's a beautiful poem. It made me want to cry. I would have done, if I hadn't remembered in time that Hannah had told me to be brave like my father. He hardly ever cried."

"There's nothing wrong with tears if they're true tears, Blue. Not the crafty self-centred type, mind you, that fall from the eyes like pieces of silver, aimed at diverting attention away from the crier's wrongdoing or gaining favour where none is deserved. I've seen my share of those – hoses turned on at will in the midst of a drought. But a fellow who weeps *truly*, from the heart, because he *loves*, because he *feels*, because he is *moved* to the very core of his being, what nobler expression of soul could the world possess than that?"

I hoped he didn't think me one of the first type of fellows, so I replied: "Mine would have been true tears, Granga, *moved to the core of my being* ones because you'd taken the time to compose a poem from the soul especially for me."

I thought I saw in his eyes the beginning of the thing we were discussing, until he looked away. Then he turned to face me again, staring hard into my face.

"I have a confession to make, Blue – will you hear it?"

I nodded nervously. I wasn't really sure that I wanted to hear a confession – I might not like it.

"On that first day, when we changed your name to *Blue*, I told you a small lie."

The idea of Granga lying to me filled me with horror, like suddenly discovering there wasn't a heaven after all.

"Why would you lie to me?" I tried not to sound as concerned as I felt. "Isn't it wrong to tell lies?" I could feel my heart pounding in my chest.

Granga put on an expression that tried to make light of it, but he didn't fool me. "There are those who would consider a lie to be a moral wrong – our friend Mr. Kant, for one. He believed we have a duty not to make false promises."

This was all very well, but I didn't want to know what an eighteenth-century German philosopher thought about lying – I wanted to know what *Granga* thought. "*You* obviously thought it was OK to lie, though, or else you wouldn't have lied to me, would you?" I asked him.

He looked at me as if I'd just beaten him in a chess game, but the trouble was, I didn't want to beat him. In fact, right then, I'd have preferred to lose. It didn't make any sense – Granga telling lies. Surely he must have had a reason, a very good reason.

"It is agreed by many philosophers that motive is important in an assessment of moral worth. My motive was a good one, Blue. I lied in order to help you – or at least, I believed I was helping you at the time. If I was mistaken in my belief, then . . . forgive me my wrongdoing."

"I can't forgive you unless you tell me what the lie was."

"Very well," he replied. "But please, refrain from judging me too harshly, boy. I am not a man to use the truth as a tool that can be put aside whenever its use is not of benefit. I value truth-telling enormously, irrespective of its consequences."

He picked up the kitchen chair he'd been standing on and moved it closer to me. Then he sat down on it, crossing his legs and arms defensively as he thought hard about what he would say next. I wouldn't disturb his silence, no matter how desperate I was to hear his confession.

Finally he said: "When I suggested you change your name to *Blue* because your real name – Rufus – was too soft, that was a lie. I didn't think there was anything soft about the name Rufus. Quite the contrary, Rufus is a fine, strong name. In fact, it is my middle name. I loved and admired the name. So much so that it was the name Sophia and I had chosen for our child if we'd had a son rather than a girl, your mother. Grace knew that. Perhaps it was why she chose the name for you."

Suddenly I remembered how I'd mistakenly thought that his poem about my mother had been written about me. I had to know whether I'd made the same sort of mistake again. "So the Rufus in your poem, was that dedicated to me or . . . to the son you didn't have?"

He beamed at me. "That's an easy question to answer. The poem was written for you, from beginning to end – although I would add, as we're being perfectly truthful, that in a way, now that I know you, the Rufus I never had and the Rufus now standing before me are one and the same to me . . . son. But as I'm not a man for sentimental nonsense, I would be grateful if we changed that particular subject to something rather more uplifting."

"Like truth-telling?" I suggested.

"What finer subject could there be?"

"So why did you say that the name Rufus was too soft, Granga?" I asked him, slightly relieved that it hadn't been a bigger lie. "Why did you change my name to Blue?"

To my surprise, the answer didn't come from Granga but

from the doorway: "'Cos he thought it'd be easier for you to start a new life with a different name, you idiot!"

The Artist turned to admire his painting *Blue* on the wall, nodded once approvingly, then was gone again.

"I liked my old name too. I was happy being Rufus," I told Granga. "So was John right, then? Was that why you lied to me – to make it easier for me to start a new life?"

Granga hesitated. "In part," he muttered, as if he wasn't completely happy with himself again. "Yes, I was thinking of what might be best for you . . . but I was also thinking of myself. And that, young man, is the hardest confession of all to make."

I had to work it out for myself this time, I shouldn't need John Thompson or anyone else to translate for me. "You didn't want a reminder of *your* past either – of your conversations with Sophia, of the son you might have had, of your middle name that you hide behind an initial."

Horatio R. Hennessy nodded, his gaze to the floor. "Old fool, old coward that I am."

I turned from Granga to take a closer look at the painting of me on the wall. "Rufus suited me," I said, still studying the painting, "but I think Blue suits me better now."

20

I WASN'T USED TO HEARING THE telephone ring in the Finca. It was morning, about seven o'clock. I was still in bed.

"Who do you say you are?" Granga sounded half-asleep and grumpy. "Never heard of you! What do you want at this hour?"

I jumped out of bed and ran to the top of the stairs so that I could hear the conversation more clearly. "Yes – John Thompson is staying with us. What of it?"

That really got my attention. I crept down the stairs to the hall and sat eagerly on the bottom step. When Granga saw me, he shrugged as if he couldn't make sense of the call at all, and pointed to the receiver for me to take over from him.

"Hello, this is Blue Ellerton." I tried to sound polite.

"Rufus – is that you?" asked Hannah at the other end – the end that was in England, just up the lane from our house, the one where we used to live, the three of us, our family, together.

"Hannah!" I cried.

"It's lovely to hear your voice, Rufus."

"Thanks," I replied. "That was Granga you were speaking to."

"I realised that, but he didn't seem to know who I was."

"I'll tell him," I said. "Was there a particular reason for your call?"

"Actually, yes. I'm ringing about John Thompson. I understand he's staying with you."

"Yes."

"There's a slight problem." She paused and I thought we'd been cut off until she continued, "His mother doesn't know where he is."

It hadn't occurred to me that he wouldn't have told her, but I should have checked. It was so like John Thompson not to tell people things. "Where did she think he was?" I asked.

"She thought he was staying with his father."

"Aren't his parents living together?" John hadn't said they were separated.

"No, they're not at the moment, Rufie," she replied. She had a way of making the most problematic situations seem straightforward. I waited for her to continue in that comforting voice of hers but she didn't.

"Would you like to speak to John?" I suggested, searching the hall for Granga, but he'd gone – probably back to bed.

"Not right now, thank you," she said, "perhaps later. First I have to telephone John's mother and tell her where he is, and that she's not to worry." Then she gave a little laugh the way she used to when she was chatting to my mother.

"I'll get John to ring her as soon as he's up," I promised.

"You're a good boy, Rufus," she replied. "We'll speak again soon." Then she was gone, like a gentle summer breeze that leaves you calmer than you were before.

I was right. Granga had gone back to bed. John hadn't even stirred. He was tucked up in his bed when I checked on him, snoring loudly. I didn't suppose there was any hurry now that his mother knew where he was, so I went back to bed too for another hour or so.

"Did you tell your mother you were coming here?" I asked John over breakfast before Granga came down. John hesitated. I didn't want to make him tell a lie, so I added, "Or did you tell her you were staying with your father?" He blushed, trying hard to conceal it by taking a sip of orange juice.

"You should have told her you were coming here!" I protested. "It's dangerous wandering around Europe on your own at our age. Anything could have happened to you. Your mother has been very worried."

I hadn't expected him to cry. If I had, I would have chosen different words to use. "Well it's done, and no harm came of it. And your mother knows you're here now." I tried to sound reassuring like Hannah, but it didn't seem to be working.

"Sorry," he said through a sob.

I passed him one of Maria's freshly-baked pastries, his favourite part of breakfast. "I said you'd ring your mother this morning."

We said no more about it after that. I gave John the time I expected he needed to compose his thoughts and decide what to say to his mother, whilst I worked out how best to broach the subject with Granga.

I needn't have worried – Granga did it for me. "That nuisance of a phone call this morning set my mind on a curious train of thought concerning young Thompson. Where is the boy?"

"He's just gone to his room," I said, waiting for Granga to swallow a mouthful of toast and marmalade then continue.

"I suspect he's been less than straightforward with me about his visit here, parent-wise – am I right?" I nodded and cleared away my cereal bowl. It wasn't easy to predict with Granga how he would react.

"Hannah will explain to his mother that he's OK here. She's good at explaining things."

As I spoke, my mind was back in England. That day again. People I'd never met, speaking without me hearing what they were saying. Strangers – all of them. Until Hannah. "Cry if you want to, Rufus. You don't have to hide. It's a terrible, terrible pain you're feeling. But it will ease – one day. I promise you. And then you'll have all your wonderful happy memories that will never leave you. You're lucky to have those – some people never have any. You'll be happy again. I know you will. Are you listening to me, Rufie?" I hadn't replied, not even a nod. Hannah had sighed a heavy sigh that lifted her floral-covered shoulders almost up to her pearled earlobes. She thought I hadn't heard her, but I had. I always listened to what Hannah had to say. She made sense, even in the midst of despair. I couldn't have coped without Hannah.

"Was she the woman on the phone?" asked Granga, watching me for clues.

"Yes," I said. "She was my mother's best friend. Don't you remember? I told you all about her when I first arrived. She drove me to the airport. She was like my guardian, she looked after me when . . ."

"Yes, yes," he said, like he was thinking about something else. "Mighty fine voice, especially for seven in the morning." He was still watching me carefully.

"She said we might speak again later," I explained, "and

in the meantime, John is to phone his mother. He's preparing for it now."

"Aha," responded Granga as if a morning haze was clearing. "An excellent plan. The woman has the makings of a fine officer. I can see you won't be needing me, not with Hannah at the helm."

"Probably not," I replied.

"Good, because I thought I'd go fishing this morning with Juan Antonio. It's time you savoured sea bass cooked with fresh herbs and served on a bed of lemon risotto. Fancy that?" Then he was gone, leaving me alone in the centre of the kitchen, licking my lips and longing for lunchtime.

John was sitting on the bed when I walked into his room. He had in his hands a scrap of paper and a pencil. "Are you preparing what you'll say to your mother?" I asked him quietly so as not to disturb his thoughts.

"No, I'm sketching your Granddad," he replied, lifting the paper so I could see it. Granga was standing as he'd stood in the entrance to our rocky shelter on the beach. He was wearing his old trilby. The brim covered his left eye, but the right one was visible, staring into the distance as if there was a lot of thinking going on. In his mouth was a half-smoked cigarette, which he held between the first two fingers of his left hand. His free hand was leaning casually against the rock.

"You've captured him brilliantly!" I enthused. "I'm getting used to recognising true works of art."

"You can have it if you like," he replied, handing it to me.

"Are you sure? It's not my birthday or anything."

"Yeah – I never keep my pictures," he said, getting up from his bed.

"If I could make pictures as you do, I'd keep them all," I said.

John Thompson shrugged. "I like giving them away," he said. "It makes people happy."

We headed downstairs to the telephone, John first. I showed him how to dial England, then stood aside as he waited for his mother to answer. It didn't ring long.

"Hello, Mum." John didn't speak again for some time after that and I guessed his mother was telling him off. John's expression stayed the same throughout so I couldn't be certain. Eventually he said, "A bloke Dad knew, a mate, was coming to Majorca for a holiday so we travelled on the plane together. Dad went to the airport with us and bought my ticket, then he was getting a train to Glasgow for a break to clear his head. He thought I'd be back before you knew about it, so please don't be mad at him."

Although I couldn't make out her exact words, I could tell from the tone of her voice that his mother was angry. It was John's turn again: "I didn't think it would make any difference to you if I was at Dad's or here. He gave me the money for a taxi from Palma Airport to the place where Rufus told me he was living with his Granddad. The address was on that postcard he sent me. It's a small village. It didn't take long to find them." His mother grew louder. "You did what?" I heard at quite a volume. "Haven't I always told you never to get into a car with a stranger? Don't you think I've got enough to worry about with your Dad and everything – do you want to give me a heart attack?"

"Sorry," John replied quietly. "Is Dad back yet?"

"No he's not bloody back!" She was shouting, then her

voice went quiet again and I couldn't hear any more. John said a few "Yeah"s after that followed by, "Bye Mum." Then he handed me the receiver to replace, saying, "I can stay a bit longer," with a big grin.

21

I WAS SURPRISED TO SEE HOW many fishing rods were needed to catch a few sea bass. Secretly I wished I was going fishing too, but I didn't say so because Granga would have suggested it if he'd wanted John and me there. Besides, I couldn't have eaten the fish for lunch if I'd seen them swimming happily hours before, innocent of what lay in store – the worst death of all.

"On the contrary," argued Granga when I expressed my concern about their death to him as he was loading the van. "Theirs is the perfect way to go – no time to dwell on it, then snuffed out like a candle in a gentle breeze in the midst of what they enjoy doing most. Exactly how I'd like to go."

"Do you really think so?" I shouted through the open window as Granga started up the van.

"Certain of it," he assured me, tilting his trilby as a signal that he was about to set off.

"*Snuffed out like a candle in a gentle breeze*," I repeated aloud as he disappeared up the drive, "*in the midst of what they enjoy doing most*." I ran back towards the Finca like a winning athlete who'd once thought he'd never walk again.

"Has he gone?" called John Thompson, coming outside when he heard me.

"Not for long. He'll be back with sea bass for lunch," I answered.

"What'll we do now then?" John asked, but I had no idea.

We decided to sit cross-legged on the front lawn. "If Aunt Lulu was still here, she would think of something fun for us all to do," I remarked lazily.

"I like her," John told me, untying his shoelaces.

"Me too," I agreed.

John lay on the grass with his hands behind his head, studying the pale-blue sky as if he was planning to paint it. Maybe he was. It was hard to tell what went on in John Thompson's mind. I should have tried harder to find out.

"What are you thinking about, John?" I asked quietly, so as not to disturb him too much.

"Nothing much," he replied, "just how me and my Mum like cooking together sometimes at home."

As I'd never made a meal with anyone, this came as a surprise to me. "You cook with your mother?"

"Yeah – what's wrong with that?"

"Nothing at all," I assured him. "It's just that my mother always cooked for my father and me at home. She was a fantastic cook."

To my amazement, John answered, "I remember." He sat up. "I had tea at your house once. She made us *spaghetti carbonara* with freshly-grated parmesan cheese on top."

To remember the occasion was more than I could manage, but actually to remember what we'd eaten, and the Italian for it, was incredible. "You must have enjoyed it," I exclaimed.

"I'd never tasted anything like it before," he replied, licking his lips.

Encouraged by my success at drawing John out of himself

so easily, I continued, "What about your father? Does he cook?" It wasn't exactly prying, even if I was curious to know why his father wasn't living with his mother any more. The question followed on naturally from the previous one – that was all.

I hadn't expected John to laugh, though. "Dad? Cook? You must be joking!" Which didn't really get me very far.

"He's probably too busy?" I made sure my gaze didn't meet his as I asked the question, but hovered somewhere casually across the lawn.

"Not any more."

There was no point in doing what I'd have done with other boys and leaving an awkward pause for John to fill, so I came right out with it this time, "Why not?"

"He's lost his job." I hadn't thought of that. I should have done. Lots of people lost their jobs, so why not John's father?

"I'm sorry," I said, "I'm sure he'll find another one soon." I'd never met John's father, but that hadn't stopped me forming a mental picture of him – tall, broad, perhaps a little overweight around the waist, dark-haired like John, with strong arms and hands that were used to hard work. But somehow, whenever John mentioned Mr. Thompson, I never pictured him smiling as I did with my own father. Maybe I was beginning to find out why.

"He says he hasn't a hope in hell of getting another job. All he's ever been is a lorry driver. He used to have his own business – employed other drivers and everything. Then when that packed up, he drove for other people again."

Poor Mr. Thompson, I thought. No wonder I never saw him smiling. "He must be a good driver," I tried to sound encouraging, "if he had his own business."

"He always said he was." John lay back on the grass again, shielding his eyes from the sun.

"Then shouldn't it be easy for him to find another job?" I was already making sense of his leaving home. He'd lost his job. He was looking desperately for another. Scouring the country, maybe Glasgow at that very moment, for the right position. Wouldn't come back until he'd found something to make his family proud again.

John moved his hand from his eyes to look at me. "Not without a driving licence," he answered.

It was getting worse and worse. The pain that the Thompson family must have been going through – no wonder John had wanted to run away to Mallorca. "Your poor father!" I sighed, patting John comfortingly on the shoulder. It was an impulse. I hadn't imagined it would upset him.

He jumped to his feet without even tying his shoelaces. "You don't understand!" he shouted angrily at me.

But I did understand. Had he forgotten the pain that I'd suffered too? "Of course I understand." I spoke calmly, like Hannah would, "At least you still have a father." He needed reminding.

"I wish I didn't." He was sobbing now, like I'd seen him that night in his sleep, perspiration clinging to strands of his hair. "I wish my father was dead instead of yours!"

"That's a terrible thing to say!" I exclaimed, standing to meet him face on. "He doesn't deserve that!" John Thompson had so much to learn, and I was the best person to teach him.

"Oh yes he does!" screamed John, his face as red as a stop traffic light.

"Just because he's lost his driving licence?" I laughed in a final attempt to calm him down. Too late. It was done. I'd reached that moment again, the one that can take you from happy to sad, life to death, the moment that can happen to you without you even being aware – until it has passed, and then it's too late, and nothing's the same any more.

"I'm not angry with him for losing his licence," he sobbed, "I hate him 'cos he killed your Mum and Dad."

22

WHEN IT HAD HAPPENED, I used to try and picture the driver over and over again. Sometimes he was old with a beard and horns coming out of the top of his head. Other times he was young and stupid and drunk and listening to music. Once he'd been the man in the dock that my father had cross-examined, speeding through the night, looking for revenge. But in all those weeks and months, never had the driver that had taken my parents' lives been Mr. Thompson.

I knew the part of the road where they'd crashed. I'd seen some glass and metal when I'd gone past. Hannah had talked and talked as she drove to distract me, but I'd already seen it lying there.

At night in bed when I'd pictured the crash as it must have happened, just as my parents' car had turned the bend, I would find myself wiping out the final details and rearranging them as they should have been. My father would take the bend just as the lorry was approaching. He'd see that the lorry was on the wrong side of the road. But instead of being too late for him to do anything about it, he'd slam on his brakes and shout to my mother, "Jump out!" Then they would stand hand-in-hand by the side of their crunched-up car, laughing at their luck in still being alive, discussing, as they went home to tell me all about it, whether a guardian angel had helped them to survive. Every time I rewrote it, something different would happen. But each new scene only made the real one worse. So eventually I'd given up thinking about it – until John Thompson had brought it all back again.

When a bigger boy tackled you in rugby and you dropped the ball, then your team went on to lose because of it, you felt like crying but you didn't, because blood mixed with adrenaline was thumping through your veins. It was only later, when your heartbeat had slowed down, and you'd replayed the moment you'd dropped the ball so many times you couldn't remember it clearly any more, yet what memory you had of it hurt more than the original experience, that tears would come.

When John Thompson had first come to our school, we'd all thought he was shy. It couldn't have been easy joining a class of boys who already knew each other. As John didn't make any attempts to start a conversation, and whenever anyone spoke to him he answered either "Yep" or "Nope", after a short while he was ignored. And I mean by me too. It was easier that way. You didn't have to rack your brains for something to say which might ignite a spark of interest somewhere inside that big, closed head of his. I'd probably tried for longer than anyone else. "I've got a tortoise called Freddy. Do you have any pets?"

"Nope," he would answer without looking up from whatever he was drawing.

"Do you like being a day boy?" I'd persist. "I do. I'd hate to have to stay on in the evenings and hardly ever see my parents, wouldn't you?"

"Not bothered," would come his lethargic reply.

"Do you live locally?"

"Fifteen minutes away on the bus, then I walk for another five."

"That's nearer than our house," I would reply. "My mother drives me to school and picks me up. It takes her about half an hour each way. That's why she's sometimes late."

"Oh."

At least I couldn't be accused of not trying. And even though it made me feel uncomfortable inside if I pretended not to have seen him in order to avoid further conversations, I told myself that I should be proud that I'd carried on beyond what anyone else would have considered necessary.

Later, when everyone had realised that everyone else was ignoring John Thompson too, it changed. Sebastian Hamilton was first. Instead of walking past John in the corridor as he usually did, he stopped right in front of him so that John was forced to do the same. I was walking behind Sebastian at the time, so I saw what happened clearly. John didn't look up from Sebastian's pair of black shiny lace-ups. He stared at them as if he was wondering how they came to be in his way. Neither boy moved. Sebastian Hamilton spoke. "Isn't the corridor wide enough for you, Fatso?" A crowd had formed on either side of them like a traffic jam. "Speak, John Thompson!" I said to myself. "For goodness' sake say something, anything!" But he didn't. The only response was a snigger from Jack Samuels – quiet but loud enough to encourage Sebastian to go on.

"What's the matter, Rain Man? Can't you speak?" This time the sniggering spread through the rest of the boys like a dose of measles. They felt like they were saying it too. A new sport was taking place and they all supported the stronger contestant. No one wanted to be on the losing team.

I shivered with a rush of adrenaline and not because I was excited by what I saw. I knew it wasn't fair – John Thompson was no "Rain Man". He was just a bit slow, that was all. But even if there was something a bit different about him, he'd done nothing wrong. He didn't deserve this. I had to think of something right to say.

"Sebastian!" I patted the taller boy on his shoulder. "I'm trying to get past – you're creating a queue. Do you think you could move on?"

Sebastian turned round to see who was spoiling the fun. A clump of greasy blonde hair fell forward as he glared down at me. "Oh look!" he said with a grin. "It's Rufus Ellerton. I thought for a minute Rain Man's brother had turned up." The laughing escalated. I knew I was now on the losing side – a team of two that had nowhere to go. I could feel my body shaking, but not enough for them to notice. I didn't dare speak in case my voice gave me away.

"Rufus Ellerton isn't my brother." So seldom had I heard John Thompson's voice that I barely recognised it at first, until he added, "Rufus is my friend."

For me, that was when John Thompson and I first became friends, although for him we already were. As far as the insults were concerned, that day was a catalyst too. Others were quick to join in. I did my best to defend John, which sometimes caused them to attack me as well. But as I was quicker than John to respond, I managed to quash their remarks before they could spread. Soon I discovered John Thompson wasn't shy, he just didn't like talking – unless he felt there was something he needed to say.

The sound through my bedroom window of wheels crunching on gravel disturbed my recollections. A van door slammed a little too loudly. Heavy boot-clad footsteps headed towards the Finca. The front door creaked open, then closed. Granga was back! It was safe at last to come down from my bedroom. I couldn't bear to face John Thompson alone. I hadn't seen him since I'd left him on the front lawn. For all I knew, he could have decided to go home.

I put down the pen with which I'd been trying to compose a letter. All I'd written so far was:

Dear Mr. Thompson,
I understand from John that you were the driver who crashed into my parents' car and killed them.

There was a lot of crossing out after that and a doodle made up of squares growing smaller and smaller, one inside another like a Russian doll, with the smallest at the centre of them all, shaded black. The doodle had captured more of my attention than the letter and distracted me from what I'd wanted to say. Every time I'd searched for the right word to express what I was thinking, my eyes had been drawn back to the black square at the centre again. Granga would know exactly what I should be saying in my letter. Now that he was back, all would be well again.

I ran down the stairs, across the hall and into the kitchen, shouting for him all the time that I ran. When I found him, he was standing by the big white sink, lining up a family of sea bass on a wooden draining board, each fish smaller than the one before, just like my squares.

"All that time for a handful of sea bass barely larger than goldfish," he declared, glancing over his shoulder to see me running in. "I expect Lulu will insist I bathe them in perfumed sea salts before she'll have one."

"Don't you remember? Aunt Lulu went home last night," I reminded him in a sombre voice, so that he'd realise that something was wrong, as my mother would have done. "John and I have been here on our own."

"Just as well – fish eyes would have frightened her off anyway," he laughed – as if this was just another day. I walked to his side and stood staring at the glazed eyes of the slimy, lifeless creatures lying like corpses waiting to be identified. "You can have the one in the middle. He took the most catching."

"I'm not hungry," I replied with a tone that I hoped would be a clue. He stopped what he was doing and turned to face me. At last, I thought, he's noticed something's wrong.

"Where's John Thompson?" he asked eagerly. "I bet he won't say no to a nice juicy sea bass and lemon risotto."

He was looking right at me but somehow he just didn't see! How could a deep-thinking poet be quite so dim as he? "I've no idea where John Thompson is and I don't care either!" This time I made sure with my voice that Granga would know. He picked up a red tea towel that had been ironed and left neatly folded on top of a gleaming white work surface and wiped his fishy hands on it. Maria would be furious when she smelt it the following morning.

"I see," he said, but the frown between his bushy grey eyebrows told me that wasn't true.

"No you don't!" I snapped. "You don't see anything about me! All you do is make it *seem* as if you understand."

I hadn't meant to sound as harsh as this. I didn't even know that this was what I'd been thinking until I'd said it. Perhaps it wasn't, or perhaps it had come from deep inside, like the black square.

Granga threw the tea towel in the direction of the draining board without looking where it was going. It landed on the body of the smallest fish, covering it like a sheet in a morgue. I could see by the way Granga stared at my face that he was concerned. "Are you drunk?" he asked, leaning towards me. "Have you two boys been helping yourself to my champagne?"

"Of course I'm not drunk!" I thundered at him in exasperation. "I'm angry and shocked and unhappy, not that you care!" This time I spoke exactly what I'd been thinking and I meant every word of it. Granga massaged his temple with the first two fingers of his left hand, as he did when he was thinking hard about something and didn't have a cigarette to inhale.

"I left to go fishing, no Lulu or Maria to distract you two boys, you quarrelled with John Thompson – not enough to do, too much to say." It was as if he was speaking to himself, not to me, trying to make sense of what I'd said without having to ask me. "The boy spoke out for once, prompted, no doubt, by your questions. A boy unlike you – not used to hearing *why*."

I had misjudged him. It wasn't that he hadn't understood, he'd seen too well, even though he couldn't have known exactly what John had told me, even though he couldn't have guessed the pain those words had caused.

"Granga," I whispered softly, "there's something I have to tell you. I only found out myself this afternoon from John."

I hesitated. Granga's frown had deepened. I feared the news would be too much for him. "The crash." I'd said that much, the rest would be easy. "The driver . . ."

". . . was Mr. Thompson," Granga finished for me.

23

G RANGA HAD KNOWN ALL ALONG — it wasn't guessing. The name of the driver, that John was his son. When John had arrived at the Finca, Granga, the man who loved truth-telling, had made him promise not to tell me. Thought it better that I didn't know. Reluctantly John had agreed — it was their secret. On the beach that day in our rocky shelter John had wanted to tell me. Granga, though, had thought that he should stop him, let me talk instead, then say we should go.

"So the boy couldn't keep it to himself any longer. I should have guessed he would tell you when I wasn't here."

I couldn't speak. I had no words, no thinking, only pictures in my head. First a crash and then two people talking — one my Granga, the other my best friend.

"I wanted to protect you, Blue," I could hear the man I'd fondly called Granga saying. "I couldn't see any reason for you to know."

I'd made a fist of my right hand but I had nowhere to put it. I could feel my nails cutting into the skin of my palm. The pain of it gave my mind something else to fix on. I closed my eyes and wished that he would go.

"The boy's fool of a father and his vile driving have

nothing to do with the son." I heard his voice quiver as he described Mr. Thompson's driving, like the strong but fragile note my father and I liked so much in Max Bruch's violin concerto. "Speak to me, Blue!" Was he ordering or pleading? "It's over now. Past. Gone. It cannot be reversed."

Then there was another voice. This one much younger. "Rufus," it said, "I've drawn your Mum and Dad."

John handed me a scrap of white paper, then ran from the kitchen. The drawing of my parents shook slightly in my hands. I didn't look at it. Instead I turned to Granga. He was standing by the window, watching where John ran. "Here!" I said. "You take it – I don't want to see it!"

He held out his hand as I passed him the paper. He didn't take it but took my hand instead. His grip felt strong. I dropped the piece of paper. It floated slowly to the floor like a dead leaf and landed on my feet. I panicked and looked down. That's when I saw them, their faces staring up at me as if they said, "Hello, Rufie, we're back!"

It was the first time I'd seen an image of them, except in my head, since I'd left England. There'd been hundreds of photographs of them at home, but I hadn't packed a single one. It wasn't that I'd forgotten – it had been my decision. I'd made it on my final night at home.

"I'd like to be alone at home tonight," I'd told Hannah. She was helping me pack my summer clothes. She'd spread them on the bed as my mother would have done, then folded them into neat piles which she'd ordered in my suitcase, light clothes on top, heavy ones at the bottom.

"Why don't you spend your last night with us?" Hannah had urged me. "You like staying at our house, and the girls love having you there."

She was telling the truth – they did seem to enjoy my company. I think my being with them made them appreciate their parents more. "No, thank you," I'd replied politely. "I'd rather spend my last night here." I knew she would understand – she'd been an only child too.

She'd cooked me supper and we'd eaten it together at the kitchen table. Steak and chips – my favourite – with peas and English mustard served from the jar my mother and I had bought. Who'd have thought that day when we were shopping that the jar of mustard would have lasted longer than she did?

"Have I cooked it how you like it?" Hannah had asked as I took my first mouthful.

"Yes thanks," I'd said – I couldn't tell her it was a bit too rare for me.

"You'll be having lots of nice new dishes in Mallorca." I knew she was trying to be encouraging, but I didn't want to hear about Mallorca. So I'd said, "What will happen to the house once I've gone?" She'd know. She knew everything – except how to cook a steak medium well.

She'd finished her mouthful before answering, "It will be sold eventually – but you don't need to worry about all that."

She was drinking red wine from one of my father's bottles he kept in the cellar. She'd drunk more of it than my mother would have done. I wondered if I should point out that she'd almost finished the whole bottle. Instead I asked, "Are you walking home tonight?"

"No," she'd replied, "I think I should stay here."

Once Hannah had gone to bed, I tiptoed quietly from room to room. The silence made the house feel empty, like when your favourite music has ended and you can't play it any more. The rooms were as lifeless as my mother's clothes still hanging on their rails.

My mother kept a chest of photographs on the upstairs landing. I'd opened the lid, half afraid to peer inside. Of course, I'd known what I would find there – the two of us had looked at them many times. On the left of the chest they started with me as a baby – in my pram, on the sofa, in my mother's arms. With each new pile I grew a little older – first teeth, first step, first day at school, first prize. What didn't change was my parents' expression – their clothes and hair might alter, but not their pride. I took out every photograph to examine it more closely. I had no idea what I was searching for. Not just a reminder of who was missing – I needed something else, something I hadn't noticed before.

I was halfway through the chest before I'd found it: a summer's day, we were all outside. I was at the top of my slide, my father pushing me down, my mother waiting to catch me in the paddling pool at the bottom, her arms outstretched. When I'd looked at the photo before, I'd seen it only with my own memory – of a birthday that I'd enjoyed, a happy moment on a slide. But now, I saw the roles my parents had played that day – my father there to encourage me gently in the right direction, my mother seeking to protect her only child from harm. This was the memory I wanted to remember. I put back the other photos and closed the lid of the chest. I would take this one with me to Mallorca. I'd held it carefully as I'd continued to walk around the house.

It felt as if I was a stranger in a museum fixing on objects that told a story from its past – but no future. That was the point. Not *there* for me anyway. Another family would probably start again. I'd lived in that house all my life and never before imagined another family living in it. Now suddenly I realised exactly what a home was. Not the building where you lived – that was as temporary as a hotel room – but the way the house was made into a home: the walls my parents had painted with colours so carefully chosen, the furniture they'd searched and searched for until they'd found, the pleasure at hanging a newly-discovered painting, the birthday and Christmas presents all around. If they'd lived, those would have included a blue drum kit in the corner of my bedroom – the one that Hannah's husband had covered with a sheet. The pleasure they must have had when they'd gone to choose it would have been part of the pleasure their present would have given me.

I had to see the drum kit again – just once more to know how it would make me feel. Would I still be able to pick up their excitement? Or had their leaving taken that as well? I threw back the sheet as if I was a matador, with a flamboyant gesture my mother would have enjoyed. I remembered the bright blue colour of the drum kit from the department store window – I hadn't known then that Blue would be my name.

The sound of the drum as I smashed the drumstick against it seemed to make the whole house vibrate. Like my heartbeat when they'd told me what had happened, and I'd said that there must have been a mistake.

The drum kit was no more a part of my home than my favourite book collection, or the leather rugby ball my father had bought for me, or the shabby teddy bear I'd said I'd never grow out of. Then why, I'd asked myself, had I chosen a photograph of the three of us to take with me to Mallorca? Hadn't I just decided to leave my home behind? I didn't need these photographs to remind me. My parents and my home were in my mind.

I'd left the photograph of us on my bedside table, propped up against another one of my mother and father in a silver frame. It had stayed inside my head without coming out ever since that night. Undisturbed, airless, like wings without flight – until I'd seen John Thompson's scrap of paper and the portrait of my parents he had drawn. Then the memory of their faces had slipped out again – I was home once more, beside a silver frame.

"You've Grace's eyes and nose." Granga picked up the drawing from where it had landed on my feet. The movement brought me back from England to Mallorca – just me and my grandfather again.

"And my father's mouth," I pointed out. We both stared at the pencil portrait as if we were reading the last page of a book we'd enjoyed so much that we didn't want it to end.

"Grace was an independent child – she liked her own company." He was reminding himself, not telling me. It wasn't how I remembered my mother – she was happiest when my father and I were around.

"I think I'll put it away somewhere safe upstairs," I said, taking the paper from him – I was afraid that he might smudge it with his big fingers.

"Good idea," he agreed. I could tell from his face that he wanted to be alone – it seemed older, like a flickering light bulb that you only notice because its light isn't flowing as smoothly as usual.

I'd reached the top of the stairs when I heard Granga shouting after me, "Well do you want this God-forsaken sea bass tonight or not?"

"Not!" I called back before closing my bedroom door behind me. It slammed shut in a way that I hadn't meant it to. I wasn't angry with either Granga or John any more, only with Mr. Thompson . . . and with God for not having kept my parents safe as He should have done.

24

I T WASN'T UNTIL THE FOLLOWING morning that we realised John Thompson was missing. When he didn't come down to breakfast I went to his room and found it empty. Granga had been in his study all morning. I could hear his typewriter, which meant he wasn't to be disturbed, but this was an emergency.

"Go away!" he shouted when I knocked on his study door. "Can't you hear I'm busy?"

"John Thompson has gone missing!" I shouted back.

The door was thrown open. Granga was still in his pyjamas and dressing gown. He looked as if he hadn't slept all night. His eyes were heavy, the lower lids swollen and he was unshaven. "Where have you looked?" he asked as he pushed past me in a hurry.

"Everywhere," I replied, following him outside.

"Including the woods?"

"Yes."

"Is his case still in his room, and his clothes?" I hadn't thought of that. I should have done. I wasn't officer material like Hannah.

"He wouldn't go – not without saying goodbye." I climbed the stairs two at a time. His bed was made, I noticed this time. He must have been missing all night. I scanned the room for his case. He wouldn't have gone back to England without that. I opened the wardrobe door. The small brown vinyl suitcase was lying inside, his big black Wellingtons covered in dried mud beside it, and his smart pair of trousers that he'd worn for Granga's birthday were on a hanger with the shirt I'd lent him to wear draped around them. John Thompson was coming back!

I raced downstairs to share the good news with Granga. "His clothes and case are still upstairs, as I suspected," I called from the front door when I saw him halfway up the drive, his silk dressing gown rippling in the morning breeze.

"Bed slept in?"

"It doesn't look like it." We'd reached the top of the drive but Granga didn't stop walking. "Where are we going?" Even in his slippers, he was hard to keep up with.

"To the village, of course," he replied.

"Don't you think you should change first?" I suggested – sometimes he needed a gentle reminder.

"No time." He retied his dressing-gown belt as he spoke, as if that would make him look more respectable to the village. "No one will notice."

He was wrong, by quite a number. Cars slowed down when they passed us, some drivers even hooted their horns. Not that it bothered Granga. "They must know me," he said, waving at their grinning faces.

The first place we stopped was Miguel's restaurant bar. Fortunately Miguel was there without his wife.

"We're looking for the other one," Granga explained, pointing at me. "Have you seen him? He vanished some time last night."

"No, I haven't," Miguel replied without the least surprise at Granga's clothes, "but come and have a drink while I ask the others."

I was glad of the chance to sit down. We'd walked quite a long way and at such a pace that my legs and feet were aching. A cool glass of Coca-Cola was exactly what I needed. Granga ordered a black coffee and brandy.

Seated at the small round table on the terrace, he didn't attract nearly so much attention. He could have been wearing a checked shirt and navy jacket, rather than pyjamas and a dressing gown. And his slippers were nicely hidden under the tablecloth. "Do you have a plan, Granga?" I asked once Miguel had joined us with the news that no one had seen *mi amigo*.

Granga sipped his brandy with his eyes closed whilst Miguel and I waited patiently. "Your Granga will know the answer," Miguel whispered in my ear. I nodded hopefully. "Did your friend have a reason to run away?"

"Not really," I replied, "unless it was because his father killed my parents."

Miguel stared at me as if he was having difficulty understanding my English. Granga opened his eyes. "Finish your drink!" he ordered. "I know where he might have gone."

Miguel offered to drive us in his black open-top jeep with the name of the restaurant *Miguel's* written in white down one side. I sat in the back, leaving the two of them in the front to discuss where we were heading and the best way for a temperamental jeep to get there.

I recognised the route we were taking, even though we'd gone much faster when Granga was driving. "It's the road to the beach!" I shouted into the wind.

"The location the lad chose for your portrait," Granga replied.

The beach was crowded this time. Bright sunshine gave the sand a light, golden hue that it had lacked in the rain. *Rayleigh Scattering* must have been hard at work – the Mediterranean Sea was striped in varying shades of blue all the way to the horizon where it met the cloudless blue sky. Only a speedboat broke its stillness, heading noisily away from the shore.

With his pyjama legs now rolled up above his bony knees, Granga could easily have passed for a bather, especially as Miguel had persuaded him to leave his dressing gown in the jeep. We stepped carefully amongst a variety of bodies, all stretched out and oiled like sea bass on a grill.

"John Thompson wouldn't lie here," I called to Granga. "He goes bright red whenever he has too much sun."

"That's why we're heading for the rocks where we sheltered," explained Granga. "I'd put money on finding the little rascal there."

"Damn!" Granga's voice echoed around the empty rocky shelter. "I'm not often wrong when it comes to predicting a hideout."

"We'll find your amigo," Miguel tried to reassure me. "Do not fear. He has probably already returned to the Finca."

"And that," agreed Granga, "is where we shall go."

There was a car in the drive when we drew up to the Finca. It was a small silver hatchback with a sunshine roof. I flushed when I saw it. The last time an uninvited car had pulled up outside my home it had brought bad news. In wartime they must have felt that way about telegrams.

"Who the devil's this?" was Granga's first reaction.

"Maybe someone has brought John back" was Miguel's idea.

"Why don't we go in and find out?" was my suggestion, so we all got out of the jeep and went inside.

"John?" I called upstairs from the hallway. "John Thompson, are you back?"

There was no reply. The house seemed empty. Maria had been there, though – the wooden floor in the hall smelt freshly polished.

"I'm going to John's room." It was all I could think of. Miguel and Granga thought they should come too.

We crept up the stairs, Granga first and Miguel behind me, then tiptoed across the landing to John's door. Granga put a forefinger to his mouth to tell us there should be no speaking. It was like being in an Agatha Christie film. If I hadn't been so worried about John, I'd have felt quite excited. Monsieur Poirot turned the handle. I took a deep breath. We all barged in.

"Who in God's name are you?" Granga should have been more courteous, as Miguel was.

"Encantado!" he said with a smile and flamboyant bow. My response could not have been more different. I threw my arms around her, sobbing into her silk floral dress.

"I should explain," she said, stroking my hair with a hand that smelt of pine forests, "I'm Hannah. Maria let me in. I've come to collect John's clothes."

It had happened again. She'd been sent like an angelic messenger to pick up the pieces when someone you needed was gone forever. She didn't have to tell me – I could read it in her expression – she'd come with bad news that she wished she didn't have to give.

"Why can't the boy collect his own clothes?" At least I still had Granga.

"Because he's gone," I cried, "gone like my mother and father. Don't you understand? Something has happened to him. He . . ."

"Rufie's right," interrupted Hannah, loosening her grip around me. "John has gone. He's back in England. He went home last night."

"You mean he isn't . . . he hasn't . . . he's alive in England!"

"I'm sorry, Rufie. He should have said goodbye."

"Are you telling me you've come all this way for the boy's clothes?" asked Granga. "We could have sent them."

Hannah hesitated – I'd seen that look before, "Not exactly." She flicked back her hair with a gesture I'd forgotten. "I wanted to see Rufus – and you, Mr. Hennessy."

25

THUNDER PASSES QUICKLY IN MALLORCA. When the sun pops back out, it's as if it had never gone away. Except for pools of rainwater and the sound of dripping from terracotta rooftops and the heavy smell of freshly-watered soil.

Miguel wasn't invited to join us for lunch on the terrace. I think Granga sensed that Hannah wanted to speak to us alone. When Granga opened the front door, then continued to hold it, Miguel knew that this was his cue to go home. He kissed Hannah goodbye on both cheeks as if they were old friends, adding that she was invited to his restaurant any time. Hannah thanked him politely but said that she wouldn't be staying long.

Granga fetched a big green garden umbrella I'd never seen before from the garage, in order to protect Hannah from the midday sun. And we each had a matching cushion on our chairs at the wooden table we'd sat around for Granga's birthday lunch. The cushions smelt musty as if they'd been in the garage too long.

Granga and Hannah shared a bottle of Granga's favourite white Rioja. Hannah said it was the best Rioja she had ever tasted. She thought it particularly suited the sea bass with lemon risotto that Granga, still in his pyjamas and dressing gown, had prepared – she had the large sea bass that Granga had reserved for John.

"John asked me to give you this," Hannah said, taking a small white envelope from her black-and-cream handbag, "and to tell you he apologised for his poor grammar but that words weren't his strength, they were yours, and to remember that he'd never laughed at your drawings."

I wished he'd been there to reassure him that I would never have laughed at anything he wanted to tell me. I was the friend who had defended him when others had laughed. I tore open the envelope while Granga and Hannah were talking. It almost felt like I had two parents again.

Dear Blue,
I hope you liked the drawing of your parents. I did it in a hurry so I could give it to you before I left. I remembered your Mum better than your Dad because I'd only seen him once at Speech Day when you went up for a prize.

I didn't want to stay in Majorka if you weren't happy with me being there. I knew you weren't when I told you about my Dad. I'd said I wouldn't but somehow it seemed like lying. Then when I saw your face I wished I'd said nothing.

I'm not like my Dad. I wouldn't have killed your parents. He said he'd been tired because he'd been driving too long. I said he shouldn't have been driving if he was that tired. I wouldn't have if it had been me and my lorry and my job. I told him your Mum and Dad were really nice people and that he was a bloody

idiot to blame for screwing up your life. He said it was
bad to use swear words and I said not as bad as killing
innocent people. My Mum's angry with him too. I heard
her shouting at him at night when I was in bed. She
said she never wanted to see his face again, then in the
morning he'd gone and she didn't stop crying. He came
back after that, then he left again and took his clothes
with him and moved into another house. My Mum
didn't try and stop him like I thought she would. That's
when I came to Majorka. I don't know if he's coming
back. I tried to draw him so I wouldn't forget what he
looked like, but I couldn't get his eyes right. So I drew
his old parrot Dirk instead and gave it to him.

I wanted to say I'm sorry for what my Dad did.
And if you don't want me as your best friend any more
I'll understand. I'm giving this letter to Hannah to give
you when she comes to see you. She met me at the
airport after I'd rung my Mum to say I wanted to leave
Majorka. She talked a lot in the car going home, mostly
about you and your Granddad. She's a bit like your
Mum but without her sparkling eyes. And your Mum
always spoke as if she was doing lots of thinking.
Hannah's nice but not as special as your Mum.

Thank your Granddad from me for letting me stay
with you in Majorka, it was the best time I ever had. If
he wants another painting write and tell me what he
wants and I'll do it. And the same with you, if you
want me to, I like painting you. Maybe you could send
me your poem when you've finished it? I might not
understand it, but I like seeing your writing anyway.
Tell Hannah not to bother bringing back my

Wellingtons that got dirty walking back from the
sheep's field.

Luv

John Thompson

I'd never received a letter from John Thompson before. He'd
drawn horizontal pencil lines all the way down the white
sheet of paper so that his writing wouldn't slope. It was easy
to read, with big rounded letters lightly joined together and
loops under the "*g*"s and "*y*"s. You could tell he was artistic
even in a letter. I folded it where John had and replaced it
in its envelope – I had to keep John Thompson's letter safe.

Hannah and Granga were still talking. Granga was telling
her how he and Juan Antonio had caught the sea bass and
which herbs he'd used to flavour it. Hannah said she would
like to take some of the herbs back with her to England and
try out the recipe on her family when she got home. Most
people would then have been led to ask Hannah about that
family – her children, her husband – but not Granga. Instead
he replied, "I don't advise it. These herbs wouldn't taste the
same in England. You need the right setting to give them
back the life that has been plucked prematurely from them
– mountains, pine forests, amber sunshine and terracotta soil."

Hannah smiled contentedly as she reflected on what
Granga had said. John Thompson was right, she wasn't as
special as my mother, but she was pretty like her.

"Aren't you forgetting the beauty of our English countryside?" she asked him. "We do have a few mountains and
pine forests, even if our sunshine isn't quite as amber as
Mallorca's."

"Indeed! And there's little to compare with smoked

salmon and cucumber sandwiches partaken on the periphery of a croquet lawn in the late-afternoon English sun. But would you enjoy them in quite the same way here in Mallorca?"

"Perhaps not," she laughed, "but we could try."

So that was how Hannah, Granga and I found ourselves on Granga's lawn partaking of afternoon tea English-style. Maria had been summoned to make the smoked salmon and cucumber sandwiches while Granga had carried his best loungers, a garden parasol and a small round table onto the lawn. It was greener grass than was usual in Mallorca as Granga had installed water sprinklers along all its sides.

"What a wonderful spot," declared Hannah, gazing sleepily into the Mallorcan countryside. Granga had shaved and changed into his cream baggy flannels and a pair of brown leather brogues for tea. I knew he'd be in his trilby even before I saw him. It gave him the distinction he deserved.

I carried the silver tray bearing the carefully-cut sandwiches and a pot of Earl Grey tea. It had taken us a lot of searching to locate the tea strainer. I'd found it behind three silver napkin rings and a matching gravy boat. Once we'd polished it up, it looked pretty impressive. I set the tray down gently on the table and Hannah poured. "Now doesn't this feel like being back in England?" she sighed.

We chatted about England and all the familiar places and what you could do on English afternoons. I learnt so much more about Granga from Hannah's questions. He'd been to almost every town she named. And he wasn't only familiar with its size or location, he knew its churches, rivers, tearooms, what it looked like in the rain. Soon I learnt he'd even visited our village. He said it had been long before I was born. I wasn't sure I believed him, though, because he described the grand pavilion on the cricket ground, and my parents had taken me to its opening when I was seven.

"Do you ever feel nostalgic for dear old England?" I heard Hannah ask Granga as I relaxed in my lounger.

"There's no point in nostalgia," he replied from under his trilby, which by now covered his entire face, "it blinds you to where you are now."

The soothing sound of their conversation coupled with the warm Mallorcan air soon lulled me into a siesta. It happens a lot in Mallorca, often when you least expect it. The sun seeps through your skin and into your head. It's not a good idea to wake too quickly, especially if you discover you're not alone. You can find yourself saying something you wish you hadn't, like, "Where's my mother?" when you no longer have one.

"Are you happy here, Rufie?" Hannah was asking.

It wasn't a question I'd asked myself all the time I'd been here.

"I think so," I answered. "It's different from being at home."

If only I'd answered more clearly it might not have happened. If only I hadn't just woken from a deep sleep. If only I'd told her exactly what I was thinking. If only I'd said, "I've made memories I'll always keep." Was that a poem? Had I just made poetry? Was that what it meant to feel your life a rhyme?

"You know, you can always come back if you want to. I'll be there for you."

She'd misunderstood but somehow I couldn't tell her. "Thank you," was all I answered like a stupid schoolboy instead of a Classicist. Hannah searched my face for what I didn't say.

"John will be going back to school soon. The summer holiday is nearly over."

I sat up straight in my chair. Hannah poured me a cup of cold tea. I glanced towards Granga, hoping he hadn't heard our conversation, sensing my inadequate answers would have made him feel let down. He was asleep under his trilby. What thoughts were being created under that hat? I had to say something to correct her misunderstanding.

"I like my lessons with Mrs. Bainbridge," I said in a loud voice that made me feel less disloyal.

"Is she your private tutor?" Hannah enquired.

"She comes from England. She used to be a Geography teacher when she was young."

Hannah moved her lounger closer to where I was sitting and whispered this time, "So Mrs. Bainbridge is an older lady?"

I couldn't lie. She was quite old. But it didn't matter. She was as good as any teacher I'd had at school. "I don't know how old she is," I said cautiously. "But John and I like her. She came to Granga's barbecue."

Hannah rested her long neck against her lounger. She looked as if she had some thinking to do. She didn't think as quickly as my mother – John Thompson was right about that too. My mother would have known without asking how happy I was to be here.

I used the time while Hannah was thinking to run back through all my answers. "Are you happy here?" she'd asked me first. "I think so," I'd answered. "It's different from being at home." She'd taken it as wanting to go back.

Why had I expressed myself as I had? Was there something I was missing? Was it loyalty to Granga that was keeping me here? I raced through all the experiences we'd had together – savouring tagines in Morocco, creating a poem together by Sophia's grave, dancing in a French village while Granga played his mouth organ to the crowd. I thought of all our conversations, of everything he'd taught me – about good taste, philosophy, poetry, art, about how to feel things, how to be alive. I thought of Maria's happy greeting when she first saw me, and of her donkey with the long grey lazy face. I remembered being on the beach that day with Granga and John Thompson, tasting the salty air with excited breath, how Granga had coaxed me gently in our rocky shelter, recognising that his grandson needed to talk. I thought of finding his published book of verses and reading aloud the poem he'd written for me. And how I'd savoured all his life's adventures – soldier, clergyman, poet, philosopher, hotelier, musician, historian, grandfather and friend. I pictured Great-Aunt Lulu in her floaty dress, her eyes that sparkled warmly as if she never wanted me to go. "*Are you happy here, Rufie?*" And all I'd said was, "*I think so.*" How much more proof could a mind need? I hadn't asked myself the question because I was the answer – and Maria, Lulu, Granga and all his friends.

Yet it wasn't home. It wasn't England. I didn't tell my mother what I'd done at school. My father didn't chase me round the garden with my rugby ball. My mother didn't catch me at the bottom of a slide. I wasn't tucked up at night in bed by my mother and told that she loved me. I didn't wake up in the morning feeling secure, like nothing in the world could ever hurt me, not with my mother and father in my life. I didn't come top of the class in all my lessons. I wasn't destined for a first-class degree any more. I wouldn't follow my father into the legal profession. I saw no one's pride in what I had achieved. Pride was what I saw in Granga's eyes when he stared at John Thompson's painting, or when he heard John say to me, "I've drawn your Mum and Dad." If there was anything I was missing here with Granga, it was my parents' look of total pride in me.

"Lots of boys your age board at school," I heard Hannah saying. "They seem to like it, from what I hear."

Granga moved his hat. His eyes were open. "How about that, Blue?" he said. "Sounds like a good idea."

26

THE LOUNGERS WERE STILL ON the lawn when I got back from a long walk in the forest. They were empty, the parasol was down and the cushions had been put away. I could hear Granga and Hannah chatting inside as I neared the drawing room's French windows. The aroma of cigar smoke filled the early evening air.

"So you say you've checked with the school and they're happy to have him back?"

"Only if you and Rufus thought it was the right thing to do." Had she forgotten my name was now Blue, or didn't she want to accept it?

"Boarding suited his mother – it's probably best for him too."

I stood with my back to the wall of the Finca, barely breathing in case I missed a word my grandfather said. His silences meant he was thinking whilst inhaling deeply. Clouds of thick smoke meant that his decision was made. "I'll ring the school tomorrow and make the arrangements. It might be a good idea if you take the boy home with you." It sounded like him, but he spoke the words of a stranger. I didn't blame Hannah – she'd left the choices to him.

The stone of the Finca felt cool in the shadows of the

neighbouring palm trees. I pressed my back hard against its old wall as if it would give me its strength. Three hundred years or more the building had stood there. For periods it had crumbled and then been revived. Granga was one of the men who had restored it. With his own hands, Lulu had said, he'd built it up again. When she'd told me, I'd thought that he must enjoy protecting what was weak from being destroyed, by giving it back what it thought it had lost through bad times. A Finca, a boy, what had mattered to me was Granga's feeling of love and protection. Was I wrong? Once it had been restored, what then? Was it time for Granga to move on – impatient – to his next project? Was that why he had travelled so much of the world and left my mother behind?

I turned to take in the form of the Finca, tall like a mighty fortress built to protect the life inside. Just like a body, I thought, as I stood before it. "Thank you, Finca," I whispered, "I hope he won't grow tired of you too."

I didn't want to hear any more that Granga and Hannah were saying, so I crept round the side and entered through the front door. Once in my room, I walked firmly across the wooden floorboards so they would be able to hear me below – I didn't want them thinking I'd gone missing, not that it would have mattered much to them if I had.

As I paced up and down, I caught a glimpse of John Thompson's drawing of my parents. I'd left it on top of my writing desk underneath the window so that I would see it when I opened my shutters each morning. I sat down at my desk as if I'd decided to join them, clutching the piece of paper in my hands.

"He wants rid of me," I whispered to them. "He as much

as told me so earlier. That's the real reason that Hannah's here. Collecting John Thompson's clothes was just an excuse."

He'd drawn them as if they were looking right at me out of the paper, waiting for me to tell them what was on my mind. "The thing is, I don't want to go back to England. I want to stay here with Granga and Lulu and Maria. I like living here. In fact, I love it."

Tears were blurring my vision, distorting their pencil faces. "You probably can't hear a word I'm saying to you, but I'll carry on just in case."

In the distance, the church clock struck six times. If I'd been in England I would have been doing my homework now. It didn't usually take me long. It was quite easy. I would finish it in time for supper that my mother would have prepared. She'd be talking in the kitchen to my father as she was cooking. He'd be telling her about his day in Chambers or in court. I'd hear them laughing as I was writing down my answers. Then my mother would call, "Supper's ready! It's on the table now!" That meant I'd have to leave what I was doing, otherwise the food, she'd say, would get cold. We'd eat at the dining table beside the door leading onto the garden. In summertime we seldom kept it closed.

"Hannah says a lot of boys are boarders," I told the drawing of my parents. "Some of them seem to quite enjoy it too. I never understood how any of them could stand it. Living at school sounds like my worst nightmare to me."

In a way, it was a bit like talking to John Thompson. Often he made no reply when you spoke to him either.

"I don't know whether Granga was asleep while I was talking to Hannah. He was certainly awake by the time we got to the end of the conversation. What bothers me most is that I don't know whether they'd planned it – or worse, is it my fault because of the answers I gave to Hannah's questions? Of course I'm happy here. I only said *I think so* and that it's different from being in England out of respect for you two – I worked that out on my way up here just now. I didn't want Hannah to think I was happier with Granga than I'd been with you. Because that's not true. It's a different happy here, that's all. And in the future I'll probably have other different happys. But I want to be happy here for as long as I can."

I traced their faces with my forefinger, careful not to press too hard and disturb them. "It's important to have friends, but they don't always have to be the same age as you. When my Spanish is better I'll make more friends if they'll let me stay. Maybe that's what's bothering Hannah, but what about Granga? Surely he can see that that's not what matters to me?"

I propped the piece of paper against my desk lamp and sat up straight. "I will be a published poet like Granga one day, you wait and see! Then he won't send me away as he did you. He said it was because you reminded him too much of your mother. Is that why he doesn't want *me*? Well if he doesn't want me either, I won't try and stop him. I'll go like you did. It really doesn't matter to me."

I'd always kept my largest suitcase on top of the wardrobe. At the beginning it had seemed like a sensible thing to do. It was there – I could pack it and leave any time if I wanted. It was the only part of my room that had reminded me of home. Then, as days had passed, the large brown suitcase had become the only part of my room that wasn't home, because it wasn't Mallorcan, because Granga hadn't chosen it. So one night I'd climbed up on my bed and covered it with one of the bed sheets that Maria had ironed and left in the airing cupboard. After that I'd forgotten all about it – until now.

It almost fell on my head as I struggled to retrieve it. I should have remembered how heavy it was. The sheet slipped from the top of it and landed in a big white heap on the floor like a parachute. I held the case close to my body as if it were a safety harness. My old English travelling companion was back. Soon we'd be on our way once more. Who knew where else it would take me? Our future would be an adventure from now on. England would be only a small part of our life together. My case would never again be hidden under bed linen.

It didn't take me long to pack. I wasn't as neat as Hannah had been when she'd helped me pack to come here. I threw my clothes into the case without folding them. Males don't take as long to pack as females. They don't fold everything into neat piles in their case. They throw their clothes in – what did it matter if heavy items were on the top or bottom as long as you could close it? None of the other boys would notice a few creases back at school.

The hardest decision was whether to take Granga's book of verses. He hadn't really given it to me. I packed it three times and three times took it out again. It didn't seem right to take it away somehow. Eventually I decided to leave it on my writing desk along with John's drawing of my parents and the one of Granga. It was the nicest place in the world I could imagine for them to be. Perhaps one day Granga would come into my empty room and see them there. And maybe that would make him think of me.

27

I KNOCKED TWICE ON HANNAH'S DOOR before she said I could enter. It was the bedroom that John Thompson had chosen – a bright room with whitewashed walls and a very high sloping ceiling covered in wooden beams. On the wall opposite the double bed hung a picture in a black frame of an enormous, vivid red sun that caught your attention whenever you walked into the room. It was signed artistically in the corner by Miró, the famous Spanish artist that Granga had told me about, who had lived in Mallorca until his death in 1983. I hadn't asked Granga whether it was an original or not, but I liked to imagine that it was, and that Miró had given it to Granga because maybe they'd been friends who'd spent long evenings together discussing the importance of art and poetry and philosophy and the symbolic nature of the sun, whilst sipping vintage Rioja.

Hannah sat up in bed when she saw me, propping a pillow behind her head. Her eyes seemed much smaller without any make-up and her hair was flatter than I'd seen it before. "Good morning, Rufie." She seemed pleased to see me, not like I was a problem she'd have to sort out. "Did you sleep well?"

"Yes thanks," I said politely, "I was wondering if you'd

like breakfast in bed — I used to bring it for my mother sometimes."

She smiled and held out a hand for me to take. "Come and sit down next to me." She made a small place in the duvet with her other hand for me. It felt warm, like being a bird tucked up in a nest. I hoped she wasn't going to talk about my mother. I shouldn't have mentioned her. I hadn't intended to.

"I was talking to Granga last night about your future." She still had hold of my hand. Her grip was tight. "We both want what's best for you, Rufie, you must understand that."

But I didn't understand it, not any more. That was the whole problem. So I didn't respond, but let her carry on. "You seemed to enjoy having your friend John Thompson stay with you." I nodded without looking her in the eye. "It's good to have friends your own age to talk to sometimes."

I knew where her conversation was supposed to be leading. I could feel it in the room like a heavy thundercloud. But I wouldn't make it hard for her — she didn't deserve that. She'd looked after me as if I was her own child.

"It's OK," I said, pulling my hand from hers, "I've already decided." I stood up and turned away from her and found myself staring right into the heart of Miró's red sun. Immediately I felt stronger. "I think it's best if I go back to England as a boarder at my old school."

Putting the thought into words made it seem less frightening. I'd taken a step — the rest was up to her.

I turned to face her again. She had crossed her bare freckled arms over her cream silk nightdress so that all I could see of it were two fine straps laced in blue.

"Well, you know how to surprise me!"

She gave a small laugh as if she was unsure what to say next. Probably planning how to break the good news to Granga. I wouldn't delay her. I had too much to do. I turned to go. The room suddenly seemed airless.

"Would you like cereal and fresh fruit salad and tea?"

"Coffee would be nice."

"I don't know how to make that."

"On second thoughts, I think I'd rather have tea."

I returned with a tray, which I placed on the floor outside her bedroom. "I've left your breakfast by the door," I shouted, not waiting for a reply.

The next thing I had to do was to find Granga. It was easy. He was sitting in his study reading a book.

"What are you reading?" My voice sounded higher than usual. He noticed it too. I could tell by the way he removed his reading glasses and peered at me.

"I am *re*-reading Aristotle's *Ethics*." He spoke slowly, as if each word was very important. "Are you familiar with his *Doctrine of the Mean*?"

I considered guessing that it was a theory about nasty people, but fortunately decided against it.

"No," I replied instead. "What's it about?"

He directed me with his forefinger towards a leather armchair. "The principle that virtue consists in pursuing a course of action between two extremes – one being too much and the other too little, or *excess* and *defect* as the two extremes are described. Aristotle believed that following *the mean* between two extremes is the principal ingredient of moral virtue."

I must have looked confused, for Granga paused enquiringly before adding, "Would an example help?" It wasn't the conversation I'd planned in my head on the way there.

"Yes please," I answered. "To be sure I understand."

He closed the big hardback book with the respect of a vicar closing a bible. "Let's take the moral virtue of courage as our example," he said. "Courage is the mean, according to Aristotle, between two extremes – stupidity, rashness, foolhardiness on the one hand and cowardice, being overwhelmed by fear on the other. Virtue consists in hitting the right balance between these two. Too much courage is rash, too little is cowardly."

It was as if in explaining the two extremes, he was describing *me* earlier in Hannah's bedroom – filled with fear that I'd be sent back to England, then rashly volunteering to go. "So in order to be courageous you should be less rash and cowardly?" I should have been brave enough to hear what she had to say before I'd volunteered to go back to England.

"Precisely!" He was pleased with me – but was I pleased with him?

"Would Aristotle have considered *you* a courageous man, Granga, or would he think that you were reckless?" Surely it was courageous of me to speak to him so?

He leaned forward on his chair so our noses were almost touching, and I was afraid that I'd forgotten courage and become cowardly. "Me? I am the Golden Mean between the reckless young man I once was and the coward I am soon to become."

"Does that make you courageous now?"

He laughed. I didn't know why – I must have said something stupid without realising.

"Today I feel brave," he said, "but tomorrow . . ."

I waited for him to finish but he didn't. He'd brought Aristotle's *Ethics* to an end. Or so he thought. "But how do you know if you've got the balance right if there's no one to tell you, Granga?"

He took out a cigarette, then put it back in its box. "You need experience, practice, reason to educate you. The mean isn't absolute – it's a moving line. It's relative to the individual and the situation. Listen to your *reason* and you won't go wrong."

"Is that what *you* do?" my reason told me to ask him.

"It's what I aspire to do, but sometimes my reason gives me conflicting answers."

"What do you do then?" I'd never asked him so many questions in one go.

"I pick up Aristotle's *Ethics* and read it again – if I'm allowed."

I was disturbing him. He wanted to be left alone. I had to tell him my decision. It would be better coming from me. "I came to say I'm going back to England with Hannah. I know you've discussed it with her. It'll be a good experience. I've never boarded before. But my mother enjoyed it, so I'm sure I will too. I've packed my things. We'll leave today. I'll stay with Hannah until term begins so that I get used to being in England again."

I remembered every word I'd rehearsed – even the order they came in. The only part I was unhappy with was the tone of my voice. It quivered sometimes. He wouldn't like that.

Granga stood up and looked out of the window towards the drive. I thought there must be someone coming, but there wasn't. His corded trousers were worn at the seat. He must have done a lot of sitting in them. The knees were baggy too. "Are you sure, Blue?" I saw his tobacco breath on the window as he spoke.

"Certain," I replied uncertainly.

"I shall make the arrangements this morning."

He didn't turn round when he'd finished speaking, so I guessed I was to leave the room and close the door quietly behind me.

It wasn't until I was outside that I realised that I'd forgotten something – the end, the part where I placed my hand on the doorknob, turned it, then said, "By the way, I assume it's OK for me to stay with you in the holidays – if you're . . . if I'm not too busy?", then left as he nodded, so that he wouldn't have long enough to change his mind.

But I couldn't go back, not in any way. So I carried on walking to the road and on to the village as Granga and I had done together when John Thompson had disappeared.

The route seemed longer alone, even though I didn't have Granga with me in his slippers this time. When I reached the village, no one stopped to stare at me as they had that day. I was just any old English boy sightseeing on holiday. Nothing special. No one extraordinary. Not a genius. Not a poet. Not a philosopher. Not an original thinker. Without Granga I was a nobody – a boy to be overlooked, a boarder at a small private school tucked away in the English countryside.

"Buenos días," I shouted to Miguel but he didn't hear me. I'd hoped he would invite me in for a glass of Coca-Cola. I hurried past the restaurant as if I hadn't meant to stop, hoping no one had noticed that he hadn't replied.

I'd never walked beyond Miguel's before. The road narrowed as it ascended. There seemed to be no more shops or restaurants, so I assumed the village had come to an end. I was about to turn back when I spotted a small shop around a bend on the right-hand side. I crossed the road to see what sort of shop it was. Through the window, I spotted row after row of bookshelves, each packed with books, mostly new but some quite old. There was only one assistant in the shop. He was sitting behind the counter, reading a book through frameless reading glasses. I guessed he was about my father's age, perhaps a little older as his black beard was splattered with grey. I went in.

"Good morning," he said in English that suggested it was his native tongue and that he recognised it was mine as well. "Are you looking for any book in particular or would you just like to browse?"

From the books I'd seen through the window, it appeared that they were in several languages, displayed under different categories around the store. "There *is* a book I'd like to find. It's by Horatio R. Hennessy. A poetry book. Quite old. It's called *Verses of a Solitary Fellow*. Do you have it?"

I'd expected him to look it up on his system, perhaps tell me it was no longer available, but he didn't have to: "Horatio Hennessy's book – I most certainly do." He got up from his chair and beckoned me to follow him to a far corner reserved for old books and first editions. "*Verses of a Solitary Fellow* – here it is. Horatio signed it for me himself."

It was darker than Granga's copy, less faded, and the cover had been bound in transparent foil to preserve it. I opened it and read the handwritten inscription: *To my dear friend James. With best wishes from a solitary fellow who has travelled far, but not yet reached his destination. Horatio Hennessy.*

"Are you sure you wouldn't like to keep it?" I asked. If he'd inscribed it to me I'd never have let it go.

"Yes, yes," James replied, "I don't believe in holding on to books. I'd be out of business if I did!"

I turned the familiar pages, hoping I could afford it – my own personal copy, to take back to England with me, and read when I was alone.

"Are you familiar with the author?" James asked.

"He's my grandfather." I wasn't going to tell him unless he asked.

"Why on Earth didn't you say so?" he exclaimed, taking my hand and shaking it. "Horatio's grandson! What a pleasant surprise!"

He looked me up and down as if to seek a family resemblance. "I've been staying with him . . . on holiday for a while." That was all it had amounted to really. A holiday in Mallorca with a relative I'd never met before. And now I was going back to the real world of school and homework and teenagers with acne and greasy hair. "How much is it?" I felt for my father's old wallet in my trouser pocket.

"Please take it!" protested James. "I wouldn't dream of charging you!" He carried the book to the counter and placed it carefully in a red plastic bag.

"Thank you very much," I beamed. It was the greatest present I'd ever had. Before I left I bought a large yellow notebook he had for sale on the counter, in case I might be inspired to write one day. I wanted to buy something from James to say thank you and to remind me of my summer holiday abroad.

28

MARIA CRIED WHEN I KISSED her goodbye. I tried not to. It wasn't easy. The best way was to swallow and close your eyes. She spoke a lot to me in Spanish, but I still couldn't understand her. This time Granga didn't translate what she said. She looked at Hannah as if somehow she blamed her for my leaving. Everything had been fine here until she'd come along. I wished I could have explained that it really wasn't Hannah's fault. If she hadn't arrived when she had, I'd still have gone. It was the virtuous thing for me to do – the Golden Mean, somewhere between having been happy to the extreme and filled with despair. Aristotle was right – extremes of any kind could not be virtues. First I'd been too unhappy and then too full of joy. My reason said that going back was the only solution. I would learn to temper my emotions better that way. And besides, it was obvious that Granga didn't really want me. Hadn't he been searching to justify his decision when I'd interrupted his reading? Wasn't that why he'd said that sometimes his reason gave him conflicting answers? Part of him thought he oughtn't to send me away, though most of his reason wanted it. So I'd given him the reason to let me go.

Hannah spoke enough Spanish to thank Maria and

Granga for having made her short stay so enjoyable. Maria nodded once, then turned back to me. There was something she had to give me before I left. She lowered her head and removed the crucifix that she always wore around her neck. I couldn't take it, I said. I wouldn't. It was too precious. She'd regret it, I protested as she placed it around my neck, and wished she hadn't been so kind. Of course I couldn't say all this to her in Spanish, but rather with gestures and tears I'd fought for so long to hide.

And then it was time for me to say goodbye to Granga. He'd been waiting patiently in silence for his turn.

"Remember which Blue you are – the happy kind like cloudless sky, not a miserable little fellow." He lifted my chin gently, "That's no way for a boy to stand! Look at me! This is how to do it!"

He removed his old trilby and tossed it to the ground. Then he threw back his head, extending both arms upward at the same time. I knew he wanted me to copy him, but I was too embarrassed. It suited him, but what would Hannah and Maria make of me?

"Back straight like a soldier," he continued, "no slumping." I pulled back my shoulders and stretched my spine. "The ground is where nature begins, Blue. Once it sees the sun, it knows which direction it should be growing in."

I raised my face towards the sun, as he demanded. It felt much better than staring at the ground.

"Upwards, Blue, that's better!" he encouraged, peeping at me out of the corners of his eyes though his head still faced the sun. I sensed my spirits rising as the sun's rays warmed my skin. Soon I felt more confident. My leaving didn't seem so bad.

We remained that way for a few minutes, until Granga said, "It's time you were gone." Maria hugged me again for the very last time while Hannah got into the silver hatchback she'd hired at the airport.

"Look after him well," I heard Granga say to Hannah through her open window.

"I promise you I shall," she half-whispered back at him. Maria hadn't said goodbye to Hannah so I nudged her arm and pointed towards the car. Maria waved once stiffly in Hannah's vague direction. "Goodbye, Maria," Hannah called to her.

It was time. I opened the passenger's door. The smell of the car's newness hit me, all hot and man-made, with no fresh air. Before I got in, I turned for one last time to Granga. I'd left it until the very last second to kiss him goodbye. His skin felt warm from all that sunshine, his cheek soft and loose like a balloon that has lost much of its air. I couldn't think what words to use for what I wanted to say to him – nothing fancy or sentimental, but truthful like good poetry. Now was my chance to whisper it into his ear so the others wouldn't hear me.

"What you taught me yesterday about Aristotle's Golden Mean, there's something I don't understand. Surely it can't be wrong, *an extreme*, to love someone too much."

For once Granga had no answer but to hold me to him, so close I could hear his heartbeat against my ear.

"Goodbye Granga," I said, "I'll miss you." He still didn't answer. I climbed into the car. "Say goodbye to Aunt Lulu from me too."

The sound of the engine starting reminded me of thunder – at the beginning, when you're not sure what's to come.

"Once we've closed the windows," said Hannah, "I'll switch on the air-conditioning." But I didn't want air-conditioning. What I longed for was fresh air.

Maria jumped out of the way when she saw we were reversing. Granga followed the car back on my side. I wished he would say something to me before we left – a word, anything – I would take it back with me to England like a prize. "I'll write to you," I suddenly thought of saying. At least that would be something to look forward to. It wasn't like my Granga to be so quiet. Had I said something he didn't like? Had I got Aristotle all wrong?

Hannah moved the handle from reverse into the driving position. She was ready to take us up the drive. It only took a second for the changeover. Time enough for Granga to whisper, "My boy."

I watched him and Maria all the way up the long drive. They seemed older and frailer than I'd ever noticed. Before long, Maria was just a small black waving figure. But Granga had turned from her and was walking away. That was when I noticed something else about him. At least I thought I noticed – from a distance I couldn't be sure. His head was forward and his broad shoulders were slouching. He was facing the ground like he'd told me not to do.

29

I WOKE IN A BEDROOM WITH pink walls and matching bedclothes, facing a square double-glazed window that was closed. I'd stayed in it before, but this time it seemed different – smaller and stuffier with nowhere to rest your eyes. I pushed back the heavy quilt. The air felt cooler. I got up – the grey fluffy carpet cushioned my toes. My suitcase was open on a white stool in the corner. On the top lay the clothes I'd travelled in from Mallorca. Underneath the stool stood my pair of walking shoes.

It was nine o'clock. I could hear the family chatting happily downstairs as I dressed. They were having breakfast together before Daniel went off to work. Katy and Melissa were still on holiday. Katy had told me so the night before. They went to school together, she and her sister, although they were in different classes, as Melissa was ten and Katy eleven. They weren't alike in any way I could see. Katy was prettier than her sister. She had straight blonde hair that went to the tops of her shoulders, and features like her mother's. She was slim like Hannah too, whereas Melissa was tall and fat with dark brown hair and a big round face that didn't say much. Katy never stopped talking. In the short time between arriving at the house and going to bed I'd heard all about her favourite subjects (English and French), her best friend (Antonia Long), and what she planned to do when she left school (read English at University and be a journalist). I learnt as little about Melissa as on my previous stay with them, although both girls were more talkative this time. Before, they'd just giggled and whispered together a lot, but now they wanted to know everything about Mallorca: what kind of village I'd lived in (Katy), whether the food was good (Melissa), what friends I'd made (Katy), if Granga let me go out in the evenings (Katy), what Granga was like (Katy), whether he'd made me walk up the mountains (Melissa), if there was a swimming pool at the Finca (Katy), a horse (Melissa), a tennis court (Katy), neighbours (Katy), or a barbecue (Melissa).

This last question had led me to tell them about my shock on the night of Granga's birthday party the day before his proper birthday. That really held their attention. Both girls listened from start to finish without speaking, their eyes as wide open as their mouths. My words held their attention like Granga's poetry held mine. It made me realise how much I'd learnt from my grandfather. His influence was with me in so many different ways.

"When the missing ewe came racing towards me," I'd recounted, "all happy and woolly and full of life, I promised myself she'd never end up as a greasy piece of meat on anyone's plate."

Now I would have to go downstairs and join the family for breakfast. I couldn't stay up here in my room all day like John Thompson would do. Like it or not, I was back in England and there was no point in moping about it. This was a new beginning – time to *seize the day*, just as Horace had written.

I could feel my spirits rising – until I cast a glance out of the double-glazed window. It was a cloudy English morning, no sun to warm me. I couldn't throw back my head and feel its rays. I'd have to find another way to lift my spirits.

"Granga's book of verses!" I said out loud. I'd put it at the bottom of my suitcase, still in its red plastic bag, with my notebook I'd bought from James.

I carried the verses carefully to the window. *A Solitary Fellow* shone out in large gold print on the cover. Was that really Granga – a solitary fellow? He hadn't seemed very solitary to me. Wherever you went with him, someone knew him – Mallorca, France, Morocco, he always had friends. As for Maria, I couldn't imagine her life without him, Lucinda too, although she would never have admitted it, at least not to him. How could a fellow be solitary with all those friends around him? I was more of a solitary fellow than he.

I replaced the book in its bag so the others wouldn't see it – I wanted to read it outside while I was alone.

They'd all finished breakfast by the time I joined them. Daniel had gone, Hannah and Melissa were washing up. Hannah had left me a bowl of cereal and a glass of orange juice on the pine kitchen table. I knew at once that the orange wasn't freshly squeezed. It didn't have the bits of fruit floating in it like I was used to. This orange juice was unnaturally flat. I tried to cross my legs under the table, but there wasn't enough room for my knee. If the wood hadn't been so new and shiny it would have scraped me. Yet I longed for it to be big and rough and old.

"Did you sleep well, Rufus?" Hannah knew my name wasn't Rufus any more. Why did she find it so hard to call me Blue?

"Yes thanks," I replied through a mouthful of sugary muesli that I'd rescued from a sea of lukewarm milk.

Melissa had returned to saying nothing. She was going riding, said Hannah, with her friend from school. She was dressed in black jodhpurs that weren't meant for so much stretching. Her hair was tied back with a rubber band.

"What would you like to do today?" Hannah asked me. But what did I want to do – eat lunch outside on the terrace, just Granga and me, go for a walk to the village gazing up at the mountains. "I wouldn't mind staying here," I suggested, "perhaps do some reading in the garden."

"Of course, if you'd like to. There are lots of good books in Daniel's study."

"It's alright," I hesitated, "I've brought a book with me from Mallorca I'd like to read." I picked up my red plastic bag and headed towards the kitchen door, which led to the garden. Granga's book was the only piece of him I had left and I didn't want to share it.

"You go and find yourself a nice quiet corner to read it in," smiled Hannah, looking at my bag. That was what I admired about Hannah – she knew when not to ask you any questions, but left it for you to decide what you wanted to say.

"Thanks Hannah," I said, tightening my grip on the handles of the bag.

There was a gazebo in the corner of the garden, which faced across the open countryside. You could just make out our house if you looked carefully, at least the back of it leading onto the lawn.

At the front of the wooden gazebo was a small veranda. From there, two half-paned doors led inside. There was only enough room for a round cane table and three matching chairs. When I sat down, a chair leg wobbled slightly. It banged against the panelled wooden floor. I moved to another, testing my weight cautiously. This one was fine, except a little hard. I got out Granga's book and placed it on the table. The sight of it lifted my spirits straight away. I opened it where it chose to fall. It was a war poem I had read already. I closed it. Years of dust wafted up my nose. I sneezed.

"Bless you," came a voice from the veranda. Katy bounced in, floppy arms and legs like a gangly puppy. "I was jogging round the garden. I thought I heard you." She was out of breath and her cheeks were shiny and pink. She had her hair pulled back like her sister, only hers was held with a clip in the shape of a flower. She was dressed in lemon jogging shorts and a turquoise top. "My feet are killing me," she exclaimed, throwing off a pair of blue-and-white trainers. One landed beside me. She stooped to pick it up. "What's the book?" she asked, trying to read the title upside down.

"It's a book of poems," I said, "I brought it with me from Mallorca."

"I like poems," she replied, sitting down on the wobbly chair next to me. I could see why it wobbled – she balanced her whole weight on its front legs then swung herself back with a thud. "Who's the poet?"

"Horatio Hennessy," I muttered.

"Isn't that your Granddad?" She picked up my book and flicked through the first few pages as if it was any old book.

"Yes – he's a poet." I spoke up this time, proudly.

"Cool," she exclaimed, curling a bare foot under her. "Shall I read one to you?"

I wasn't prepared for an intrusion such as this. I hadn't the words for it, so I said nothing. Unfortunately Katy read my silence as an invitation for her to recite one of Granga's poems, the ones I'd been longing all morning to read to myself – in private.

"This looks like an interesting one," she announced, her small fingers smoothing a page about three quarters of the way through the book. She cleared her throat, made sure I was watching her and began:

"See that clearing
In the woods
Beyond those fields of yellow?
They say that once
A man lived there –
A solitary fellow.

He lived alone,
Had many friends
Would always say hello
But in his head
He knew he was
A solitary fellow.

He read good books,
He liked good food,
Good music stirred his soul.

He always sought good company
That solitary fellow.

He lived his life
As if he feared
The pains of growing old
Yet as he aged
He found those fears
Were not as he'd foretold.

The tears he wept
Were not of joy
Not even tears of sorrow.
His tears
Were of a tender kind
That solitary fellow.

He wept because
His knowledge grew
With every passing year.
And what he learnt
As he grew old
Was that he need not fear.

The pain of death,
The pain of loss,
The pain of being alone
Had lessened
In his ageing heart
As solitude had grown.

'Twas not
The solitude of man
Whose lonely heart
Is worn.
His was an understanding
Of why mankind is born.

To love
To live
To think
To feel
To have
And to let go
To realise
That who we are
Is all we need to know.

I understand
That man who lives
Beyond those fields of yellow
Because, you see,
I am that man
That solitary fellow."

One of us said, "Wow!" whilst the other hid tears of understanding from his eyes.

"I'm not sure that I know who I am yet – do you, Rufie?"

The book lay between us on the table. "I think I do," I replied, replacing it in its plastic bag before she could read any more. "I'm a poet too." I was pleased with the way it sounded, as if my future was as clear as a cloudless sky.

Katy leaned forward on her chair again, "Would you write a poem for me?"

I hadn't expected that. "I'm not sure," I said, getting up to go outside into the fresh air. "Poetry doesn't work like that. You have to write what inspires you."

Given the awkward circumstances of a girl asking for her own poem, then following a boy outside, I was quite pleased with my answer, until she added, "Don't *I* inspire you?"

She'd left her trainers in the gazebo and was running barefoot alongside me as I increased my pace. "Of course not," I said, keeping my gaze firmly ahead of me to where I could see the road. "You're a girl."

"Then what *does* inspire you?"

It was hard to think of an answer whilst working out an escape route at the same time. "My grandfather," I told her, "I wrote a poem about him."

We'd reached the road. If I turned left and kept walking, eventually I would come to my old home. It seemed like the obvious choice, especially as the roadside was rough so Katy couldn't follow me without shoes on.

Before I could get away, she asked another of her silly questions, "Why on Earth would you find an old man more inspiring than a girl?"

I had to give her an answer before I left. It would have been rude not to. "Because my grandfather's more interesting than any girl I've met."

I thought she would understand. "Oh, I see," she said sternly before walking away.

It took me less than ten minutes to reach our old drive. It wasn't a long drive like Granga's. In fact, it seemed shorter than before. I opened the iron gates and walked tentatively towards the house. The front lawn had grown so long that it covered the footpath, which led to the black-panelled front door, and my mother's climbing rose bush had swallowed up my father's study window.

I strode on, carefully avoiding the nettles like a soldier avoiding landmines, until I reached the back of the house. It had always been my favourite place to be. I needed to find something that had stayed the same, something strong enough to have survived without love and attention. I found it – the mighty oak, standing like a general observing his dead in the aftermath of battle. I ran towards it as if it were a friend I thought I would never see again. When I reached it, I flung my arms round its dark musty trunk, pressing my cheek hard against its bark until it hurt.

This was the tree whose biggest branch had barely ever swayed under the weight of my swing and me. This was the tree that my father had climbed in order to secure the two ropes that held the wooden slab I sat on. I may no longer have had my mother to push me, but I could still use my legs and feet to pick up speed. As I did so the branch creaked for once as if to warn me of its ageing frame. I forced myself higher and higher into the air.

When I closed my eyes I was back home again, my father in his study, my mother in the kitchen preparing something nice for us to eat. When I opened my eyes I was alone in the overgrown garden of a deserted house on a swing whose ropes were beginning to decay.

I jumped off while still in mid-air. My mother would not have approved. I landed on the ground with both feet parallel and knees slightly bent like an Olympic gymnast. I watched the swing sway back and forth until it reached its resting point, its Golden Mean. It was a day of little breeze and heavy cloud. Within minutes rain would penetrate the earth and water the wild flowers that splattered the lawn like colourful brush strokes on a John Thompson painting. I was ready to leave.

30

"**H**ELLO, JOHN. IT'S ME – Blue. I'm back in England."

"Where are you staying?"

"With Hannah."

"How long for?"

"Till I go back."

"Back where?"

"To my old school."

"As a *boarder*?"

He could have sounded less horrified.

"Yes – why not?"

There was a pause before John answered, "No reason."

"Do you want to meet me at the school gates tomorrow before we have to go in?" I asked.

"What time?"

"Eight o'clock?"

"OK."

"See you then."

"Bye."

I'd asked Hannah if I could use her phone but I hadn't realised there was someone else in the hall listening to me.

"Who was that?" Katy was starting to get on my nerves.

"A friend," I replied sharply.

She'd done something funny with her hair. It was sticking out like a scarecrow and it looked like there was some sort of gel on it. She must have seen me looking at it because she ran her fingers through it, probably to try and tidy it up a bit.

"What do you want to do on your last day?" she shouted after me as I walked upstairs.

"I haven't thought about it yet," I said, "I've got some letters to write this morning."

I shut my bedroom door to block her out. It was important that I wasn't disturbed whilst I was composing a letter to Granga. I'd said I would write but he hadn't said he would write back. He probably would, though. He liked the written word.

There was no desk in this bedroom so I took the writing paper and pen that Hannah had given me to the bed. It was easy to begin,

Dear Granga,
I thought I'd write and let you know how I'm getting on in England.

My difficulty was how to continue. Should I describe Hannah and her family, or would he be bored with that? Should I tell him how much I missed Mallorca and the Finca and him, or would he think me too sentimental? Should I attempt a poem to impress him? But what if it didn't? I hadn't imagined it would be as hard to write a letter as a poem. I thought back to the time in France when we'd composed a poem together. At first I couldn't decide what it should be about, just like now. Then Granga had told me to write for myself, what I wanted to say, not in order to please him. I held my pen to the paper and waited for the words to flow out.

> I went back home yesterday. It was empty and
> overgrown and not home any more.

If I hadn't been on such a flow, I wouldn't have minded the knock on the door quite so much. "Who's there?" I called impatiently.

"Katy," she replied.

"What do you want now?" She was becoming a nuisance, like a mosquito around your face when you're trying to rest.

"Can I come in?"

"No. I told you. I'm writing a letter." Didn't she understand privacy at all?

"I'm going swimming at a friend's house." Thank God, I thought, but I didn't say so. "I thought you might like to come?"

As much as I enjoyed swimming, there was no way I was going to join two silly girls on a cloudy day. "No, thanks." I tried to sound polite. "I hope you have a good time."

I thought that would be final, but Katy didn't take it that way. "I'd have a much better time if you were there too."

There was something about the way she said it that caused me to panic and drop my pen. I got up as quickly as I could and placed my suitcase in front of the door. Then I sat on it. Neither of us spoke and I hoped she'd gone away. But I wouldn't risk it. "Bye then," she said eventually. "See you later." I didn't reply.

By the time I returned to my letter, the flow had gone. I

tried for half an hour but it wouldn't come back. I'd have to do something else – but what? I could hear Hannah singing happily downstairs. Melissa had gone riding again. Daniel was mowing the lawn.

My notebook I'd bought from James was still in the plastic bag unopened. I tucked it confidently under my arm and headed outside. The gazebo would be safe as Katy had gone swimming, and it wasn't warm enough to sit outside.

Her trainers were still on the floor where she'd thrown them. I picked them up by the laces and threw them outside. It was important to a poet to create the right atmosphere before he began. I made sure I avoided the wobbly chair.

The cover of the notebook was brighter yellow than I'd remembered. There were thirty-three lines on every white page. On the first, I wrote in capitals "SELECTED POEMS OF BLUE ELLERTON". Then I turned the page and waited for inspiration, something that moved my soul. To my surprise, I didn't have to wait long:

My home is over there
Where the chimneys point Heavenwards
That's where I used to live
When I was blessed
With false belief
That
Now
Would be
Always.

That's where I used to play
In that garden you glimpse through the trees.

Neglected
Forgotten
By everyone
But me.

Hear those church bells ring beyond,
Calling worshippers to prayer?
That's where we used to kneel
We three
My father, mother and me.

If you wait till it grows dark
That's when you'll see
The star I used to wish upon.
It listened then
It heard each plea
Will it shine still?
Or has the world
Forgotten me?

I was pleased with my first poem in the notebook. It expressed what had moved me that day. And even if Granga read it and disapproved, it would still be important to me. That was the lesson he'd tried so hard to teach me. I hadn't completely understood it then. Now I did. I dated the poem in the bottom right-hand corner of the page. I wanted to remember this day. It was the day I became a true poet.

• • •

Dear Granga,

I was going to tell you how it felt to be back in England, but I thought I could explain it better in a poem. So here it is. I wrote it earlier today in Hannah's gazebo in the garden. I'm going to bed now. I want to make sure I get up early in the morning for my first day back at school.

Love,

Blue

P.S. Give my love to Maria and Lulu.

P.P.S. The sky here is blue – but cloudy.

I copied out my poem on its own piece of writing paper. I'd forgotten about a title. I decided to call it "Overgrown".

HANNAH HAD BROUGHT MY SCHOOL uniform from home. She'd ironed it for me too. It all felt a bit tight, so I must have grown while I'd been away.

No one else was up when I went downstairs. I wasn't surprised – it was only seven o'clock. I poured myself an orange juice from the carton in the fridge and ate a piece of toast covered in Hannah's homemade marmalade. It was delicious. She'd made it the evening before, while the rest of us were watching television. She told me she'd used Seville oranges all the way from Spain. She'd thought I'd like that. Katy had returned to saying very little but whispering a lot with Melissa, which was a relief. Also it enabled me to talk to Daniel about rugby and football and cricket without her trying to join in.

Before I'd gone upstairs to bed, it had been agreed that Daniel would drive me to school on his way to the office. I'd explained that I wanted to get there early to meet my friend before school began. Secretly, I had another reason for wanting to leave early – Katy. I dreaded her insisting on coming with us, which she would have done if it had been later and Hannah had been taking me. I was getting used to

Katy's ways. She'd have seized the opportunity for a big embarrassing farewell and might even have tried to kiss me.

I left a note for Hannah on the kitchen table. It said,

Thank you, Hannah, for looking after me so well. I know why my mother chose you as her best friend. Blue x. P.S. Say goodbye to Melissa and Katy from me. I should have said it myself but I was very tired last night, which was why I went to bed so early.

Daniel smiled when he read the note, "Are you ready, Blue?" he asked, picking up his car keys. It was the first time I'd heard my name since I'd left Mallorca. Somehow it didn't sound the same in England.

"I think so," I replied. Daniel placed my suitcase in the boot of his car and I kept my satchel in the front with me. I had no books to put in it so it looked strangely empty, especially next to Daniel's big black leather briefcase.

He made sure I was wearing my seatbelt before he started the car. It was too wide for me so I had to adjust it.

"Off we go," he said, pulling into the road, "a brand-new adventure!" If I'd been a nicer person I'd have let him believe that he'd managed to cheer me up. But for some reason, his attempts only made me more remote. "You'll make lots of new friends," he continued after several minutes of silence.

"I know them all already," I reminded him, which shut him up again until I said, "I'm meeting John Thompson by the school gates."

"He'll be pleased to see you again," tried Daniel, checking his wristwatch without removing his hand from the steering wheel. I don't know why – he had a clock right in front of him on the dashboard. It was ten to eight. "Just in time," he said as we pulled up to the gates.

"I'm early," I pointed out. Then we sat staring out of the windscreen as if we were watching a film at the cinema, only without the popcorn.

"You're very lucky," it took me till five to eight to say.

Daniel turned to me. He seemed taken aback. It wasn't part of any conversation he'd expected. "Why's that?" he asked.

"You found someone as good as Hannah," I explained, "and you still have each other."

I didn't wait for him to reply – John Thompson had arrived. I climbed hastily out of the car. Daniel carried my case to the pavement. "Thank you," I said, "for everything."

"Bless you," he replied softly, like I'd made him sad, which I hadn't wanted to do. He was back in his car and driving away before I even had time to introduce him to John Thompson.

"Was that Hannah's husband?" John asked as we watched him disappear.

"Yes," I replied.

"Nice car."

"I didn't notice."

We took it in turns to carry my suitcase up the school drive. When we reached the front lawn, we sat under a chestnut tree on our school blazers.

"Shouldn't you have checked in before today?" John asked.

"Hannah and Granga organised everything," I explained. "They said today would be OK under the circumstances."

"What does that mean?"

"I'm not sure exactly," I replied, "but I think it's got something to do with me having no parents any more."

"Oh."

Before, when I'd been a dayboy, I hadn't paid much attention to the school building. It was a place where I did my lessons, then waited for my mother to take me home. It was different now.

The walls of the school were made of old red bricks that ivy clung to. There was an arched entrance to a porch the size of a room, which led to heavy wooden double doors. The front of the school was older than the back, which was attached to it at the sides like artificial limbs. Most of our classes were in the modern part. The classrooms had big windows that looked out over mown lawns and open fields beyond. The dorms were upstairs in the old part of the building. I'd only ever seen them when I'd had to go for an eye test in the Sick Bay – the dorm was next to it, filled with single beds in two lines facing each other. At the time, as I'd peered in, it had seemed like stumbling upon a spaceship from another planet.

"What are you looking at?" John asked as I stared at the upstairs windows, wondering where my bed would be.

"Home," I replied.

"I wouldn't have come back if I'd been you," he said. I didn't respond.

We watched as a stream of delivery vans drew up to the front porch, then drove back down the *out* drive on the other side of us. The postman was the last to arrive. He had sacks full of mail to deposit. Before long, some of it might be from Granga for me.

"I sent a letter to Granga yesterday," I told John, "with a poem in it."

"He'll like that."

"I expect he'll write back soon," I went on, trying to sound confident.

"He might send you a poem!" John exclaimed. I hadn't thought of that. A Horatio Hennessy poem written especially for me, like the one in his book, only better, because this new one would have been written since he knew me. It might even be called "Blue".

"How long do you think the post will take from Mallorca?"

I didn't know why I'd asked John. He would have no idea.

"I dunno. Your postcard from France only took a few days." He hesitated, then added: "Did Hannah give you my letter?"

"Yes, thanks," I replied. "I've kept it."

"What for?"

"I don't know really – to remind me of you, I suppose. It must have been a difficult letter for you to write."

"Yeah, the spelling was hard and the straight lines," he replied, not looking at me.

I smiled at him. "I wish I had your gift for being so straightforward. When I had to say goodbye to Granga, I couldn't do it, not properly. I couldn't say the things I wanted to say to him. You'd have found it easy, but when I tried my best, all I could do was to dress up what I really wanted to say and ask him in other ways."

"Like what?" he asked with interest.

I thought about my answer for a while – I wanted to be as straightforward as John. "I suppose, like trying to find out whether Granga really wanted me to leave without actually asking him the question."

John pulled a face: "So why didn't you just ask him, then?"

I took even longer to answer him this time. I knew I had to, for my sake as well as John's. The trouble was, I didn't have an answer.

Eventually John spoke for me: "I asked my Dad if he was happier living on his own."

"What did he say?" I asked.

"I'll have a beer, please. We were in a pub at the time."

Sometimes it was hard to tell with John Thompson whether he was trying to be funny or just telling it exactly how it was. So I didn't laugh in case it was the latter. "You're braver than I am," I said instead, "like when you asked me if I'd still be your best friend."

"You haven't given me an answer yet," he replied, retying his shoelaces.

This time it was easy to give him an answer. "Of course you are! Like Granga said, you're not to blame for your father's driving. It was the shock that made me run away from you, that was all."

He beamed, then asked: "So what shock made you run away from your Granddad, then?"

Since his stay in Mallorca, John Thompson had started asking a lot more questions.

"Or did your Granddad run away from you?"

I had to be direct, I promised myself. I wouldn't do what I'd done with Granga. I'd be just like John Thompson. "I was hurt because I'd heard him tell Hannah that he thought it was a good idea for me to come back to England to board. I hadn't expected that. I should have, because that was what he'd done with my mother when she was about my age. But I thought we were different, Granga and I. I thought it might be easier for a man like him to look after a boy than a girl in some ways. And I didn't remind him of his dead wife the way my mother had."

I worried that John Thompson might have lost interest by the time I'd finished speaking, but he hadn't. "You must've reminded him of *your* dead Mum, though – you're the spitting image of her. That's why I could draw her so easily."

"I have my father's mouth," I felt I needed to add in a whisper. "Everyone says so."

"Well, you didn't ask your Granddad why he thought you should leave, so you won't know now, will you?" He stood up and shook grass from his blazer. "All you can do is guess." He put his blazer back on. "I'm not like you, I don't like guessing. That's why I like animals – they tell you what they're thinking."

I could see that, for John Thompson, we'd reached the end of our conversation, so I stood up too. "I should probably go in now. I'll see you later."

"Good luck," he said through a mouthful of chocolate he'd brought with him as breakfast.

"Thanks," I replied, picking up my suitcase, my travelling companion, my passport to new adventure.

When I reached the entrance porch, I stopped. "Excuse me," I said to the postman. "Could you tell me how long it takes for a letter from Mallorca to get here?"

"Mallorca?" he repeated, scratching his chin. "I'd say about a week, maybe less, depending on whereabouts in Mallorca it's posted."

"Thank you," I said with a smile. "That was all I wanted to know."

32

BOARDING WASN'T AS BAD AS I'd feared it might be. My bed was comfortable and I was next to Philip Newman and I quite liked him, except that he snored. Also, I was able to play sports in the evenings. Tennis soon became a favourite, which surprised me, as I'd never particularly liked it before. Sometimes I would climb up the hill that led to the oldest tennis court with a pavilion at the back of it, and practise my serving on my own. I was good at hitting the line and I hardly ever double-faulted.

In my letter to Granga from school I asked him if he played tennis. I thought I'd write again before I'd heard back from him to my first letter to set a fast pace like a good rally. It was a brief note, really, to give him a flavour of my new life.

The first week had passed quickly. I'd spent more time on my homework than I used to, as I liked being in the library. It would have been Granga's favourite place to be too. There were so many old and new books to choose from. I checked the poetry section, but his book wasn't there. I hadn't really expected it to be. Anyway, I had my own copy with me under my mattress.

I did manage to find a copy of Aristotle's *Ethics*, though, with a commentary about the Golden Mean. As I read it I wondered how much of it Granga would agree with. Did he aim at achieving the right balance, harmony, in his moral decision-making, as Aristotle had suggested, or did he sometimes value the extremes, which Aristotle opposed? What would Aristotle have thought of Granga's appetite for fine food and wine, for instance, or his passionate enthusiasm for life? And what of the extremes in his professional career – killing men in battle one day, preaching to men and women in a congregation the next? Did that show courage or recklessness? Was he courageous to send away his daughter and then his grandson, or was he a coward? If neither, then what had he achieved in between – what exactly was the Golden Mean? Several times, I picked up my pen to ask him, but as I hadn't yet received a response to my first two letters, I decided against it. Three would be extreme. Two was the perfect Aristotelian balance.

I hadn't received any post at all yet, not even from Hannah, as she'd promised. I was relieved not to have heard from Katy. She'd have written on pink writing paper with a matching envelope, and put circles above the "*i*"s instead of dots. I knew exactly what Granga's letter would look like. I'd seen his stationery in his study. The writing paper was cream and thick like parchment paper, and the envelopes were lined in burgundy. He always wrote in ink, with a big black fountain pen, which he dipped into a silver inkwell. I would recognise his writing – scrawled, as if he'd done it in a hurry.

Sometimes, when I was in bed at night and all I could hear was Philip Newman's snoring in the bed next to me, I tried to picture my first Granga letter. It was hard to predict whether it would make me laugh or cry, but I knew it would make me think. No one here did that, not even the teachers. They gave me knowledge, they told me facts which it was my duty to remember, but that was all. Day after day, I sat at my square desk by the wall and longed to hear something original, something that would teach me a new way of viewing the world. Perhaps about a king who had fought for what he believed in, what moved him, and who'd suffered as a result, or perhaps an unusual contradiction concerning a geographical fact, or whether numbers could exist without objects, or why poets preferred fewer words. All I heard was when or where, but never why. I came away from my lessons able to list the names of kings and queens sequentially, countries relatively. I could conjugate, multiply, summarise, translate. But what I longed for was to *reflect*. Granga had shown me how. It had been his legacy to me, like a magic box that took you somewhere new and exciting every time you lifted its lid.

Yet what was the point in a gift that required someone else to make it work? Surely that was not a true gift at all, but a loan that could be withdrawn at any time? He'd left me with my magic box, but he'd taken away the key.

"There's a letter for you, Rufus." John was panting. He must have been looking for me. "Is it from *him*?"

He sat down next to me in the pavilion. Sebastian Hamilton was playing tennis with Philip Newman. Sebastian was serving at our end. He didn't throw the ball up straight enough and so it went into the net.

"Shit!" he shouted, picking up the ball to try again. "Bloody wind!" While Philip waited patiently to receive a second serve, Sebastian checked that his baseball cap was correctly in place back to front.

"Aren't you going to open it?" John asked excitedly.

"In a minute," I answered, not daring to look down at the envelope in my hands.

"The stamp's come off," he went on, "so you can't see the postmark."

"Sebastian's serving for the set," I replied, trying to sound as if nothing else mattered to me.

"It had been left on your desk. I thought you'd want to see it straight away."

Sebastian threw the ball higher this time – an *up the drainpipe* action, just as we'd been taught. It landed on the line. Philip returned it with a strong forehand stroke that hit the baseline in front of us.

"Out!" Sebastian shouted. "That's my set, 6–4."

"No, it's not!" I shouted, leaving the pavilion and John Thompson and my letter and walking towards the court. "The ball was on the line!"

Sebastian turned and glared at me through the tennis court fencing like a panther at the zoo whose tail I'd just pulled. "Are you calling me a liar?" He pointed at me with the head of his racket as if it was a machine gun. I took a deep breath and contemplated the Golden Mean.

"No," I said calmly – not too loud, but not too quiet either. "I'm saying I saw the ball clearly from the pavilion and it definitely hit the line."

John was beside me now, and Philip Newman had joined Sebastian on the other side of the fence.

"I thought it was good too," Philip said, looking at me.

"How could you tell from the far side?" Sebastian asked, laughing as if suddenly it all seemed very amusing. But it wasn't.

"Why don't we play the point again?" Philip suggested,

which seemed like the perfectly-balanced solution to me.

Sebastian walked towards the chair at the side of the net and picked up his sweater and racket cover. "I can't stand bad losers," he said, loud enough for us all to hear.

"Leave it," John said to me when he saw Sebastian walking from the court and approaching us. "Open your letter instead." He passed me the cream envelope I'd left in the pavilion. It felt warm in my hands. But I couldn't bring myself to look at it, not when all the others were around.

"What's that – a letter?" Sebastian snatched the envelope from me and waved it in my face like a fan.

"Give it back!" I roared, forgetting suddenly the danger of extreme. "That's my letter – take your filthy hands off it!"

Sebastian used his locker key to tear open the envelope, saying, "Let's see who it's from."

Every day I'd waited for a letter from Granga. When it hadn't come, I'd convinced myself that it would arrive the following day. I knew the postman's van registration number. I knew which channel he listened to on his radio. I knew the sound of his rubber-soled boots on gravel at eight o'clock every morning. I knew what the top of his head looked like from the small window beside my bed.

"Dear *Blue*," Sebastian spoke the words I'd imagined myself reading. I reddened as he emphasised my other name. "*Blue*?" he sniggered over the top of the piece of cream writing paper that he held between the forefinger and thumb of each hand. "So you're *Little Boy Blue* now, are you?"

"No, I'm Blue like cloudless sky on a summer's day actually," I answered him, emboldened by his mimicking of Granga's name for me, "and *Rayleigh Scattering*, but you've probably no idea what that is."

Philip had heard enough. "If you're not prepared to replay the point, then I'm going," he said to Sebastian who appeared not to have heard him – he was too absorbed in the contents of Granga's letter, which he continued to read aloud.

"*I'm looking forward to reading the poems of Blue Ellerton one day.*" He'd adopted a tone to suggest that such an idea was ridiculous. "Little Boy Blue – the poet!" His laughter was so exaggerated that it failed to hurt me. "Let's hear one of your great poems – *Blue.*" Philip had walked away. Sebastian was ready to go on.

"What's this bit? *You have the talent to be a great poet.*"

I didn't care how much it amused Sebastian – my grandfather thought I had the makings of a great poet! Let him read my letter if he wanted to – I was proud of it.

"*There was just one other thing I wanted to write and say to you, Blue. And that is – I miss you.*"

In those few words he'd given me back the key to my magic box and now the world was mine. I would be a great poet. I would move people's hearts with my words as Granga had moved mine. I would write back and tell him that I missed him too. Read on, Sebastian Hamilton – and learn!

"*If you have time, write back to me. Tell me what you're doing, what you're thinking. I'll wait for your letter.*"

Sebastian had reached the end but he wasn't letting go. "I think I'll keep it," he said, folding the paper in half.

Moments earlier, I'd worried that my excitement may have been too rash, an Aristotelian extreme, a fault that I should try to curb if I wanted to be virtuous. Yet now my anger was a far greater extreme, and I didn't care what

Aristotle would have said. I took a step towards Sebastian and tightened my right fist. "If you don't give me back my letter . . ."

Sebastian folded it in half again so that it fitted into the palm of his hand like a little square paper box. "What will you do, *Little Boy Blue*?" he laughed into my face. "That rhymed! Is it poetry? Am I a great poet too?" I swung back my arm as if I knew exactly what I would do next. Sebastian thought I knew. I could tell by his change of expression.

As did John. I'd forgotten about John Thompson till then. All I could see was Sebastian Hamilton and Granga's letter. Then suddenly, from nowhere, John was there, pushing his wide body between Sebastian and me. "That's Blue's letter in your hand," he said in a tone that Aristotle would have approved of. "Give it back to him right now or I'll have to take it from you."

John's hair at the back was cut in a straight line. My eyes focussed on the skin between his hair and his collar. It was pink and sweaty. I couldn't see Sebastian Hamilton any more, but I could hear him. "Take the bloody letter," he was saying, "what would I want with rubbish like that?"

I heard the tearing of paper before I saw the pieces floating to the ground like the soft white underfeathers of a bird who has just been trapped in a predator's mouth.

Once Sebastian had gone, John and I fell to our hands and knees and picked up the pieces of my letter. John found most of it, "Dear Blue" first. It was upside down by my left foot. Then he managed to piece together "the talent to be a great poet". He was pleased with himself for finding that.

But I found the very last piece. It was sticking out of the soil of the rose garden, which I was careful to brush off before I read it, just once, aloud, so there could be no mistake. Then I pushed the pieces of my letter into the rose garden, and kicked soil over them with my foot until I couldn't see the paper any more. The last piece of my letter read, "Love Katy x".

33

"WHO'S KATY?"

"I told you before, John. She's one of Hannah's daughters."

"Do you fancy her?"

"You must be joking."

"Why not?"

I hadn't thought of that. The answer felt so obvious but it wasn't easy to put into words, like knowing you don't like school dinners without needing to reflect on the reason.

"She's a ham salad rather than a seafood paella," I said, happy with the metaphor. That should be enough.

"I like ham salad," John replied.

"She's a ham salad," I explained, "that's been in a luke-warm plastic container."

"Oh right," John nodded.

He had his towel around his shoulders but I preferred to let the breeze dry my skin. It wasn't hot air like in Mallorca, but it didn't make me shiver as it did the other boys. I'd found that if I kept my shoulders back and my head up as Granga had taught me, soon I felt warm and invigorated from my swim.

We'd been competing for places in the school's

swimming Sports Day in two weeks' time. I'd won my
heat, but John had come last. In fact, he hadn't finished at
all because he'd got cramp in his foot halfway down the
pool. Fortunately I'd been ahead of him and hadn't noticed
or else it might have put me off and I wouldn't have come
first, just beating Sebastian Hamilton. I was pleased to beat
him. He'd tried to put me off by shouting, "Katy! Katy!"
when he'd been level with me. It hadn't worked though.
I'd known he must have been struggling to resort to a tactic
like that. Unfortunately he'd come second so he'd qualified
for Sports Day too. But I would beat him again. He was
longer than me but my co-ordination was better. And his
ears stuck out.

"Do you think Hannah will come to Sports Day?" John
asked, drying his hair with the corner of his towel. It hadn't
occurred to me till then – I had no parents coming to cheer
me on. No mother to throw her arms around me when I
came first. No father to boo quietly if first prize was given
to someone else. No one to go home with afterwards and
laugh with about the other boys' shorts or the faces their
parents had pulled. No special supper to celebrate my magnif-
icent victory or my glorious defeat. Win or lose, the result
for me now would be the same – an empty achievement or
a hollow defeat.

"I shouldn't imagine she'll have time," I said, "and I
wouldn't want her bringing Katy."

"So won't you mention it?"

"No."

I wanted to ask him if his parents were coming, but I
couldn't. His father's presence would be too much for me to
bear – watching me with eyes that had been the last to see

my parents alive, eyes that had been responsible for their death.

"My Mum's coming, but not my Dad." He must have read my mind.

"What's she like?" I asked, as if the news hadn't mattered.

"My Mum?"

"Yes."

"She's got a nice smile," he said. "But her face is too big for her body." He tipped his head to the side and used his little finger to try to clear out the water. "She'll cheer for you," he declared proudly, "and she's got a loud voice when she wants to."

I tried not to picture Mrs. Thompson with her big head and small body, shouting loudly as I battled to outswim Sebastian Hamilton in his long baggy black shorts, but it was no use – I'd already seen the whole scene, like when you're dying and your life is supposed to flash in front of you. "That's nice." I tried to sound convincing. "Something to look forward to."

It was the end of the school day, the time when John and the other boys went home as I used to. I always stayed away from the drive as they were leaving. There was a small parking place at the side of the entrance porch, only just big enough for my mother's sports car to squeeze into. She'd always waited for me there, except when she'd been late and I'd waited at the top of the drive for her to come speeding up towards me, hooting her horn and waving to let me know she'd arrived. One day, when the school coach had blocked her way, she'd driven right across the front lawn to reach me. Her tyre marks had stayed there for days. Miss Crosse, our English teacher, had given my mother one of her disapproving looks and shaken her head as I'd got into my mother's car. But Mr. Gilbert, who taught Geography, had laughed and waved at us, which had made Miss Crosse even crosser. I don't think it was only my mother's driving she didn't like, it was my mother too. She was pretty and confident and popular. And Miss Crosse wasn't. And my mother had a husband who doted on her. And Miss Crosse didn't. And my mother had everything to live for. And now she didn't. Since I'd come back, Miss Crosse smiled at me a lot as if we were friends. But I'd never smiled back. I looked down at my feet. I wouldn't smile at anyone who hadn't liked my mother.

As soon as John had left, I went up to my dorm on the first floor. My bed was by a small window that faced the drive, but I didn't look out in case the others were still leaving. I could hear the slamming of car doors and the occasional "Hello!" from my bed.

The dorm was empty, as I'd hoped. On the wall behind me I'd pinned a wildlife calendar that Philip had given me. It had been his up until the end of *September*, which was the month of a grizzly bear. When he'd flicked ahead and found that *October* was an orangutan, he'd shouted, "Quis?" And I'd shouted back, "Ego." Then the calendar had been mine. Unlike Philip, I had nothing against monkeys, but I hadn't been bitten on the nose by one as he had whilst on holiday in Spain with his parents and having his photograph taken by the monkey's owner.

Every night, before I got into bed, I placed a tick in the box under that day on my calendar. There were twenty-two days remaining until half term. Surely I'd have heard from Granga by then. He'd have written to me with arrangements for my flight back to Mallorca for the week-long holiday. Perhaps he would even come to England to take me back with him. Maria would throw her arms around me when I climbed out of Granga's Land Rover. Then the three of us would spend the evening chatting happily in our curious mixture of Spanish and English and sign language as we enjoyed the supper that Maria would have cooked for us.

I placed a tick under today's date even though it was only afternoon. As I leaned forward, I felt Maria's crucifix knocking against my chest. I never took it off. It stayed where she'd placed it the day I'd left. I knew she wouldn't write to me, she spoke so little English. But I had expected to hear from Granga by now.

I felt under my mattress for his book of verses. The springs had left marks on the transparent cover in which James had bound it. As always, I let the book choose where it fell open. I propped up my pillow against my iron bedhead and made myself comfortable. The poem was at the end of the book – the final poem. Fate had pressed a tiny fly between the last two pages. It lay there, preserved beside the title, "The End", like an illustration.

> In the beginning
> In the very beginning
> Before life
> When everything
> Was nothing
> When yesterday
> Was now
> A voice said
> "Let there be!"

And there was
Movement
Heartbeat
Joy and pain
Creation
First breath
First sound
First smell and taste and sight
First man then woman
First human understanding
Of divine delight
First naked moment
As the world unfolds
First sun
First moon
First heaven and earth
First stars.

Time passed
First days and nights
Became first years
And soon
First false temptation
Bore first fears
New eyes
Saw good and bad
And were ashamed
First purity
First innocence
No more remained

As if
Life first begun was at an end
And what
Once might have been
Time could not defend.

And a voice said
"Let there be!"
And there was
Void
The stars
The sun
The moon
The earth
Destroyed.

Where life?
And yet
'Twas not an end
But end of the beginning
Change
Altered state
New understanding
Came.

Mistake
Not sin
That set
New world
In motion.

Mankind
Imperfect
Now stronger
Than before
And what had started
As beginning
Was now existence
By a human law.

Then a voice said
"Let there be!"
And there was
Death
Final
Cold
Unfathomable
End.

An end
To time
An end
To space and motion
An end
To years
Of growing
With devotion
An end
To dreams
A final
Separation
An end

To joy
The start of
Desperation.

In the beginning
In the very beginning
When I look back
To how it was before
When everything was nothing
When my life had not begun
No heartbeat
Joy or pain
No creation
No first breath
No naked moment
No first sun
Or stars
In that beginning
When this man
Knew not
That woman
Had not tasted
Human understanding
Of divine delight
As if
Life first begun
Could know no ending
As if two
First created
Were made one
In that very beginning

Now
I see an ending
Set in motion
Just as time began.

Without that end
There would be
No beginning
Without her life
I would not know
My own.

And a voice said
"Let there be!"
And there was
Ending
Beyond this world
To life
We cannot see
For once begun
There cannot be an ending
Once ended
Then comes true reality.

The first time I read the poem I thought it was about Adam and Eve and Creation. When I read it a second time I thought that Granga was talking about his relationship with Sophia. On my third reading, I realised that he was describing both, binding them together into one, like a bouquet of wild flowers.

What I liked most about it was that it made me reflect on important subjects in a way I'd never thought of them before. Life and death, beginnings and ends, the pain of loss, the joy of understanding, love, a growing kind of love that teaches about yourself as well as the other person. I especially liked the last four lines, the way they seemed like a contradiction at first – how can you say "once begun *there cannot be an ending*" and then go on to say "*once ended* then comes true reality"? Eventually I saw that Granga was meaning that life begun had been given ending – death, like my parents were given – but that our lives continued after that ending into true reality, so it really wasn't an ending at all. The only bit I didn't yet understand was what exactly he meant by *true reality*, but maybe he didn't know yet either.

I hid Granga's book under my pillow this time so there would be no marks from the bedsprings. Then I lay back on the pillow, closed my eyes and reflected.

Losing Sophia had taught Granga so much. A terrible event that had changed his life had also added to it, like dead leaves that nourish the tree they fell from.

But what had the loss of my parents added to my life? Had it made me a different person from the one I'd been before? I tried to remember the old Rufus – loved, protected, confident in the false belief that everything would be that way forever, I hadn't realised at the time how lucky I'd been. And now that I did, it was too late. Or was it?

Without that end
There would be
No beginning
Without her life
I would not know
My own.

What my parents had given by their example was still with me. Without their love, maybe I wouldn't have been able to recognise my own. The old Rufus might have accepted it quite selfishly – the Blue I'd become wouldn't do that again.

I could feel the corner of the book sticking through my pillow into the back of my head. It made me picture the dead fly that had been pressed between the pages, preserved in death.

But could I really be certain that Blue was so different from Rufus? Or had Rufus lost his parents and Blue gained Granga instead? I couldn't exist without something of Granga around me. I needed him just as I'd needed my parents before. Was that learning by loss, as Granga had described in his poem? Yet where would I be if I found that Granga had died too?

Void – the stars, the sun, the moon, the earth, destroyed. That's where!

I opened my eyes. Philip Newman was standing at the foot of my bed, half a chocolate éclair in his left hand. "Are you alright?" he asked, wiping some cream from the corner of his mouth with the back of his right hand. "You looked as if you'd just had a heart attack."

"I'm fine, thanks," I smiled to let him know just how fine I felt. "I was thinking, that was all."

It seemed like the end of our conversation because Philip didn't reply but finished his éclair in one go. I'd just climbed off my bed to go downstairs when suddenly he said, "Your parents died in a car crash, didn't they?"

I hadn't expected that. No one but John had referred to it before. "Yes," I replied.

"That's what I'd heard." He was staring quizzically at

me. I waited for him to say something more, but he didn't. So I spoke instead, "I like the calendar you gave me."

"I don't," he said, "I'd rather have one with girls on it." We both laughed, but I didn't really find it funny. The wild animals were beautiful. I'd looked ahead to *November* and found it was a white leopard.

"Do you think about them a lot?" Philip asked once we'd stopped laughing.

"Quite a lot," I replied, "especially at night."

"Me too," he said thoughtfully.

"Have your parents died too, then?" I asked – no one had mentioned it to me.

"No, stupid!" he laughed. "I was talking about girls!"

34

DEAR GRANGA,
        I haven't heard from you yet, but that's probably
        because the post is slow from Mallorca. I
thought you might like to know that I've qualified for
our school swimming Sports Day in a week's time. I'll
be swimming crawl. I was the fastest in my heat. If I
win, I'll get a gold medal and a small cup with my
name on it. Rufus Ellerton – not Blue, as everyone here
still calls me Rufus. Unfortunately, John didn't qualify,
but he and his mother will be cheering for me. I'll let
you know how I get on.

How is Maria? Tell her I wear her crucifix around
my neck all the time – even in the shower and the
swimming pool.

I read your poem "The End" the other day. It's
extremely moving and clever. It made me think for a
long time afterwards. I wanted to ask you a question.
Sometimes you speak as if you don't believe in God any
more but I think you must because otherwise you
wouldn't have written after Sophia's death about an
afterlife. "Once ended, then comes true reality." What
else could you mean by that? It's just that I want to

understand you better. And I think there are some things you're afraid to discuss with me, and you needn't be. I know how you felt when your wife died – not exactly, but almost. As if the world had ended. Then you accept it hasn't and you have to carry on. Gradually you understand that you only have such unhappiness because you've had great joy. And you wouldn't swap that happiness for anything that might happen in the future. And when you realise that, you start to feel stronger. And you don't exactly need people the way you used to any more. I thought I needed you, like I used to need my parents. But now I realise I don't. I enjoy being with you and learning from you and getting to know you better and better (I hope), but if I never saw you again, I would still have all the happy memories of you in my mind, like a photo album I could take out and look at now and again. Because those memories have become part of me – they influence who I am. Blue like cloudless sky sometimes and like a miserable little fellow at others, soulful like the blues. Sometimes when I'm about to do something, like write a poem or a letter (this one, for instance) I wonder what you'll think when you read it and at first that makes me cross parts out. But then I remember what you've taught me, to write for myself, what moves me, instead of trying to write what I think you would like. So that's what I'm doing. I still hope you like it, but I wouldn't change a word even if you didn't. Because it's me – Blue. And I've learnt from you – lots. I want to say, thank you, Granga for who you are and who you've helped me to be.

With my love,

Blue x

P.S. My half term starts on Friday 26th October and lasts for a week. I was wondering what you were doing then? I understand if you're busy. I could stay with Hannah if I wanted to.

I read it over to make sure I was happy with what I'd written. I decided to delete the P.S., which was easy as it was squashed at the bottom of the page. So I got a pair of scissors from my chest of drawers and cut along the pencil line that I'd drawn with my ruler. He would never know.

"I'm walking up the road to the postbox, Philip. Do you want to come?" It was noisy in the dorm and I wasn't sure whether Philip had heard me until he shouted back, "OK."

The postbox was only a short walk from the entrance gates. I could have posted my letter at school, but I thought it might go faster from the public box. I'd noticed there was a collection from there at 5.30 every day except weekends, and it was only 5 o'clock on Friday. I wasn't sure how much postage cost to Mallorca. On my previous two letters I'd placed two first-class stamps, which I thought would be more than enough, but as I hadn't heard back yet from Granga, I decided to stick the entire contents of the packet on the front this time, which was six first-class stamps.

"Who's it to?" Philip asked when he saw the white envelope in my hand.

"My grandfather," I told him. "He lives in Mallorca."

"Lucky sod," Philip said. "Is he Spanish?"

"No – English. He's my mother's father," I explained.

"Then what's he doing living there?"

"He likes it," I said, glad of an opportunity to talk about Granga. "He lives on the north of the island, in an old finca he restored himself."

"Is he a builder?"

"No – he's a poet. His book of verses was popular some years ago. I have my own copy. It's very good."

"What's he called?" Philip had taken my envelope from me to read Granga's name for himself. "Horatio Hennessy. What a funny name. I've never heard of him."

I wished I hadn't started this conversation. Philip wasn't the type to understand about poets. "I'll show you his book if you like." It wasn't exactly bragging – Philip Newman needed to know just how important Granga was.

"No, it's alright," he replied. "I don't like poetry."

"That probably explains why you haven't heard of him," I felt compelled to point out for Granga's sake. "I've been staying with him for a while in Mallorca up in the mountains," I went on.

"Weren't you bored?" he asked, his eyebrows rising above his superficial eyes. "I mean, staying with an old bloke up in the mountains?"

"Of course not!" I answered indignantly. "I had a wonderful time. My grandfather's a very interesting, intelligent man."

"Then he can't have been pleased having a boy to look after."

I hadn't thought of my arrival that way before. Philip was right. It must have been a shock for him. I'd been so selfish that I hadn't given enough consideration to Granga's point of view. A twelve-year-old must have been a burden to a man like Granga. What experience did he have of young boys, after all?

"He enjoyed my company," I said half-heartedly. Philip noticed.

"He probably did at the beginning," he suggested, "before the novelty wore off."

We'd reached the shiny red postbox by the side of the road. It was slightly raised on a grassy bank like Father Christmas on his throne, waiting to see what you're asking for this time. "I've just remembered," I said, "there's something I've forgotten to put in with the letter. I'll have to take it back." I turned and headed back the way we'd come.

"What have you forgotten?" he asked.

"A photograph of me," I said, reddening to the colour of the postbox. "He asked for one in his last letter to me."

I crumpled the envelope and its contents into a ball in my pocket, then threw it into the bushes when Philip wasn't looking.

35

ARISTOTLE WOULD HAVE THOUGHT THAT Mrs. Thompson's face was too extreme. Her mouth never stopped smiling, not even when she spoke (which she did a lot), but it didn't seem to be in harmony with her eyes. I was used to eyes that reflected whatever was happening with the rest of the face. Mrs. Thompson's eyes were like two sad strangers who'd wandered accidentally into someone else's party.

"We'll sit here at the front, where we can see your race clearly," she grinned, nudging John towards the first row of seats beside the swimming pool. "We'll wave as you swim past."

John did as he was commanded without saying a word to me, not even "Good luck". He was too busy helping his mother arrange her denim coat around the back of her chair. I joined the rest of the competitors, who were gathered behind the diving boards using their towels to keep them warm. It had been raining earlier, which had caused chaos amongst the staff, who had relied upon the weather forecast for a sunny Sports Day, even though it was October. Fortunately the sun had come out long enough to dry the wooden seats, which the parents would be sitting on. But now that they

were arriving and the first race was about to begin, a cool
wind had begun to blow. The crawl, my race, was first. There
were six of us competing. I was in lane 3 next to Sebastian
Hamilton in lane 4.

Once all the guests had sat down and the members of
staff who were acting as judges had taken their positions at
the other end of the pool, our headmaster, Mr. Collins, made
a short speech. I didn't hear what he said because I was too
nervous.

It was time. I walked to my position as directed by Mr.
Long, our P.E. teacher. The concrete was cold against the
soles of my feet. I shivered. Sebastian Hamilton adjusted his
goggles. He hadn't worn goggles in the heats. I should have
worn a pair too. They would probably give him an advantage.
Andrew Curtis on the other side of me was swinging his
arms as he leaned forward towards the clear blue water.

If only my parents had been here like the other boys'
parents. I'd seen Mr. and Mrs. Hamilton in the front row, a
few seats away from John Thompson and his mother. Mr.
Hamilton was wearing an expensive-looking suit. His wife
was dressed smartly in a navy woollen dress and long beads.
They lived in Switzerland most of the year. Perhaps they'd
come back to England especially for this event. I should have
been brave enough to have at least sent Granga an invitation,
even if he'd ignored it. I'd have felt more confident if he'd
been watching.

"On your marks," I heard in the distance. What would
Granga have told me? "Enter the race for yourself, not for
anyone else. The only winner is the boy who enjoys his swim
the most."

"Get set!"

The sun had come out. I tilted my face towards it, feeling its rays warm my skin. For a second, I was in Mallorca again. I crouched forward, like November's white leopard ready to pounce.

"Go!"

The water was colder than I'd expected, and I hit the surface with too much force. I swam on, conscious of Sebastian Hamilton ahead of me. "It shouldn't matter," I said to myself, but it did. When I reached the other end, I twisted my body and pushed with my feet against the pool's wall. I picked up some speed and before long Sebastian and I were neck and neck – only his neck was longer, so he was slightly in the lead.

I thought I heard John Thompson's voice shouting, "Blue," but I could have been mistaken. Water was brushing in waves against my ears and eyes. If only I'd worn goggles like Sebastian, I'd have been able to see John sitting there. It might have been the encouragement I needed. "Swim for yourself, Blue, not for others," I kept thinking. But I didn't want to let myself down. I knew I was a better swimmer than Sebastian Hamilton. I'd entered the race because I wanted to win.

I kicked my feet hard and soon I'd overtaken Sebastian. As I passed him, he shouted "Orphan" into my left ear. I carried on kicking. The race was nearly over. I could see the judges waiting by the edge of the pool. So close, I began to picture the gold medal and wonder if they would put it over my head.

It must have been that very thought which made me feel it, slipping from its place around my neck. I saw it for a second as it was falling – Maria's crucifix that I'd never taken off.

"No!" I shouted, loud enough for everyone to hear. "My crucifix! It's fallen off! It's gone!"

Sebastian swam past me, but that didn't matter. I no longer cared if I won the stupid race.

My toes just touched the floor of the pool where the crucifix had fallen. Once the race was over and the other boys had all climbed out, the surface was still again. Only I remained – alone in the water, orphan that I was. I dived down to the bottom of the pool with my eyes closed and used my hands to feel along the tiled floor. I couldn't find it. I came up for air then dived quickly down again. I tried opening my eyes this time, but I couldn't see clearly because the chlorine stung them. I stayed underwater for as long as my lungs allowed.

When I emerged again, a crowd had formed along the edges of the pool all around me. There were even some older boys standing on the diving boards. "Can anyone see my crucifix?" I shouted – they had a better view than mine.

"You need a pair of goggles," someone shouted back.

He probably felt more charitable now that he'd won his gold medal. Or perhaps he just liked being a hero in front of a crowd. Whatever his motives, Sebastian dived into the water to join me. "I'll find it, Rufus, don't worry," he said, as if he was my best friend.

I stood on my tiptoes as Sebastian combed the pool's floor. He was down there so long that some of the parents began to sound worried.

"Sebastian will be fine," called out Mr. Hamilton who, along with his wife, was the only parent to have remained seated.

"I'm afraid," announced our headmaster, "that if Sebastian

doesn't find the necklace soon, we'll have to continue with the next race."

I must have been shivering because Mrs. Thompson suggested I got out of the water. "Come and sit over here, love," she shouted, holding out a towel. I did as she said – I was glad to have her big arms and a warm towel around me. "What a shame," she sighed, "when you'd so nearly won the race."

"You were great," said John. "You couldn't have swum any better."

"It was Maria's crucifix," I explained. "She took it off to give me on the day I left Mallorca."

I wasn't sure if they heard me – Sebastian Hamilton was climbing out of the swimming pool. His expression as he approached us made me think he'd been unsuccessful. When he reached me, he removed his goggles and stood dripping onto the lawn.

"Any luck?" Mrs. Thompson asked for me – I was too anxious.

"Is this the crucifix you were looking for?" He opened his right hand to reveal a palm of silver.

"Yes. Thank you," I said, taking the crucifix from him. It didn't seem right that he should have been the one to find it. I wished I'd stayed longer on the bottom of the pool.

All the parents started to applaud, except for Mr. and Mrs. Hamilton, who were sitting close by me. "Is that what all the fuss was about?" asked Mr. Hamilton. "If I'd known, I'd have offered to buy you another one so we could have got on with the races." Mrs. Hamilton laughed quietly as if her husband was only being funny.

Mrs. Thompson got to her feet. "There are some things,"

she called loudly, "that money can't buy." I noticed that this time her eyes were matching the rest of her face, and again, when she turned and gave me a great big hug. I liked Mrs. Thompson. I hoped what her husband had done to my parents hadn't made her too unhappy.

"Would you fasten it around my neck again?" I asked, passing her Maria's crucifix.

"It would be my pleasure," she beamed, turning me round. It may not have been the gold medal going over my head but it was the greatest award I could have won.

36

"Hello, Hannah. It's Rufus."

"Rufus! What a lovely surprise!"

I probably wouldn't have phoned her if it hadn't been such a sunny morning. I was used to waking to cloud and October rain. This day would be different, I'd told myself as I'd thrown open the curtains and waved to the postman, a Saturday that I would make sure was special somehow.

I'd given up hoping for a letter from Granga. There was no point in wasting time thinking about what I couldn't have. I'd left the past behind once before, I could do it again.

"I was wondering if it would be alright for me to stay with you over the half-term holiday. It would be for nine days, starting on Friday."

"Of course, Rufie!" she replied. "We'd be delighted to have you here again. I'll pick you up on Friday afternoon."

I was about to thank her when she asked, "Have you heard from your grandfather?" I hoped she didn't think it was why I'd phoned. I wanted to see her anyway – I'd always liked Hannah. If it hadn't been for Katy, I'd have contacted her sooner.

"Not yet," I replied. "He's probably gone off travelling. I'm sure he'll write to me soon when he gets back."

Pauses in telephone conversations always seemed longer than they really were – I'd noticed it before. It was one of the reasons I didn't like them, that and not knowing when to say goodbye.

"I could phone him for you if you'd like." Hannah was the first to break the silence. "Ask him how he is, that sort of thing."

"No, no!" I spoke louder this time so there could be no misunderstanding. "Don't do that! He'd think it was my idea that you'd phoned."

"It was just a thought." She sounded disappointed, as if she'd hurt me without meaning to.

"Thanks anyway," I replied, trying hard to think of a way to change the subject. "I nearly won the gold medal at our swimming Sports Day." It was what I'd planned telling Granga if he rang.

"How wonderful!" she said. "Silver is something to be proud of."

"I wasn't second," I explained. "I didn't finish the race at all."

She couldn't think how to reply to that, and I wished I'd chosen something else to say.

"How's Daniel?" I asked, relieved to have had such a brainwave.

"He's fine," she said, "he'll be looking forward to seeing you again. So will the girls."

"I'd better go now. I'll see you next Friday."

As I hung up, I could hear her saying goodbye. I put the receiver back to my ear but there was only a dialling tone. I'd tell her on Friday that I wasn't very good with phones.

Now that it was all arranged, I wished I hadn't rung her,

and not just because the sun had disappeared behind a big grey cloud. I could have stayed at school. Not everyone was going home. Or I could have accepted John's invitation to stay with him and his Mum. But it was too late. I'd made my decision. Hannah would make sure there was a lot for us to do. It wasn't as if it would just be Katy and me. Hannah and Daniel and Melissa would be there too.

As the day progressed, the more I regretted my phone call. I'd been too hasty, just like when I'd told Granga that I thought I should leave Mallorca. I still couldn't hit Aristotle's Golden Mean.

"It's all your fault, Granga!" I shouted into the net as I served an ace to an imaginary opponent. "You're my mother's father – you shouldn't ignore me this way!"

It began to rain, strong, blustery rain falling diagonally towards me across the tennis court. I blinked hard as I served again. The ball went into the net. "Is this how you behaved when you sent my mother away?" I ran to the net and picked up the soggy yellow ball. As I threw it into the air from the baseline, I heard the first clap of thunder. "Just one letter. That's all I wanted. Just one word from you."

I couldn't see where my ball landed – the rain was too heavy. I ran from the court down the path that led to my dorm. Perhaps I could ring Hannah back, tell her I couldn't make it, that there'd been a mistake, I'd been given a project to do. She wouldn't believe me. She'd know I was making excuses. I'd have to go. She was my mother's best friend after all.

I was leaving a trail of rainwater across the dormitory floor. I took off my tennis shoes and swung them by their laces as I continued towards my bed.

It was probably because I was barefoot that Philip didn't hear me approaching. He was sitting on his bed, facing away from me. I couldn't see what he was reading until I drew closer. When he noticed me, he jumped to his feet. The letter fell to the floor.

"I was just having a look." He spoke quickly like when you're embarrassed by something. "I've never seen a stamp from Mallorca before."

As he handed me the cream envelope, a drop of water fell from my hair and smudged the ink writing. I could still read it though. "Blue Ellerton Esquire."

"It had been left on your bed. I hope you don't mind me looking."

"Of course not," I beamed as if nothing could bother me. "It's from my grandfather," I said proudly, not daring to open the envelope.

"I remember," said Philip. "The poet, Horatio Hennessy."

"Blue is his name for me," I explained, pointing to the envelope.

Philip laughed, "Funny names must run in your family." He was waiting for me to open my letter – I could tell by the way his gaze went from it to me. "Aren't you going to open it?" he asked finally.

I placed my forefinger in the small opening in the corner of the envelope and tore it carefully along the top. I wiped my hands on the bedspread before I removed the thick, cream writing paper. A single sheet slid past the burgundy lining that had held it there. It was folded once in the centre across his bold handwriting, created, no doubt, with the ink from his silver inkwell.

The letter had no beginning, it had no ending. It referred

neither to himself nor to me. No address to mark the top, no
date, no elaborate signature. In fact, it wasn't a letter at all
– it was poetry.

> Harmony in measure is what I taught you,
> The way to Virtue through the Golden Mean.
> A midway point between excess and defect,
> Courageous acts turn reckless in extreme.

> "But is it wrong," you asked, "to love too deeply?"
> Your tutor's voice was silenced like the grave,
> So wise – yet could not give a balanced answer,
> So strong – yet feared that he could not be brave.

> For days and nights my mind explored your question,
> I asked in vain for Reason to help me
> Forgetting the importance of Emotion
> Without whom Reason has no eyes to see.

> A measured love cannot be Virtue's answer,
> Like reaching for the stars – but not too high,
> Else all Man strives to be and feel and offer
> Is nothing but a wise man's foolish lie.

> "Then what is love?" I asked of Aristotle.
> "If I've misled, I'm guilty of a sin."
> I opened up his work, found parts on Friendship:
> "Books Eight and Nine – a good place to begin."

> By love, he says, we mean extreme affection.
> In friendship, this is felt t'wards but a few.

The good man needs good friends to share his love
    with,
Good virtues that reflect in one or two.

Love is excess that can't be shown to many.
First you must trust and know him through and
    through,
A man who's worthy of your true affection,
A friend whom you can bring your troubles to.

The good choose intense pleasure for a short time
Over a quiet pleasure that will last.
They choose one glorious deed to many petty,
Choose one fine year to long indifferent past.

It takes a wise man to be truly loving,
Someone reflective who pursues Virtue,
Who shares his thoughts, discusses with the
    other,
Who loves himself as much as he loves you.

Without self-love man cannot love another
First *in himself* he must find true virtue
So that he recognises in the other
That very love the friend sees in him too.

I fear I've failed you is my own conclusion,
I've used wise words, I've shown you fine new
    things,
I've introduced you to life's brave adventure
But, in the midst of flight – I've clipped your wings.

'Twas always my intention, Blue, to love you,
To offer up my thoughts to your pure mind,
But in my zealous quest for the right answers
I see now that my actions weren't all kind.

I taught you courage – yet I don't possess it
I preached friendship – yet in your need, where's
      mine?
I spoke of love – yet when you asked your question
"Love" was a word that I could not define.

It took *you*, child, to help me see my problem,
Perhaps in union with your God above,
'Til, with the help of Aristotle's reason,
I saw my fault . . . I could not find self-love.

In you I saw fragments of a reflection
Like stepping stones to a forgotten past
Through you I'd make amends, appease my
      conscience
Wipe out my painful memories at last.

But selfish love is not the same as self-love
The latter grows from deep within the soul
The good man loves his friend for who that friend is
Not as a means to further his own goal.

I sent you off, just as I had your mother
With no real chance for you to have your say
A brave man would have discussed your opinion
For in my heart I longed for you to stay.

I've shared my imperfections for a reason
So that you'll understand these flaws one day
For love is not a state of shared perfection
We love once we throw our ideals away.

"What does it say?" Philip asked when I looked up.

"It's about Aristotle's *Ethics*," I replied. I could see he was disappointed.

"Boring!" he exclaimed, then left the room.

All these weeks while I'd thought he'd forgotten me, Granga had been struggling with an answer especially for me – and for himself too. It was a poem for both of us to share.

37

"THANK YOUR MOTHER FROM ME, John, for her invitation, but I'm staying with Hannah over the half-term holiday. It's all arranged."

"OK," John answered, closing a textbook on his desk. "You probably wouldn't have enjoyed it anyway."

I'd hoped he might at least have sounded a bit disappointed.

"I'm sure I would," I replied, "I like your mother. But Hannah's sort of my guardian while I'm here."

It was Monday. We'd just finished our last lesson of the day – English Literature – nothing that Mrs. Bainbridge couldn't have taught me equally well, except that in Mallorca we'd have been sitting in the fresh air on Granga's terrace, surrounded by pine forests and palm trees and brightly-coloured flowers, rather than being in a stuffy classroom, perched on hard chairs.

"I got a letter from Granga on Saturday."

I'd been waiting all day for an opportunity to tell him.

"You did? Can I read it?"

Until I saw John's smile, I hadn't realised quite how much he admired my grandfather. I didn't often see John Thompson smile. He seemed much younger when he did, more enthusiastic. And he had nice teeth – not too small, but not too large.

"He wrote a poem for me." I felt for the folded piece of paper in my trouser pocket. I'd taken it everywhere with me since Saturday, except in the shower, when I locked it in my cupboard and placed the key on the floor of the shower cubicle where I could see it.

"Did he call it *Blue*?" I think John had in mind his painting – a fellow artist seeking to compare.

"He didn't give it a title."

He looked surprised. "What's it about?"

"Virtue," I replied, uncertain whether or not to show it to him, "and love – something I asked him about Aristotle's Doctrine of the Mean when I was leaving Mallorca. He's been thinking about his answer. That's why I hadn't heard from him sooner."

John said nothing. I knew he wouldn't understand even before I told him. I'd have to express it differently somehow.

"Aristotle thought that moral virtue was about getting the balance right. Not too much of something, not too little either. Somewhere in the middle."

"Like a beautiful painting," John replied, "when you know you've got it right because everything blends together."

"Exactly," I said, happy with the success of my explanation and wondering if I should show him the poem after all. "On the day I left Mallorca, I told Granga that I couldn't see how it could be wrong – a fault, without balance or harmony – to love someone to an extreme. How could loving ever be too much?"

"I could have answered that," John replied, which was not what I'd expected him to say. "It's wrong because if you love someone too much and then they disappoint you, it makes you really unhappy and then you hate them too much as well."

Could John be right? If Granga hadn't written to me, would my love have turned to hatred?

"I don't think I could ever hate Granga," I said after a moment's reflection. "If I did, it wouldn't prove I'd loved him too much, but not enough."

I hesitated, then lifted Granga's piece of paper carefully out of my pocket. "Would you like to read the poem?"

John nodded. I watched him as he read it slowly to himself in the empty classroom. The paper didn't shake in his hands as he read it as mine had done. His face didn't break into a smile when he'd reached the end. It wasn't until he looked up that I noticed he was crying.

"What's wrong?" I asked, taking my poem from him in case he splashed tears on it, and replacing it in my pocket.

"I wish my Dad would write a letter to me."

"I expect he will," I tried to sound reassuring. "Look how long I've had to wait for mine."

"He's not coming back," he said, wiping his nose on the sleeve of his blazer. "He wrote and told my Mum the other day."

We were discussing the man who'd taken the lives of my parents, the man whose face I'd tried to picture every night. I'd wanted him to suffer the way he'd made them suffer. Yet now I sat hoping that he'd come back one day.

"Granga sent me away, but I know that he still loves me."

"That's different," sobbed John. "I don't think my Dad loves me or Mum. Not really. That's why he'd rather live on his own and go travelling."

I thought of my own father and how he wanted to spend as much time with my mother and me as he possibly could. John Thompson had a point and I didn't know how to reply.

"I'd better go home. Mum will be waiting for me." He'd stopped crying but his face had stayed swollen and wet. "She's doing me fish fingers for my tea."

"You'll enjoy that."

I stood up to leave with him, but I could tell from his expression that he didn't want me to – he was regretting already that he'd let me see him cry. I had to think of something helpful to say or he'd be gone.

"Granga would tell you to pull your shoulders back," showing him what I meant, "stretch your head towards the sky and not go around like a miserable little fellow."

It worked. John's smile returned. And his eyes came back to me. "See you tomorrow, Blue," he said cheerfully. Then he walked across the classroom, his back stretched like a soldier, and closed the door behind him.

As soon as the sound of John's footsteps along the corridor had disappeared, I took out Granga's poem, smoothing it gently along the crease in the middle, and read it again to myself, slowly this time, feeling every word as if it were a chord of music. Then, when I'd reached the end, I picked up my pen and at the top of the page, I wrote "Love" where the title should go.

38

M Y ROOM AT HANNAH'S DIDN'T seem as bad this time. She'd put a photograph of my old house in a wooden frame on my bedside table. She must have remembered that I'd written and asked her for one when I was in Mallorca. My parents were standing outside by the front door smiling and waving – I'd no idea who to, maybe Hannah had taken the photograph. I didn't remember having seen it before.

In a way, English houses suited the winter more than they did the summer. They felt cosy and safe, even when they weren't really your home and you were only being looked after in them by people who felt sorry for you.

Except for Katy. I don't think *she* only liked me because she felt sorry for me. Even she didn't seem so bad this time. She let me have my space and didn't ask me loads of questions any more.

"Thanks for your letter," I said to her on my second day there. I'd been expecting her to ask if I'd received it for the whole of my first day.

She didn't giggle, but smiled quietly and replied: "Oh, that! I'd forgotten I'd sent it." Which really surprised me.

"Sorry I didn't write back," I went on, just as I'd planned. "I've been very busy at school."

"No problem," she said. "I didn't really expect you to."

We'd just finished lunch and I was about to go for a walk. The lanes between Hannah's house and ours were very familiar to me. I'd missed them – the hedgerows between the lanes and the fields where I used to try and spot different birds calling to each other, the holly bushes splattered with bright-red berries, the horses munching cautiously at hay bales as you called to them and patted their manes if you were lucky.

"I thought I'd go for a walk," I said to Katy. "Would you like to come?"

"Sorry," she said, "I'm due at a friend's house – Dad's about to drive me there. Maybe next time?"

"Fine," I replied, heading to the front door. "See you later."

I'd only asked her out of politeness, so I was really quite relieved that she'd said no.

I waved to her and Daniel as they passed me along the lane. They waved back. I didn't intend to walk far, not as far as our old house. I couldn't face seeing that again, not yet anyway. When Hannah had driven me past it from school, I'd noticed that there was a *For Sale* sign sticking out of the ground by the entrance gates like a white flag. Soon it would be another family's home. Maybe another boy would have my room. I hoped they wouldn't change it too much. "What happened to Freddy?" I'd asked Hannah. "We found a wonderful home for him," she'd told me as we'd drawn up to her house. "The family don't live far away – I'm sure they'd be happy for you to visit him if you'd like to?" "No, it's OK." I'd said hurriedly. "It might upset him seeing me again. He's got a new home now." Hannah had patted my arm before we'd got out of the car. "You're a wonderful boy, Rufie," she'd said, "very kind and sensitive. Your parents would be proud of you."

Not many cars drove along our lane, even fewer lorries. It was wide enough for them to pass, but only if they both slowed down as they got near to each other. My father used to pip his horn on the corners to let other drivers know he was there. He was a good driver.

At the top of the hill, there was a small village green. At the centre stood a wooden bench that I'd never noticed before. The wood was light oak, not weathered, so I guessed it was new. I strolled over to inspect it in more detail. It was a bench big enough for two, with carved arms that made it look welcoming. I walked closer. I was about to sit down on it and enjoy the views across the open meadows, listen to the stream babbling along the wayside down the hill. But I didn't. Because there was something else about the bench I hadn't seen until I drew closer. It was about fourteen inches long and screwed into the back of the bench at the top. Gold, with the words carved out of it:

IN LOVING MEMORY OF
GRACE AND JONATHAN ELLERTON.
MAY YOU REST IN PEACE.

I traced their names with the forefinger of my right hand. The letters were deeply engraved.

"Did you enjoy your walk?" Hannah asked when I ran into the kitchen, out of breath.

"I saw the bench," I told her, "with the plaque on it and their names."

Hannah stopped washing up and beckoned for me to sit with her on a pale-yellow sofa in the breakfast room.

"Would you like to talk about them, Rufie?" she asked in that voice of hers.

I knew there was no one else in the house. It would have been a good time to tell Hannah what I was thinking, maybe share some memories of them with her, listen to what she had to say, like I used to with Granga. She'd be a good listener, I was sure. She'd helped me so much before I'd left for Mallorca.

Suddenly I remembered the poem that Granga and I had composed together by Sophia's grave. Line by line, we'd shared what we were thinking, the painful memories of our past, our uncertainties about the present. In those few words we had understood each other far more than in a conversation.

"I don't think so," I said to Hannah, looking down at the floor. "Thank you anyway."

Hannah continued to watch me. Finally she said, "I don't like to see you so sad, Rufus. Now you have to be honest with me . . . are you missing your Granga?"

I could have burst into tears and thrown my arms around her neck like I used to do with my mother when she guessed what I was feeling, but I didn't. "Yes," I replied quietly instead.

Then we sat in silence for a while until she said, "Why don't I make you a nice strawberry milkshake? You go and read a book upstairs and I'll bring one up to you – how about that?"

I nodded and went upstairs. I didn't know how she knew that strawberry milkshake was one of my favourite drinks – I hadn't told her. Maybe she was good at guessing like I used to be with my mother.

There was only one book I wanted to read right then – had Hannah guessed that as well? I took out Granga's book of verses from my suitcase and carried it to my bed. The fly was still pressed between the last two pages as if to highlight the poem "The End". I read it again. Then I took out the pen that I always kept now in my pocket and wrote the following on a notepad by the bed:

It seems we've reached an end, our last verse over,
Yet there is one thing more I'd like to say:
If you are right about ends and beginnings,
Then you're the yesterday in my today.

I gave it a title, "The Beginning", and placed it in Granga's book beside "The End". Hannah knocked at the door before she came in with my milkshake. "I've made it with vanilla ice cream," she said handing it to me. "What's this?" picking up Granga's book. "*Verses of a Solitary Fellow* – your Granga's poems, how lovely!"

She sat next to me on the bed and flicked through the book, reading one or two. "He's a talented man, your grandfather," she said. "I had no idea he was such a fine poet."

"We wrote poetry together," I told her. "He taught me. We composed our first one by my grandmother Sophia's grave. And he taught me all sorts of things – about the thoughts of different great philosophers and about art and how to appreciate good food and use your senses. I even learnt how to dance while he played my mother's favourite song on his mouth organ in front of a whole crowd in France."

I would have carried on, but Hannah had found the poem I'd just written and asked, "Who wrote this?"

"I did," I replied nervously, unsure what she would think of it, "just now, while you were making my milkshake."

"It's beautiful, Rufus. It's so . . ."

She didn't get to finish telling me what she thought of my poem because we were interrupted by the telephone ringing in the hall.

"Rufus, answer that, would you?" she asked with a smile.

I ran downstairs, while she carried on reading Granga's poems.

"Hello?" I panted into the receiver.

"What kind of day is this?" came the booming reply. "Describe the blue to me."

My hands and voice shook just a little as I said, "Right now, it's like Miró's blue."

"Aha!" he exclaimed. "Miró's *This is the colour of my dreams*. An unreality, then? A sense of the magical realm of the unknown?"

I hesitated. "It's just that I didn't expect to hear your voice again, that's all."

He was silent after that and I worried that he might have hung up. "Granga?" I whispered. "Are you still there?"

"I am here," he replied quietly, as if he was distracted by other thoughts in his great big brain, thoughts too deep for someone like me to understand. "But my question is where do we go *from* here?"

Was he asking for my opinion or asking himself? If the latter, then why now, why . . . "Hannah rang you, didn't she? That's why you called now. You didn't really want to speak to me, you just felt sorry for me because I told her I missed you!"

My voice was too loud again, like in the restaurant in

Morocco. But I couldn't help it. I was angry, with him, with Hannah, with the world.

"Lower your voice, will you? Your temper is a trait in your character that I do not admire. You need to work on restraining it. But you're young and the young are prone to extremes, as Aristotle would have told you. Too angry, too emotional, love too much, hate too much, everything to excess. Aim at finding that Golden Mean we discussed."

"Sorry, Granga," I muttered, which didn't make me feel any better at all, but at least my voice was quieter.

"No need for apologies, Blue," he replied. "It's yourself you let down, not me. We all do it from time to time. It's how we know which areas we should be working on. Take mine, for instance. A man of a mountain of years, my weaknesses, extremes, are those of the old. Aristotle was swift to assess those too. He thought that the old were prone to cowardice through their fears, distrustful as a result of experience, and small-minded because they've been humbled by life. Unlike the young, who have a long future ahead of them, the old know that their future is short. The young have exalted notions – life hasn't yet humbled that out of them – they are joyfully hopeful that they will achieve great things. Read Aristotle's *Rhetoric* when you have a moment. He spells it out in Book two, Chapters twelve and thirteen."

"I found some books on him in the school library," I told him enthusiastically. "I didn't know that he'd been orphaned too, when he was about my age."

"Indeed," Granga replied, "and it might interest you to know that he was also brought up by a guardian, Proxemus, his uncle, who encouraged him towards poetry, amongst other things, before Aristotle went off to study at Plato's academy."

"Wow!" I exclaimed, which didn't sound very philosophical, so I added, "We have even more in common than I realised."

"But to return to our main topic of conversation, you see, Blue, that I recognise my own weaknesses as well as yours. The difference between us is that I was young myself once so I understand you better than you, who have never been old, understand me. One minute you think you love me, the next you think you hate me, and Hannah for having contacted me. You probably even blame your parents from time to time for having left you. No need, boy. We're all in this together, this world of which we know so very little. You and I just happen to be at opposite extremes of age's Golden Mean, that's all."

It seemed to make sense, what he said, at least the bits that described *me*. I wasn't so convinced by his description of himself, though.

"I don't think you're distrustful," I said, "or small-minded . . . even if you may have seemed cowardly once or twice."

He laughed and replied, "I must hide my weaknesses better than I thought. But they're there, nonetheless, deep within my chest, fed by the duplicitous air that I breathe."

I didn't understand the last part, so I didn't say anything and let him carry on. I knew he would – he was on a roll. The right foot of his crossed leg would be swinging backwards and forwards in the duplicitous air.

"You know, Blue, it feels good conversing with you again. You encourage me to reflect far more than I would have thought possible for one so young. Never underestimate the value of applying the mind to worthwhile ideas – Aristotle put it well when he described thinking in his *Metaphysics* as the most divine of things in our experience – Book twelve, Chapter nine if my memory serves me well."

"*You* taught me how to think," I said, "it's what you do."

"A task that helps *me*, boy, as much as you."

I was sure that he'd made his reply rhyme on purpose – he still wanted to share poetry with me.

"I miss being Blue," I felt ready to confess, "even the Blue who's a miserable little fellow singing the blues. I'd rather be him than a grey cloud."

"A cloud, you say? Come, come, I suspect a hue of youthful exaggeration once again. You have your schooldays, do you not, fine opportunities to learn, and you have all your friends."

"I thought I wasn't to trust a fellow with too many friends," I reminded him. "Isn't that what you taught me when we were in France?"

He laughed and replied, "You remember your lessons too well!"

This time *I* was on a roll rather than Granga, so I felt confident enough to say, "Granga, how you just described my extremes wasn't quite correct. I never really thought I hated you . . . or my parents. I was angry, but I didn't ever hate you."

"Well said!" he exclaimed. "I stand corrected. And perhaps you also had a right at times to be angry with me. It is so easy to be angry, is it not? Any fool can be angry. But to be angry with the right person, and to the right extent, and at the right time, with the right motive, in the right way, as The Greek explained in his *Nicomachean Ethics*, Book two, Chapter nine, is not possible for everyone, nor is it easy – that's why goodness is so rare and worthy of praise and noble. In your case, it is perhaps the *degree* of anger that is faulty. Whereas, in *my* case, it is perhaps that my anger has been aimed sometimes at the wrong *person*."

"You mean by blaming my mother for Sophia having died?"

"I mean that very sin. And not dissimilar to your own of being angry with me on occasion for no reason, and with poor Hannah, perhaps even with your parents for a departure that was not in any way of their making. Our anger would be better aimed at ourselves for having been so very foolish, would it not? But to experience is to learn."

"I'm not angry with my parents any more," I thought I should tell him, "or with you or Hannah."

"Nor I with dear Grace," he thought he should tell me. "In fact I applaud her for having reared a child as wise and loving as you."

I didn't often receive praise from Granga like I had from my parents, so it came as a bit of a shock and I didn't know what to say.

Fortunately, Granga spoke first: "The gentle breeze called Hannah will be awaiting your presence. She's a good woman, don't forget that, nor take it for granted."

It felt like the drop in temperature when the sun is disappearing and I knew our conversation was coming to an end.

"And to answer your question, boy, yes, Hannah did telephone me earlier and mentioned in our conversation that you missed me – you were correct in that part of your vociferous assumption. As to your subsequent suggestion, that I didn't really want to speak to you and that I only called you because I felt sorry for you, I can only presume that an absence of sunlight and Maria's paella has caused you some form of cerebral deficiency."

I guessed that meant I'd got it wrong, but I had to be certain. "Then why *did* you phone me?" I asked. "And why didn't you phone me before?"

"One is confronted from time to time with a question – *explanandum*, you may recall – to which there is more than one answer."

"*The thing to be explained*," I translated – I still couldn't help wanting to impress him.

"Correct," he replied.

I waited for more, but soon realised that I'd had the only explanation to this *explanandum* I was going to get.

"I suppose what matters most is that you've phoned now," I murmured. "You probably didn't want to speak to me until I'd had a chance to read the poem you wrote for me. It's a beautiful poem. I'll keep it always. I understand Aristotle a lot better now . . . and love."

"A poem shared, dear Blue, is a problem halved."

Of course he was right – we'd both halved our problems by sharing poetry together – but only Granga could have thought of altering a proverb that way.

I had to think quickly or he'd be gone. I couldn't let him go just like that – I'd made that mistake before.

"Before you go, Granga, shouldn't we discuss your question?"

"What question is that, Blue?"

"You asked where we go from here," I reminded him.

"Did I say that? I could have sworn I'd only thought it."

I hoped Granga noticed that I managed to restrain my anger this time and keep my voice down as I replied: "Do you mean you don't really *want* my opinion?"

"On the contrary," he replied. "Your opinion on the matter

is one that I would value enormously . . . once you are in a position to give it."

"Maybe I'm in that position now," I said, trying to sound confident.

There was silence in Mallorca, but that didn't prevent me from picturing Granga at the other end – sitting at his big desk in his study, fountain pen in hand, a dusty old book open in front of him, massaging his forehead gently with the fingers of his left hand, as he did when he was thinking hard. It was the sort of silence that only a fool would disturb, and I was no fool. Granga's silences were as sacred to me as the quiet stillness of prayer in a church when you bow your head and wait, unsure what you're expecting at the other end, but knowing there'll be an answer eventually, even if it isn't the one you'd hoped for.

"I hesitate to hear your opinion now, today, in this manner," he told me finally. "I'd prefer to hear it when it is accompanied by your face. I want to see the expression in those intelligent, sensitive eyes of yours as you give it. I want to judge whether what you *say* is identical with what you *feel*. In short, I want to be certain that what you describe as your *opinion* is more than a string of hastily thought-out words, clouded by an excess of emotion. It must be a combination of reason and feeling – neither one without the other, mind you! It is a task that I would only ask of a fellow whose mind and soul I admire enormously. And I shall ask it of myself at the same time. Take as long as you need, Blue. I will be here – do I make myself clear?"

"That last bit rhymes," was all I could manage in reply, and it wasn't even what I was thinking.

"The best thoughts often do," he replied. Then he hung up.

"Was that your Granddad you were talking to?" I hadn't noticed Katy come in through the front door.

"Yes, he rang from Mallorca. He wanted to make sure I was alright."

"And are you?" she asked.

I hesitated. "I'm not sure. Sometimes I think I am."

"When I'm not sure how I feel, I usually go for a jog around the garden – want to try it? It works most of the time."

"OK," I said with a smile that I hadn't expected.

"Cool," she replied. "Fetch your trainers and I'll meet you at the back door."

She jogged quickly for a girl, which didn't really surprise me. It wasn't so much a jog as a sprint. I won, though – at least the first lap around the gazebo and back. The second time, she cheated and took a short cut I didn't know about. After the third lap we were both exhausted and collapsed in a sweaty heap on the lawn. I hadn't laughed so much since I'd left Mallorca.

"You'd like Mallorca," I told her once we'd stopped laughing. "There's a lot to do there. You can swim in the sea and climb the mountains covered in pine trees and eat Maria's paella outside in the sunshine. Maria is Granga's housekeeper. She has a pet d . . ."

I stopped myself just in time – Katy might be a good runner, but she wouldn't understand about donkeys, not in a million years.

39

"**Y**OU WANT TO GO BACK to Mallorca, don't you, Rufie?"

"Yes," I replied.

"Shall I take you there?"

"Yes, please," I replied.

There was silence after that as Hannah cleared away the breakfast plates, until she asked: "Are you quite sure that's what you want?"

"Yes," I replied.

"I understand – leave it to me."

"But please, Hannah, promise me you won't tell him I'm coming. It has to be a surprise."

"I promise, Rufus."

It wasn't an impulse, I'd been thinking about it ever since my conversation with Granga the day before. It didn't seem right that I should spend the holiday with Hannah and her family, not when Granga was waiting in Mallorca for my opinion.

It hadn't taken me as long as I'd expected to reach that opinion. I'd begun, as Granga had instructed me, with what my reason told me. That part was the hardest. I'd examined my future from every angle I could think of – what my parents would have wanted me to do, where I would receive the best education, who my real friends were, what I wanted to do when I grew up, and so on. But each time I thought I'd reached a conclusion, another answer popped into my head that made me less certain. Did I really know what my parents would have wanted for me? Who were my real friends? John Thompson – yes; Hannah and her family – yes; Granga – most definitely, but how did that help me? And who could say whether I'd be better educated in England or in Mallorca? Didn't that depend on what I wanted to do with my life? Be a poet – that was what I wanted more than anything else. But mightn't that change as I grew older and more experienced about life and its practicalities?

I hadn't imagined it would be this hard to listen to my reason. When I'd been in Mallorca, my reason had told me that I never wanted to leave. But now that Granga had instructed me not to cloud my opinion with excessive emotion, I wasn't so sure.

So I turned instead to my feelings, again trying not to be too emotional. It turned out that those feelings were identical with the thoughts I'd expressed in my poems. There was my poem "Overgrown", that I'd written after visiting my old home, there was "Yesterday I Dared", that I'd written in the South of France after I'd danced to Granga's music, there was the poem "The Crumbling Wall", that I'd created with Granga beside Sophia's grave, there was "The Beginning", that I'd written most recently about Granga being the yesterday in my today. None of these poems were excessively emotional, they contained no "extremes", as Aristotle had described. In fact, I would call them measured, balanced poems that summed up exactly what I was feeling.

I concluded, therefore, by the end of the day that I would only reach a measured, reliable opinion, a mixture of reason and feelings, with the right amount of emotion, if I wrote it down in the form of a poem that I could share with Granga. So that is exactly what I did.

Perhaps it would have been more sensible of me to stay with Hannah and her family, but it wasn't a *sensible* decision I was making. I hoped Aristotle wouldn't have thought that made me a coward, like a soldier who runs away from the army to be at home with his family, because in a way I felt that my decision was quite a brave one – except for one part, that is: I'd reached my own opinion, of that I was certain, but what would Granga's be? Whenever my thoughts went to that question, I wasn't brave at all.

• • •

Hannah brought the silver hire car to a halt by the gates at the top of the driveway to the Finca. I'd told her that I didn't want her to take me all the way to the front door. I had to make my own way on foot down the moonlit drive. My arrival had to be a surprise.

I'd tried to explain to Hannah that as soon as I saw his face – the expression in his eyes when I'd read him my poem – I would know whether or not he wanted me to stay, not just for the school holiday, but permanently. If I walked inside the Finca with him, she could go home to England. If I didn't, she would have to drive to the front door and take me back to England with her, just a wrongly-addressed letter being returned to sender. I thought it was quite straightforward, but Hannah didn't seem to understand.

"Don't you think it would be more sensible for us to knock at the door together?" she suggested. "Discuss the situation with him over a cup of Earl Grey? He'd like that."

Hannah wasn't a poet – that was the problem.

"Poets don't look for what's sensible," I said. "They listen to their reason *and* emotion. Granga put it best in his poem to me when he said that without emotion *reason has no eyes to see.*"

"I understand," she replied, but she didn't really – I could tell by her eyes. "You know, I'm always here for you, Rufie. I've so enjoyed having you stay with us again – we all have."

She tidied my hair neatly with her fingers the way my mother used to do. "Now promise me you'll let me know if you need me – I'll wait here for as long as it takes."

"I promise, Hannah," I told her, undoing my seatbelt. "Thank you for everything you've done for me. After Granga, you're my best friend."

"You're a brave boy – a son to admire," she said, brushing away her tears.

We both got out of the car. Then she opened the boot and passed me my suitcase.

"I packed your Granga's book of verses on top of your clothes so that you'd see it when you opened your case," she told me, as if I hadn't watched exactly where she'd put it. "I'm glad you shared your poetry with me – it's a great gift you have . . . you both have."

She kissed me on the forehead then climbed back into the car.

"Take care," she called through her open window. "And don't forget those wise words you wrote in your poem to

Granga, *you're the yesterday in my today*. You know, we're all still part of your yesterday – your mother, your father, me. We all want what's best for your today. Remember that . . . Blue."

"I won't forget," I assured her. "I'll never forget."

I picked up my case and began the solitary walk down the drive.

● ● ●

All the way to Mallorca, I'd planned what I would say when he opened the front door and saw me standing there. "I thought I'd surprise you" didn't sound interesting enough. And what if it wasn't a happy surprise for him? He might not want to see me. Or perhaps he'd have gone out, or worse, have gone away.

Too late for hesitation – I was at the front door. It was ajar and all the lights were on. I knocked hard. The door creaked. I closed my eyes. When I opened them again, Granga was standing there.

"Hemos llegado," I said – it was the Spanish he'd taught me for "we've arrived" – here on this very spot when we'd first reached my new home. I looked towards my suitcase in my hand. "Me and my suitcase."

He didn't reply, but stood staring at me for several minutes. Just as I'd remembered him, I thought, like a proud and mighty oak tree stretching up to the sky. I stared back at him in silence. That's when I noticed that he wasn't quite as proud and mighty as he'd been before.

I put my case on the doorstep between us. A frown remained between his wiry grey eyebrows. "You're shinier

A MAN OF UNDERSTANDING | 309

than I remember," were his first words to me. "Like a horse
that's been prepared for dressage."

"Sorry, Granga," I said, reddening. "Hannah combed my
hair for me so I'd look smart for you."

"I thought the woman had more sense," he replied. "What
time is this?" he asked, gazing at the dark moonlit sky.

This was my moment – if I had the courage to carry on.
Not too much, not too little, I told myself.

"It's the time for my opinion," I told him, trying to sound
measured.

"Aha!" he said, tightening the belt around his dressing
gown. "I'd like to hear it."

"And then will you give me *your* opinion?" I asked.

He nodded once. That was enough for me. I reached for
the piece of paper in the back left pocket of my trousers and
unfolded it carefully. I knew I didn't need it, but I wanted
it in my hands just in case.

"I'll read it, then, out here. It won't take long."

"I'm listening."

He knew I wouldn't go inside unless I'd read it. Poets are
like that. They understand the silence between the words.

"It's in the form of a poem," I explained.

"I thought it might be," he replied with a smile.

I held my poem so that moonlight shone on it. I took a
deep breath of the night air. "I think it's my best so far – I
hope you'll agree."

As I cleared my throat and focussed on the page, I remembered what I'd told Granga on the day I'd read his poem
"To Rufus", that he'd written for me in his book of verses.
"One day," I'd said, "I shall create a poem all for myself. It
will express what I truly feel about something or someone.

And when I've finished it, true judges of taste might even appreciate it. I won't have written it for that purpose though. It will be my greatest ever achievement. And I'll dedicate it to you."

"*To Granga*," I said, not daring to look in his direction:

"Is this the hour, is this the day
When, stumbling up the long driveway
Where tidy corporal pine trees
Heralding my return
Stand ready for inspection,
I stop and pray?

Is this the moment
As the sun goes down
And whistling crickets
Make me turn and frown,
That my body warms
With uneasy sweat
And a heart aflutter
Lest I soon regret?

Is this the way
You'll see me when
With work-rough hands
And shoulders broadly back
You open up
That wooden door
And see me stand
Where you'd thought no more?

Is this the time
To stand and stare
And celebrate
With mutual delight
The other being there?

Is this the time, is this the day,
The God-blessed, heavenly mortal day
To tell you
In my fledgling, half-baked way
That my return
Is something I have dreamt of such a while?

Yet now I stand here
With my boyish, panic-stricken face
And gaze upon
The wisest, truest member of the human race
I fear I'll wake,
Find you and all this gone
'Til from the shadows of unknowing night
A voice cries out . . ."

I paused, just as I'd planned, for Granga to end the poem. It
was for him to decide what he would cry out:

"You're home, my little one."

He picked up my suitcase with one hand, wiped away
my tears with the other and said:
"These eyes of yours tell me that what you've expressed
in your fine poem is identical to what you feel. And the

symmetry of that, dear boy, is poetic – for your opinion happens to be identical to my own. It's not a dream, Blue. You *are* home at last. This time, I hope, to stay."

Then two humbled poets turned their steps towards a moonlit finca, and walked inside, as a shiny silver hire car drove slowly away.

EPILOGUE

I woke to a familiar room that welcomed my return like a long-lost friend. I was back home, a place where my heart beat like a drum to a rhythm I hadn't known before – until my grandfather had shown me how to listen.

Soon the beat of the music began to echo again. The world was in place once more, only calmer and wiser and stronger than ever before.

I passed my days of youth like stanzas in an unfinished poem, needing no conclusion, seeking no goal – but one: to live and feel and see and breathe and touch and hear what my grandfather taught me. Nowhere in the world could I have been more contented. No one in the world could have loved me more – but two, and they were gone. But by their end, they had created a beginning. Their legacy in death had been new life.

My life. But not just mine – there were so many others. I like to think that Granga's life was furthered too. And dear Maria, she grew ever more contented, if contentment can be measured through a smile. As for Aunt Lulu, like her brother she did not age but rather grew in fascination, like an ancient leather-bound book, which holds within its fading pages the key to life.

Two other lives were enhanced through my homecoming – John Thompson's and his mother's too. I'd thought of it even before I'd left England for Mallorca, before our old house had been sold and the money was mine. This was the place for an artist to live and paint and sell his paintings. To buy a house here for them was a privilege to me. Not just because I could see my friend almost daily, I also saw the reward as his talent grew.

Our village became a colony for accomplished artists – painters, composers, sculptors, novelists, poets. John Thompson was one, Blue Ellerton another, published by the time I was twenty-one. And there was one more poet in the village, who had his second collection of poems published at the same time – Horatio Rufus Hennessy's *Verses for Blue*.

With each passing year, I've understood more clearly those lessons Granga taught me. But of them all, there's one that still stands out to me: *Once begun, there cannot be an ending, once ended, then comes true reality*. A story, like a poem or a painting or a piece of music, must have an ending, a man-made moment when a work of art concludes. A final brushstroke, a final note, a final word and the work is over – as finite as a life that must end one day. Yet, as Granga would say, what matters most is "the aftertaste" that follows. Therein lies the true reality.